In the End

Donna H Duhig

Editor: Viv Ainslie
Asssitant Editor: Dave Power

Printed in the United Kingdom

First Printing, 2020

ISBN: Print: 978-1-912677-43-6
Ebook: 978-1-912677-75-7

Published by Purple Parrot Publishing

www.purpleparrotpublishing.co.uk

Acknowledgements

In the End is a work of fiction. None of its characters exist and any similarity to any person, living or dead, is coincidental and accidental. Many locations and venues in the story do not exist and they are also not intended to portray any real places or businesses.

The journey to publishing *In the End* has been a memorable and enjoyable one and this would not have been possible without the help of a few very special people.

I would like to thank my mother, Lorraine, who has always encouraged my passion to write. If it was not for her continuous support, honesty and guidance, I would not be the person I am today. She read the very first draft of the book and her invaluable feedback gave me the confidence to develop it further. Thank you again, Mum, for believing in me.

I am grateful to my husband, Phil, for his patience. For many months he listened to my tapping away on the keyboard while I wrote. He endured chapter after chapter being passed over to him to review and was forced to read a genre he would not normally entertain.

I am thankful for Jennifer Duhig, Samantha Dawson and Helen Jennings, who each took the time to read and review the final draft of the book.

A special 'thank you' goes to my publishing team. Firstly my editor, Viv Ainslie, who has made the whole publishing experience an enjoyable and interesting one. In the time I have known her, we've shared many laughs, a few tears, breakfasts and puddings. But her knowledge and expertise goes without saying. Secondly, to my proofreader, Dave Power, whose eye for detail further enhanced the book.

Last, but by no means least, a huge 'thank you' to my talented friend, Alexandra Fisher, who created the beautiful illustration for the cover.

To all of you, we got there *In the End.*

Dedication

In loving memory of Muriel Small.

Contents

Part One

Chapter One

There was nothing notably different about that bleak and gloomy day back in December 1919; nothing to warn me or prepare me for what was about to change my life forever. Yet my most vivid memories will always be attached to that winter, and every minute detail would stay with me, forever embedded in my mind.

All day, an endless waterfall poured down on the town. The icy rain whipped hard against the buildings and hammered against the brittle panes of glass, streaming into our home through the smallest of gaps.

I was relieved to be home, escaping from the ferocious wind that howled and whisked through the streets, screeching through the gaps under the door and rattling the loose windows. The comforting smell of my mother's cooking wafted over from the stove, filling the air with the savoury aroma of mixed vegetables and freshly baked bread. I welcomed the warm blaze from the only fire in the house; defrosting my chilled body, still numb from the cold classroom I had been trapped in all day.

My moments alone rarely lasted for long before I was taunted by my older brothers, Bert and Frank, who found great pleasure in frightening me with spooky ghost stories of the Headless Widow and The Revengeful Baron. They had either made up or adapted stories from the ones they were told, giving the characters their own unique, eerie, scary voices. My brothers performed so well and, combined with the sound of the weather outside, created the perfect haunting atmosphere.

I was easily scared and never enjoyed the ghost of the Headless Widow creeping up behind me asking for 'a needle and thread to fix my head.' Bert was arched over me wearing one of Mother's dresses, the ribbons of the neck pulled tightly above his head, hiding his face and creating the illusion he was headless, whilst strands of his short hair poked above the collar.

Bert carried Frank's head under his arm and the rest of Frank's body trailed behind, like the back end of a donkey. It was all very convincing, especially in a room where there was more shadow than light. The only light came from the fire and two candles, strategically placed to provide the most light possible, with their dancing flames casting flickering shadows against the wall.

Despite knowing that it was only my brothers, they often succeeded in terrifying me. Frank's face, barely visible under the brim of Mother's hat, made him look sinister and the cackling shriek of an old woman's croak came out of his mouth as, once again, he repeated the words, 'a needle and thread to fix my head.' In a slow, jerky movement Bert reached out towards me with his free arm and in a stricken panic I clung on to my toy doll, screaming as loud as my lungs enabled me to.

I always screamed. In my childlike imagination, I lived in a world where there were fairies, unicorns and angels, but surely ghosts and demons had to exist too? I always thought, *what if it actually is the Headless Widow?'* I screamed again, ducking under his arm and running towards Mother.

'Leave her alone,' May, my sister, scolded them.

Bert was the eldest son, but May was the oldest child; she was eleven and very much an adult – mature, helpful and responsible, as a result of Mother always involving her in everything to do with the house. Aside from assisting with the washing, cooking, baking and cleaning, she often supervised us. I had been bathed and tucked into bed more times by May than I had by Mother.

Bert was nine and Frank was eight, and they were a similar height, which frustrated my mother, Florence, as normally Bert would outgrow shoes and clothing to pass down to Frank and then to me. Being the fourth born I wore shoes that had been re-heeled many times and clothes that had been repaired equally as often.

I am Betsy Colborne. I was six years old and my duties were to darn socks on a wooden darning mushroom. It was a tedious chore I carried out frequently, as the wool on the socks wore down quickly in our house. I often wondered if holes were made deliberately to divert me from doing other things. When I asked Mother once, I was scolded for being ridiculous, 'I have enough to do without making holes in socks for you, young lady.'

For a change, I sometimes rolled the wool up into a ball for Mother when she was knitting. She was a fast knitter and I was fascinated by the clicking sound the needles made, watching in awe as she produced something spectacular.

For my fifth birthday, Mother made me a beautiful doll from left over material; with brown wool for hair and blue embroidered eyes. The doll wore a red knitted dress, boots and had a thin red line of stitching for the mouth, curved into a smile. I absolutely adored her and she went everywhere with me. I named her Dotty.

I had asked Mother many times to teach me to knit, but she didn't have the time or the patience to show me. I was too slow and too clumsy. My fingers were too short and chubby to hold the needles, and I often dropped a stitch or knocked a stitch off when I tried to push the needle through. Likewise, with other chores around the house, it was faster if May or Mother carried them out instead of stopping to teach me, and so I was left darning socks. Mother always said, *'Speed comes with age,'* when my face dropped to a sad and rejected expression after her instant refusal. However, in my head I would question this and doubt it was truthful, with the contradictory words of a teacher once saying to me, *'speed comes with practice.'*

We were fortunate to live in a two-up, two-down property, which Father rented and paid for weekly. We, the children, slept upstairs; my sister and I shared a bed in one room and our brothers slept in the other. The rooms were small, allowing for a bed and a set of drawers, nothing else would fit in comfortably without creating an obstruction in the space available. The windows were small, allowing very little light in and no fresh air, resulting in a permanently smoky room from the coal fire downstairs. The rooms remained bitterly cold and felt a similar temperature to that outside. Many mornings I woke up to ice on the inside of the windows, yet with a few layers of blankets and clothing we were able to keep warm during the winter.

Our parents slept downstairs. It was safer for Father to stay on the ground floor, as the stairs leading up to the first floor were narrow and steep, more like a ladder than a flight of stairs. They were unsafe, and if Father were to fall he would be unable to work, and no work, meant no money; not a risk he wanted to take. Father had to work, *always*, even when he was unwell.

At home, we spent most of our time in the living room; a small square room, where everything happened. Furniture was crammed in, wooden chairs, a table and a bench. The walls were cluttered with pots and pans hanging from hooks, and shelves filled with crockery above the large cast iron range. The largest item hanging was the tin bath that stuck out and took up a large part of the room.

'Come along, wash your hands,' Mother called out, placing a bowl of water on the table. The boys pushed in front as always, their hands barely touched the water as they dipped their fingertips in and splashed around. The water was cold, but I scrubbed my hands vigorously with the bar of soap, in case Mother did her routine inspection of making sure our hands and nails were clean.

Once my hands were washed, May removed the bowl from the table and my brothers continued to frighten me. I clutched Dotty tightly, pulling her close to my chest for protection.

'Here comes the Revengeful Baron,' Bert said in a creepy voice, arms outstretched as he walked slowly and jerkily towards me.

'And we like little girls' blood, ha-ha,' Frank said, joining in and mimicking Bert.

'Dotty will save me,' I said, holding her out in front of me, 'she can defeat all evil.'

'She has no power over me,' Frank said, as he leapt towards me.

Before he had a chance to attack, the door swung open. It was dark outside and the shadow that stood in the doorway was that of my father. He stepped inside and rain dripped from his coat, gathering in a pool near the entrance, as he forced the door shut against the wind.

He removed his cap slowly, much slower than usual. He unbuttoned his coat with difficulty and hooked it on the peg behind the door, lifting it as though it was made of lead and taking several attempts to catch the hook. He didn't speak as he tugged on the laces of his boots and slipped his feet out.

He was only thirty-three, but he seemed to have aged two decades in a day. His face was pale, his eyes were dark and his body was leaning over in a rigid and uncomfortable way, as though he was carrying an invisible, heavy weight on his back.

My mother noticed how weak Father looked; she stopped preparing dinner, cleaned her hands with her apron and dashed over to him.

'Alfred, dear,' she fretted, placing her supporting hand on his arched back. 'You are unwell, this has gone on long enough, I should fetch the doctor. You look frozen. Come, sit by the fire.'

'Don't worry about me dear, it's just a cold,' he reassured her.

Father stiffly straightened his back to plant a tender kiss on her forehead and forced a smile. He was a man of perseverance and resilience; a survivor of the Great War, who carried on regardless of pain, discomfort and illness.

His feet, like lead weights, dragged along the floor towards May, and a kiss that mirrored Mother's was placed on her forehead. He cupped her face and whispered a few comforting words, for her ears only.

Father always greeted the family in age order and next in line were my brothers, while I waited impatiently behind them on hopping feet. Another day he would have treated Bert and Frank like men, ruffled their hair and passed a few gentle punches and dodges. On this day, exhaustion had overcome him and just the ruffle of their hair would suffice. He asked them about their day and praised them for growing into big strong men.

Last of all he turned to me, spreading his arms wide, an invitation for me to run into his grasp, as he swooped me up in the air with what little energy he had left and held me tightly.

'How is my angel today?' he croaked.

'Happy, Daddy,' my smile so wide, I could feel his cool breath wafting against my face.

'Have you met the fairies of the Secret Wood today?' He spoke with difficulty, as though he was struggling to breathe.

'Dotty was there too,' I said excitedly, with one arm around his neck and the other, waving my doll under his nose, 'and we rode on a white stallion. We were searching for the lost Fairy Princess of the Secret Wood, but the evil Headless Widow knocked me off the horse. She's a witch and needed blood to cast a spell on all the fairies. Then the Revengeful Baron came.'

Father raised his eyebrows at Bert and Frank, fully aware that my imagination was usually magical with happy stories and no evil villains. 'Headless Widow and Revengeful Baron?'

Bert and Frank shrugged, looking at one another and smiling awkwardly.

'Well, I'm sure Dotty's magical powers kept you and all the fairies safe. She's a special doll, for a special girl.' Father gave me three big kisses on the forehead and lowered me to the floor.

As he released me he let out a groan, he could not conceal his pain; a grimace engulfed his face and he lifted a shaky arm to grasp his chair by the fire. He slipped into the seat and slouched back; his eyes pressed tightly shut. His hands were trembling; they had turned a pale blue from the cold and over his knuckles the skin pulled tightly, looking transparent, as though his white bones were protruding through.

'Alfred,' my mother grew more concerned, 'let's get the doctor, you don't look well!'

Father lifted his head up with difficulty, barely able to support the weight on his shoulders, and he shifted himself into a more upright position. She handed Father his tea, a winter warming vegetable broth and a slice of bread. Mother always managed to make the most delicious broth with very few ingredients. Taking the bowl with one hand, he took hold of her wrist with the other and his thumb grazed across her rough hand.

'Not to worry, Florence,' he responded, 'it's just a cold.'

Father worked as a coalman, delivering coal on a horse and cart throughout the town. His hours were long, working most days for a small wage, and he always left for work before we were awake. Sometimes I would hear him shuffling around in the mornings, and the soft whispers of Mother talking to him as she prepared him a simple snack for later, and I would run downstairs to give him a kiss goodbye, before he began his long day.

His values made him a true gentleman; to be polite and a good man to everyone. A trait he encouraged in all of us, 'manners cost nothing,' he often said, and 'do unto others as you would have them do unto you.' He never left the house without wearing his cap and he nodded his head and touched his cap to greet everyone who passed him. Although we were poor, our wealth was our health. This was his belief, and as long as we were good decent people, things would work out *in the end.*

My siblings and I sat on stools around the table to eat our tea, while Mother sat on a chair at Father's side; this was the time to whisper about *their* day and have a few moments where they could relax in each other's company. Normally we would squabble at the table. May would try and resolve the situation before our mother intervened. Often there was no need for words, Mother's face would say it all, and if we didn't take heed we'd all receive a hard clout across the back of our heads, after which she would return to her seat and sit in silence, and no one would dare to speak for the remainder of the meal.

Father would laugh at how annoyed she was; to him, it was always healthier if we bickered. He was normally very talkative, asking Mother questions, telling her about his day and showering her with beautiful compliments. Then, once he was satisfied he had given Mother enough of his undivided attention and to mainly distract us from our fighting, he would raise his voice for our ears, showing interest in what we had learnt at school or what we had been up to, whether we had been good and helpful to Mother or anyone else.

This meal was different. We ate in silence, looking down at our food. We all sensed something was wrong – something was missing – the usual sound of our father's deep voice, like a pleasant bass sound that flowed across the room, was not heard.

The room seemed awfully quiet, just an orchestra of spoons clinking against bowls as we slurped the broth. Frank and Bert made small talk at the table, a desperate attempt to draw Father into their conversation, but he remained quiet. His grey face and his pale lips parting just enough to slowly take a small mouthful of broth, as though each spoonful was rotten. With most of the broth untouched, Father passed his bowl to May.

Usually this was my favourite part of the evening; after Mother and May had tidied up, we would drink warm milk and sit by the fire. Father would tell the most exciting stories of wonderful adventures that he made up or remembered from his childhood. He would often include fairies for my benefit and the occasional ghost or ghoul for the boys. May had no preference, she enjoyed the break and feeling like a child again. She was often lost in her thoughts, staring into space, a smile on her face, and I often wondered, *'what was she daydreaming about?'*

Like normal, I crawled onto my father's knee, waiting for the stories to begin, my head rested under his chin and my tiny arms curled around his neck. He held me tightly, I could hear his heart beating in his chest and I found comfort in his arms. I adored my father.

'Let your father rest, Betsy,' Mother ordered, disrupting my moment with him.

At first I ignored my mother's demand, not wanting to let go, but she soon broke the embrace. He had fallen asleep and his arms flopped down by his side as she dragged me from his knee.

For a long while I played with my doll on the rug close to his feet and we all made a conscious effort to keep quiet. Father appeared to be sleeping peacefully, both his hands rested where they fell and, although washed, his nails were permanently outlined with black dirt from the coal. He had rough hands that would grate my skin when he stroked my face, chapped from the cold and coarse from his labour. One leg was stretched out in front of him, the other tucked under the chair, his socks were wearing thin on the soles and I sighed knowing that darning them would be my next chore. His trousers were dirty from the heavy rain and splashback from the puddles. Father was a small man, slim, but strong from carrying heavy sacks of coal. He wore the smell of coal like a perfume, embedded in his clothes and skin; a smell I had become fond of. He still had a thick head of hair, dark brown with a slight wave. Wisps of curls would poke out from underneath his cap and when he removed the cap at home the top of his hair would be flattened. Bert, Frank and I were the ones to inherit the dark, wavy hair and brown eyes, May was more fair-haired and her eyes were pale blue.

His face had flopped to his right shoulder, facing nearer to the warm flames of the fire and his eyes were tightly shut.

'Darling,' Mother said to him, as she carried a tray with a cup of warm milk, for each of us. I sat in position facing my father, certain the stories would begin and I reached for my cup before my siblings.

Father was still asleep. She placed the tray down and gently shook him. When he didn't respond, her shaking became vigorous and increasingly desperate. She screeched his name, 'Alfred!' in a plea to wake him and continued to cry out his name.

May was the first to sense something was wrong and she alerted Bert. While I continued to wait by Father's feet, dancing Dotty around with excitement, I was unaware that the man I adored was vanishing forever into eternal sleep. It was the shriek, the scream, the devastating cry in Mother's voice as she fell to her knees in hysterics, that made me look up at Father and then across at the others. I was confused, not understanding what was happening.

May began to cry, but after a few sobs she swallowed hard and bravely said to Bert, 'get Dr Oxley.'

At first Bert didn't hear her, he stood still and stared in horror at Father.

'NOW Bert!' The urgency in May's voice snapped him from his trance and within a minute he had vanished out into the cold.

'Daddy's sleeping.' I breathed the words that were barely heard or acknowledged by the others.

I rose to my feet and my legs were shaking. I knew about death. The year was 1919, death was all around us; people died when they were poorly, and the war had brought thousands of deaths. A child could not be protected from death, but I had never seen death myself. My paternal grandparents had died before I was born, my mother was an orphan, and Father only had his sister, Lily, and brother in law, Matthew Cooke, who were both perfectly well.

'Daddy,' I whispered, 'wake up, it's time for a story.'

I leant closer to him and held my hand out to touch his face.

'Don't touch him!' Mother screamed, whacking my hand away.

The venom in her voice caused me to step away. I hadn't heard this harshness in her voice before. Taken aback by this new scolding, I began to cry and May took me in her arms.

The door swung open; the wind howled into the room, the candles started to flicker and Bert ran in panting, with Dr Oxley following behind.

He was an old man, wearing a black suit and carrying a black leather bag. Specks of rain nestled in his thick, white beard, yet his head was bald and round, like a polished ball. He spoke only to our mother and didn't seem to notice us stood by, watching.

He was tactless when he confirmed Father was dead and proceeded to cover his face with a rag. Everything was happening quickly, and his word 'dead!' echoed in my ears, ringing around inside my brain, bouncing from side to side. I had heard him right, but Father was not dead, he had missed gunfire, dodged explosions and walked past the enemy completely invisible during the years he was at war; *'how could he die, now? He was sleeping like he always did; he would wake up soon.'* I kept telling everyone that, but, other than May, no one listened to me.

'No, Betsy,' May said, 'he won't wake up.'

Father's body was there for a further four hours. I remained by his side, believing he was still asleep, waiting for him to wake up and tell one of his stories. I promised him, 'if you wake up, Daddy, I'll darn your socks.' I found my wooden mushroom and waited to fulfil my promise.

Mother sat in her chair by his side, her hand rested on his arm and she watched him. She had removed the cloth from his face. I thought Mother knew he was sleeping too and perhaps the doctor was wrong. Father always said, 'people don't get it right all the time,' and my favourite was when he said, 'people make mistakes, why do you think you write with chalk on slate? To rub out your mistakes!'

'I am so sorry, Alfred,' Mother repeated over and over again.

Her eyes were red from crying, her face was drained and she said to Bert, 'put some coal on the fire, keep your father warm.' She was heartbroken, a widow at thirty-two with four young children.

May sat on the floor next to me. Occasionally she stroked my hair, more when I spoke to Father. She had stopped crying and had developed an inner strength to hold the family together, making everyone a drink and, most of all, supporting Mother. The maturity in her showed, she was an eleven-year-old behaving like an adult; she was taking over the role of Mother, like she was trained to do. She told a story to the boys and me, the boys sat on their stools by the table, and I stayed close to Father.

The story was not the same, the pirate's voice was nothing like Father's, she was not scary or masculine enough, and the magical feel of the fairies' world was lost, but we listened to her efforts. She paused every few minutes to swallow hard and close her eyes, inhaling deeply, before she continued.

'Father never paused, his story always flowed through each adventure, and each adventure sounded new and exciting.' May just retold a story we knew, and Mother continued to stare at Father, his face highlighted by the dancing flames.

The hardest part came when the men knocked on the door to take Father away.

Mother didn't move and muttered the words, 'goodnight my love.'

'No!' I screamed, wanting to stop the men as they carried Father away, but May held me back, her arms locked tightly around my chest. Bert and Frank assisted, as I tried to wriggle out of her hold, crying and screaming through my struggles. Frank was crying, even though he had been told many times before, 'boys don't cry,' he could not repress his sadness any longer.

'Betsy,' Frank said through his tears, 'don't make it worse.'

Through surrender and defeat, I watched as my beloved father was taken from his home. He was carried like a sack of potatoes through the front door by two men, immune to their work, they were not subtle or compassionate; to them this was not a man, *just a body, just their job.* The door slammed shut putting a permanent barrier between us and him. Mother howled through the night, like a wounded animal.

May ushered us to bed, and once in our own rooms, the boys failed to be the strong men Father encouraged them to be, I could hear their weeping through the walls.

For the first time in my life I felt the pain of a broken heart and I clung on to Dotty, whispering 'things will work out *in the end*, that's what Father says.' May hearing my words of comfort, wrapped her arms around me and buried her head in my hair, her body trembling from her sobbing.

Chapter Two

Mother used the money she had saved for Christmas and Father's final pay packet to fund the funeral. 'He will not have a pauper's funeral,' she said, as she counted out the money on the table one evening, 'he will be buried with a headstone.'

The funeral was a week later and only a few people came. Aunt Lily, Matthew and Father's boss, Mr Dawson, were amongst the small gathering. Mother stood alone during the service and she didn't cry. She had spent all her tears the night he died and since then she had become distant and emotionless. She resembled a living puppet, pulled by the strings of society doing what was expected of her; to behave like the heartbroken widow, to speak when spoken to, to move, to breathe and to live. She showed no animation, she was just an empty shell with a cold, vacant expression being drained of her love and stripped of her happiness.

Aunt Lily held on tightly to mine and May's hands, whispering to us as she choked on her own grief, 'be strong, things will get better and time is a healer.'

The boys stood either side of Matthew, his supportive hands on their shoulders, and that was all they needed to comfort them. Their uncle's firm, heavy grasp was a reminder to stay strong like Father would have wanted them to. They held their heads high and proud, presenting themselves as the sons of the late Alfred Colborne, who, although working class, was as much a gentleman as anyone above him and a well-known, respected man to all.

After Father's coffin was lowered into the ground and the dirt was scattered on top, I cried the hardest. This was my final goodbye. His body was being given to the earth, he was trapped in his final resting place; a wooden coffin in the earth's bed. That was it; he was dead, he was not going to wake up and he was not going to come home again.

I reached for my mother's hand, I wanted to be held by her, I wanted to feel her love, her comfort, her support; but she pulled away and looked with icy cold eyes, like glass marbles, at the coffin. The grief on her face had faded, and her expression had turned to anger and bitterness. Her gesture caused me to freeze. From shock, my body stopped producing tears, and I stepped away from this woman I no longer recognised as my mother. This woman scared me.

When the mourners began to leave and offer Mother their condolences, Aunt Lily waited patiently, she wanted to be the last person to speak to Mother, 'Florence, let's not grieve alone, please, come to our house any time, if you need us, we want to help.'

Aunt Lily grasped my mother's hand to express her sincerity. She was very much like my father, with a short, strong build and dark hair, that she pinned back neatly, twisted like a bread roll on the back of her head. My mother snatched her hand away from Aunt Lily's warm touch and placed them both on her chest, with a scornful look that read, 'how dare you touch me?'

'Can you bring back Alfred?' she spoke out loud, 'can you pay the bills, pay the rent, pay to feed *his* children?'

Aunt Lily didn't respond. She gave a supportive smile and nodded, acknowledging her defeat. She crouched down and held me tightly. I wondered when we would see her again; my beloved aunt and my father's treasured sister. Mother had become bitter in the week that had passed and I hoped it would not keep Aunt Lily from us.

'Be strong, little one and you too, Dotty,' she said, stroking the face of my doll and mine too.

She embraced the other three and, with regret, said her

goodbyes. Mother summoned us to follow her, 'stop your moping around,' she scornfully said, 'your father is at rest now, we're not, life goes on. Those that stand around and weep for the dead after they've joined God, may as well join the dead.'

We returned to our dark and empty house. Christmas was a week away, and no one felt like celebrating. Mother sat on her chair and picked up her knitting. She didn't speak or look up from her busy hands, except when Bert threw coal onto the fire, she shouted 'No! We do not light the fire; we wear coats and extra clothing in the house, is that clear?'

Days passed and she continued with her silence, ignoring our questions and efforts to talk to her. Neighbours and friends of Father showed their respects by calling around the house with bundles of food. Mother managed to thank them and accept their offerings. It was left to May to ration the food and make it last, as well as trying to stretch the small amount of money we had left.

There was a glimmer of hope when Christmas day arrived. We had agreed to celebrate Christmas as Father would have wanted us to; remembering how much he enjoyed the day.

The morning was bitterly cold, but I didn't notice as I crawled down to the bottom of my bed eager to investigate my stocking and explore what Father Christmas had brought me. It took me a moment to find the old woolly socks May and I had left out the night before.

Last year, the socks were bulging when we found them on Christmas morning, stuffed with various items, the wool stretched to house the wonders inside peeping through the stitches. Only this time, they were empty. They had both fallen to the floor, just lying there and looking no different to discarded dirty washing.

I jumped down from the bed and knelt down beside the socks. I carefully picked them both up and in turn, reached inside, until my fingers touched the end. I was hoping to find something, anything, but there was nothing there. My heart shattered; the individual pieces fell from inside me and landed somewhere at my feet.

I resisted the urge to cry. At first, I questioned my behaviour over the year, but I could not recall being naughty.

I stood up and, with heavy feet, I slowly walked around to the side of the bed to wake up May. Her eyes eventually opened, but I couldn't speak and instead I waved the socks under her nose. There was a sad look on her face when she took one from me.

At that moment, Bert and Frank barged through the bedroom door. They too were holding up empty stockings.

We all looked at one another in disbelief.

Great disappointment weighed us down like heavy stones piled up in the pit of our stomachs, built up of lost excitement, lost belief, lost hope and lost happiness, just ripped from inside us. We all felt it.

May was the first to react. She shrugged her shoulders, a sympathetic look fell from her eyes and she forced a brave smile, throwing her sock onto the bed, like a useless rag. She stepped out from the covers and wrapped an arm around my shoulder, and with her other arm, waved the boys to join in with our embrace.

I wanted to still believe in magic, to escape to a world of fairies and mythical creatures, to wait for a man who rides on a sleigh delivering presents across the world in one night, and to believe angels guarded me; just to know there is something more to life than to live and to die.

When we broke away, I noticed Dotty lying in the middle of the bed and I seized her up by her arm. The doll who had been by my side since my fifth birthday. *'How could I believe now?'* I gave her one last look; a tear fell down my cheek before I let her go. She fell quickly to the floor and I buried her face with my sock. She had no importance to me now, her value was lost. I turned around and wiped my tears and nose with the sleeve of my nightgown, with a triumphant 'hmph.'

We dressed quickly in our Sunday clothes, our coats worn on top for extra warmth and together we climbed down the stairs. I followed last.

Mother was sat at the table taking sips from her freshly poured tea. I wished her a 'Happy Christmas,' but she ignored me.

To Mother it was just another day and we went along with it too. She had pulled a dozen mince pies and the Christmas pudding from the larder, that she had made early in December when life was perfect. They were left on the table, untouched. They looked delicious, but we were too frightened to look at them, let alone take one.

Our empty stomachs churned as we left with Mother to go to church. The only thing she was willing to do; more for keeping up appearances to the town folk than for herself or our benefit.

The ground was lightly frosted with snow and tiny flakes fluttered down as we made the short walk to the church in absolute silence. It was an impressive building that stood proudly on a mount in the centre of the town. Several streets branched off from the grounds and directly in front was the road where all the shops were.

On a normal day, this road would be filled with workers and customers bobbing about as they carried out their daily business. There would be the fishmonger yelling, trying to sell his catch of the day, the paper boy bellowing the headlines, and many other people trying to make a living. The buses and trams would drive along the centre of the road, and the occasional car too, diverting the town folk as they wandered across dodging the vehicles.

All the shops were closed and there were no buses or trams running. Just people pleasurably strolling and smartly dressed, as they greeted one another with festive cheer, embarking on the same journey to the church.

After the service a few people expressed their sympathy, they shook my mother's hand and said how sorry they were again before wishing us a Happy Christmas. Mother smiled slightly, thanked them for their kind words and wished them a Happy Christmas. The same sentences were repeated to the next family, friend or acquaintance that knew us. Under her breath she muttered to herself, 'they've sent their condolences once before, how many more times do I have to hear it?'

Aunt Lily and Matthew weaved their way through the congregation, greeting people with festive wishes and good health, as they made their way towards us. Mother was last to catch sight of them approaching and attempted to slip away, but we remained still, eager to greet our aunt.

'Happy Christmas, my darlings,' Aunt Lily kissed each of our cheeks, followed by Matthew. Seeing her young, friendly face, slightly red from the cold weather, sent butterflies fluttering in my stomach; she was a breath of fresh air. She rejoiced and found comfort on this day, which she so clearly enjoyed, just like Father would have done. I felt uplifted and so happy to see her. Mother stopped trying to escape and waited with folded arms, her face as hard as stone.

'I'm so glad you're here,' Aunt Lily said, 'I have something for you.'

Aunt Lily was carrying a woven basket over her arm covered with a cream cloth, which she eagerly pulled back and in turn handed us each a gift. She gave May a book; *A Christmas Carol* by Charles Dickens. She was thrilled with the gift – books were so expensive and we only owned a few that had belonged to Father. May had a smile that stretched from ear to ear as she scanned through the pages, she could not thank Aunt Lily and Matthew enough for their generosity.

The same gratitude was equally expressed by Bert for his gift, a hand-crafted wooden soldier and Frank's magnificent, red wooden train.

Aunt Lily studied me for a while smiling and her eyes sparkled. She slowly pulled out a teddy bear; a beautiful brown fluffy bear, with brown glass eyes and a black nose. His fur was so soft and cuddly, his arms and legs rotated. I had never seen anything so wonderful.

'This is for you, Betsy,' Aunt Lily said and made an exaggerated kissing noise, as the nose of the bear pressed against my cheek.

'I love him,' I cried, holding him tightly, 'thank you.'

I threw my arms around her waist and she held me with her free arm. The emotional strength behind a loving embrace and the affectionate stroke of Matthew's hand on my head, overwhelmed me. My face pushed into the harsh material of her coat that coarsely brushed against my cheek, as I wept.

'Thank you for making it feel like Christmas,' I cried.

'You're very welcome, you're all very welcome,' Aunt Lily said. She tried to release my hold, but my grip was firm and not without a little difficulty, she wormed round to face my mother while my arms remained locked, like a belt, around her waist. She reached inside her basket and pulled out a pie, wrapped in cloth, to hand to Mother.

Mother took the pie and nodded to show her gratitude.

'You're more than welcome to spend Christmas with us,' Aunt Lily continued, 'we have plenty and it'll be nice for all the family to be to-'

'We have plans,' Mother cut her off. The four of us all looked so disappointed. I released my hold on my aunt and cradled my teddy bear, using his paws to wipe away my tears.

'Thank you,' Mother quickly added, not to come across as too harsh to Aunt Lily's kindness – there were too many people nearby.

'Well,' Matthew said, 'once again, Happy Christmas and goodbye to you all.'

Matthew replaced his hat and touched the front with a polite nod, before taking his wife's arm, prompting her to bid her farewells and leave. Aunt Lily reluctantly walked away with her husband, glancing back before she left the church. My eyes followed her until she disappeared through the thick wooden doors.

The journey home was as equally quiet and dismal as the one to church. Mother walked briskly ahead, not concerned if we were keeping up or falling behind. May was able to match her quick pace, keeping at her heel, and the boys walked for a while, then jogged to close the distance. I ran the whole way home; my legs were too short to match their stride. I was exhausted.

'In,' Mother barked, holding open the door for us to enter the cold house. Once we were inside, she threw the pie on the table in disgrace, it made a loud thud and bounced once. She untied the belt on her coat and hung it up by the door next to Father's brown coat. I was the only one to see Mother stand motionless when the fabric brushed against her hand. She massaged the material with her fingers and pressed her face up close, deeply inhaling the last scent of him.

'How could you Alfred? How could you leave me?' She spoke to his coat, 'remember what you promised me?'

The others were sat on the floor still wearing their outdoor clothing and looking content, completely oblivious to Mother's whispers. May had begun to read her book, Bert was marching his soldier along the stone hearth, and Frank was pushing his train along the floor.

I realised how closely I stood behind Mother and I made a few slow shuffles back. I had become petrified of her new ways, I panicked at the prospect of her turning around and finding me there, for fear of receiving a strike of her hand for being too intrusive.

Before I had fully escaped her shadow, the silence was disturbed with a knock at the door. The noise caused me to jump backwards in fright and I could hear the pounding of my heart in my ears. I remained still, taking in deep breaths in an attempt to calm myself down. Mother didn't notice me, she snapped out of her trance and turned the doorknob.

'Hello, Mr Irving,' she sounded cheerful.

Mr Irving was our neighbour from two doors down. He lived with his wife and two children, Mark, aged nine and Beatrice, aged seven. We knew the children well, we went to the same school, and we often played together outside on the street. Mark and Bert's birthdays were close together, with only a few days apart, and Mark often took pride in knowing he was slightly older than his friend.

'Happy Christmas, Mrs Colborne,' he said, touching his hat. 'My wife and I would very much like you and the family to join us for Christmas dinner.'

'Oh,' Mother smiled, in a playful way, her hand touched her heart, as though touched by his generous gesture. 'That's awfully kind of you, but really we couldn't be a burden.'

'Please, we insist; my wife will not take 'no' for an answer, and she has prepared extra.'

After more persuasion from Mr Irving and much exaggerated hand gestures from Mother, she agreed.

We were thrilled with the invite for a traditional festive feast and my stomach roared with the possible delights that would soon fill it. We joined the Irvings once Mother had dictated her orders for us to 'behave, be grateful and remember your manners. Show me up and it'll be the last thing you do.'

Mother offered her mince pies and Christmas pudding to Mrs Irving, as a thank you token. Mrs Irving graciously received them with a thin smile. The children were told to play outside until dinner was ready, the house was too crowded with the six of us crashing and running about.

We all went outside to play in the cold, wet street; the thin layer of snow had now turned to slush. A few other children were on the streets playing farther up the road and Stanley Rhodes, a quiet boy who lived down the street, came outside when he saw us all. He was eight, like Frank.

'We are playing tig,' Mark said, 'so Stan, you're last to join in, you're *It.*'

'Here I come,' Stanley said, agreeing to his position in the game.

We all started to run in different directions trying to avoid Stanley's grasp; he was a swift runner, the fastest one out of us all. He targeted Mark, the most competitive contestant and a pathetic loser. To his annoyance he was grabbed instantly, and Stanley cried out an elated 'Ha!'

'No,' Mark disagreed, 'you have to say 'tig' for it to count.'

'Right, I'm still on,' Stanley said, rolling his eyes at Mark's pettiness.

Beatrice stood still making herself an easy catch for him, waiting for him to get close, before she darted away, knowing she had no chance of succeeding. With no effort at all, he touched her arm and said 'tig,' looking at Mark as he did so with raised eyebrows.

'Oh, no,' she smiled, sounding more pleased than disappointed, 'I'm *It.*'

Without giving Stanley a chance to run away, in a quick and sly move she tapped his arm and cried, 'tig!'

Stanley laughed at her sneaky playing. Beatrice expected him to chase after her again, she stuck out her tongue and waved her hands above her ears, before darting away from him. He did not follow, he turned around and chased after me. Being the slowest runner, I was not much of a target and within two strides I was caught.

My turn at being *It* was long and tedious; everyone was far faster than me and could dodge my grasp with ease. After many failed attempts, May felt sorry for me and slowed her pace down. Once she was caught, everyone upped their game and darted away, with her long legs and speed, she targeted Bert and his turn to chase was upon him within seconds.

'I'm bored, shall we play hide and seek?' Mark said, sounding more like an order than a suggestion.

Out of breath from running, we agreed.

'The rules are,' he dictated, 'we can hide down this street, that street and that street,' he pointed left and right. 'Nowhere else. I'm *It* and I'll count to twenty. One...Two...Three...'

Everyone started to run in different directions. Unsure of where to hide, I watched the others disappear down the road to seek the best location.

Mark continued to count his numbers loud and clear. I caught sight of Frank nearby, and I followed behind him as he disappeared down the passageway leading to the back of the houses. A yard gate was ajar, he peered over to see if anyone was home, not wanting to be caught trespassing and, satisfied it was empty, he crept inside. I stayed behind him, to his annoyance.

'Betsy! Find your own hideout,' he whispered.

'Please, Frank,' I begged, crouching down beside him, 'I'll be quiet.'

'Right, be quiet, don't breathe.'

I nodded and agreed to his orders, my index finger pressed firmly against my mouth.

We heard a faint cry out from the distance, 'ready or not here I come.'

A few minutes passed, possibly ten, I had no concept of time, but my legs were beginning to ache from crouching down. The ground was too wet to sit on the floor, and I knew

Mother would be angry if I spoiled my dress on Christmas Day, especially as we were dinner guests. I poked my bottom in the air to stretch my legs, my hands pressed on my feet trying to keep my body below the short wall.

'Betsy, what are you doing?' Frank laughed, 'we don't want your backside giving us away.'

'They can see the top of your big head; you need to get down,' I said back in defence, as I squatted again on the floor and Frank lowered his head as much as he could.

'They're coming,' he whispered, when the footsteps drew closer and the sound of laughter became louder.

Frank held his finger to his lips to urge me to stay quiet and we were still, like statues. I held my breath and covered my mouth, adamant they could hear nothing.

'I bet Betsy is with Frank, she's such a baby, she can't hide on her own,' Mark said.

'Shut up, Mark,' May scowled.

They were close now, I could hear them over the wall, but I could not hold my breath anymore. The sound of me panting for air when my lungs failed to hold it any longer did not escape the nearby ears of the others.

'Hang on,' Stanley spoke, 'I think I heard something.'

Frank glared at me for giving away our location, and I mouthed 'sorry.'

Stanley leant over the wall and his hand patted my head.

'Got you,' he said, 'found them, Mark.'

'We won,' Frank said, as we left the yard, 'you found us last.'

'No,' Mark said, 'she cheated, she didn't find her own spot, so you don't count.'

'You're making up rules now,' Bert said.

'So, who did you find last?' Frank asked.

'Beatrice,' Mark replied.

'Ha!' May exhilarated, placing her hand on her hips, 'she was with Stanley.'

Stanley nodded in agreement with May.

Mark looked at everyone, he knew he had lost the argument

and unable to admit it, he walked off saying, 'I told you Betsy was a baby.'

'Enough, Mark,' May warned.

'We're playing *blind man's bluff* and the baby is on,' Mark said, pointing his bony finger at me.

We made our way back onto the street, I was sulking and held my head low, feeling hurt by Mark calling me a baby. May used her scarf to cover my eyes and whispered, 'you're not a baby,' and then asked me, 'how many fingers am I waving?'

'She probably can't count anyway,' Mark, with a spiteful laugh, said scornfully.

'You're an idiot,' I heard Stanley say.

I was asked again how many fingers were being waved at me, I was unable to answer, and May spun me around twice. I was released and ready to find my catch.

Relying on only my hearing and touch, I walked towards the voices, sensing their movements as they slipped passed by me. My arms were outstretched and my fingers, twitching, feeling certain someone was there, but an 'oooh,' sound was made as they escaped my grasp.

Mark taunted me, 'come on, it'll be New Year when you get us.' Everyone laughed at his joke.

I stopped and listened. Someone was nearby and I was going to catch them this time. I accelerated forward towards the movement and just as I did, I tripped. Something had caught my foot causing me to tumble and, in a natural defence, I held out my hands to break my fall. The impact caused my head to follow and bang the ground hard.

My head was throbbing and feeling wet, the palms of my hands were grazed and beginning to sting. I tugged on the scarf, freeing my tear-filled eyes and I heard laughter.

Mark was laughing, 'she can't even play the game.'

'That was *mean*,' Stanley said, 'you tripped her, I saw you do it.'

'Yeah, what you going to do?'

Mark towered over Stanley, and Stanley backed down, knowing he stood no chance in a fight against Mark. They were an unusual match for friends. Mark was filled with aggression; he liked to battle and looked for conflict, playful or not, and gained great satisfaction from winning. Stanley, however, had a gentler nature.

May found a handkerchief in her pocket and pressed it firmly against my head. A ring of blood stained the white cloth when she pulled it away. Bert, on seeing this, charged towards Mark. He rarely lost his temper, normally he was calm and in control, but seeing my injury and being in the constant front line of Mark's bullying, caused something to snap.

'You hurt my sister,' he yelled, punching Mark hard in the ribs. The boys rolled about on the floor, dirtying their clothes on the wet ground.

'Say sorry to Betsy,' Bert demanded getting Mark in a headlock.

'It was a joke,' Mark managed to splutter out.

'Say it,' Bert squeezed him tighter.

'Sorry.'

'To whom?'

'Sorry, Betsy.'

Mrs Irving came to the front door at the right time and called us in for dinner, diffusing the rising tension between us all. She was farther up the street and didn't notice Bert and Mark were fighting. They were quick to break away from one another and rise to their feet, but their cold stare remained much longer.

'You're mean,' Beatrice said to her brother as we headed to their house, 'you deserved that.'

'He's a bully,' Stanley said to me when we reached Mr and Mrs Irving's house, 'picks on anyone smaller than him.'

We said goodbye to Stanley and made our way into the house, feeling let down by how the games had turned out. Mrs Irving was busy serving dinner and Mother was looking cosy sat by the roaring fire. She was too engrossed in conversation with Mr Irving to notice the cut on my head, or the blood that trickled down. Mrs Irving responded immediately to my wound and stopped the bleeding. When she asked how it happened, we just said that I had fallen rather than telling tales.

However, Bert and Mark failed to keep the tension between them shielded from the attention of the adults, as they stared sharply at one another throughout the meal. It was difficult to separate them as the space was limited. The grown-ups were sat at the table and we were huddled together on the floor, the boys were sat opposite each other with crossed legs, and their knees almost touching. Rude and offensive comments were batted back and forth to one another, until Mrs Irving intervened with a sharp 'stop it now!' which was enough for them to end their quarrels.

Mother and Mr Irving were not distracted by the squabbling of the boys and they continued to talk quietly while Mrs Irving sat looking distressed. I thought the sadness was due to Bert and Mark, and I brought it to May's attention, 'they need to stop it, Mrs Irving looks upset.'

May didn't respond, she studied everyone, and her face appeared troubled by something I could not see, my immaturity against me.

Aside from Bert and Mark at war with one another; the meal was delicious. We had chicken and I savoured every mouthful. Mr Irving kept his own chickens in the garden, he had six, which gave him a good supply of eggs and, this one time, a good meal.

He worked as a cobbler and owned his own shop in town. A business that once belonged to his father and would one day be passed down to Mark.

'I must apologise for the small feast,' Mrs Irving said, 'I had only prepared food for four.'

I looked at May feeling confused, remembering what Mr Irving had said about the extra food Mrs Irving had cooked in the hope we would join them. May raised her eyebrows, she was thinking the same too.

'I'm starving with half a plate,' Mark grumbled.

May looked at Mother in a plea for her to say something to assure Mrs Irving and show her gratitude, but Mother didn't speak. 'Thank you, Mrs Irving,' May soon said on Mother's behalf, 'we appreciate it.'

'It's all right, dear,' she collected our plates, her voice sounded shaky.

Mrs Irving brought over the Christmas pudding, 'thank you, Mrs Colborne, for the pudding and mince pies,' she said and then addressed her husband, 'dear, would you like to do the honours?'

Mr Irving caught a flame from the fire and placed it over the pudding, which glowed a bright blue.

'I hope there's a lucky shilling in here,' Mrs Irving smiled weakly as she sliced into the pudding.

The room was getting darker. Mrs Irving turned on the oil lamps, filling areas of the room with warm yellow light. The corners of the room were still dark and shadows fell where the light failed to reach. The brightest light came from the fire, the flames flickered and danced merrily as we tucked into the Christmas pudding. I ate mine slowly, enjoying the spices and fruit in each mouthful, I could smell the richness of the pudding, and it satisfied my stomach.

It was May who found the shilling, she held it in her hand, closed her eyes and thought for a moment. Mr Irving noticed she was the lucky one and raised his glass to her, 'well done, May, you must keep that safe,' and then said to my mother, 'we have a lucky woman there.' With a hopeful smile, she tucked the coin safely away inside her petticoat.

Mrs Irving stood up from the table and busily started clearing pots.

We stayed up late that night and went home with a tipsy mother who was singing Christmas carols loudly and cheerfully all the way. We were happy too, we'd had a heartfelt warm Christmas after all, restoring our Christmas spirit.

Chapter Three

When Mother flung herself down on the chair in Father's spot by the fire, she sang quietly in a jumbled-up murmur and quickly drifted into a deep sleep. We left her there snoring next to a dead fire, with her coat and shoes still on.

'Come on,' May beckoned us to bed, after ensuring Mother was safe downstairs.

'Will she be all right?' Frank asked.

'She'll be fine,' May promised.

We tried not to laugh when Mother's loud snore caused us to jump as we climbed the stairs.

'I'm not sleepy,' Frank said.

'Me neither,' Bert agreed.

I shook my head.

'All right,' May said, and we all climbed into the same bed, snuggling up under the blankets to keep each other warm, and we talked for what felt like most of the night. We reminisced about the happy memories we had, but mostly we spoke about Father.

'Mother forgot Christmas,' I said, after all it was still playing on my mind.

'I know,' May said.

'We would have gone to Aunt Lily's for dinner,' Bert added, 'if Father was still here.'

'I miss Father and I miss Aunty Lily; I want to see her.' I was fighting back the tears as I spoke.

'Why don't we go and see her tomorrow?' Bert suggested.

Frank and I sat up with excitement, almost jumping on the bed at his wonderful suggestion.

'Mother won't let us,' May dismissed the idea.

The room fell silent. May was right, Mother would be furious if we went there, she disliked Aunt Lily, but we didn't know why; she wouldn't give a reason for it. We thought it was due to Father's fondness for his sister. In the past, Mother had grumbled at Father over the closeness of his relationship with Aunt Lily. Mother would raise her voice, accusing him of preferring his sister over her and the children. He never rose to her accusations; he just laughed at her foolishness and reassured her. Father wasn't a man to lose his temper.

We didn't believe Mother. Father's visits to Aunt Lily always involved my brothers, sister and me. Sometimes Mother would attend, but more often than not, she made excuses that there was too much work to do around the house. If anything, she isolated herself.

May and Bert continued to talk in a whisper, their voices fading as my eyes grew heavy, and I succumbed to my tiredness.

I woke the following morning to Bert frantically shaking me with one hand while in the other he held a candle in front of my face.

'Betsy,' he said, 'wake up.'

I slowly came around; my eyes were heavy and I was barely able to open them fully. I yawned, looking around the still dark room, the candle doing little to add anything other than a dim, flicker of light.

Once my sight adjusted to my sudden awakening, I noticed Bert was fully dressed.

'Quickly,' he said, 'get your clothes on.'

I was used to following instructions, it came from being the youngest – everyone ordered me about – and, without questioning, I slipped out of bed into the bitter cold room.

I was quick to dress in my day-to-day clothes that were waiting for me at the bottom of the bed, hearing the constant, 'quickly, come on,' from Bert wanting me to move faster.

'Now be quiet,' Bert said, as we climbed down the stairs into the living room.

Where we had left Mother the night before, she was no longer there. Frank waved a finger in the direction of her bedroom, signalling where she was. He was stood by the door with his coat and boots on, May by his side dressed in her outdoor clothing.

Bert slipped into his boots and coat, while May helped me into mine.

'Sshh!' she whispered, tying a scarf around my neck and pulling a woolly hat over my head, 'it's cold out there, we must wrap up warm.'

She glared at the boys; her words aimed at them. We were very quiet, the boys scurried around like mice, gathering their woollies, taking notice of their older sister for the first time.

We crept outside, quietly closing the door behind us and stepping out into the freezing cold. The icy air hit our faces, and the few inches of snow that had fallen during the night chilled our feet. We moved quickly through the dark, cold morning; the white powdered snow crunched beneath our steps.

'Where are we going?' I eagerly asked.

'To Aunt Lily's,' May said, 'we have to move quickly, it's cold.'

We still whispered until we were in the centre of town, afraid Mother could hear us, or worse, she was following. The journey seemed longer with the temperature so low and the deep snow slowed down our strides. Running was difficult and pointless, but we enjoyed every footprint we made. You could hear the excitement in our voices as we laughed, a mixture of defying our mother and reuniting with our aunt.

May held my hand, aiding me when we trudged through the deeper snow. In parts, the white powder was so deep it rose above my boots and flakes crept inside, finding their way to my feet. I soon became numb to the coldness that encased my toes and the squelching pools of water that had formed around my feet.

Frank and Bert attempted to run ahead, their strides exaggerated as they leapt over the snow and sunk into their next step. In shallower parts, they scooped up round white balls and launched them at one another. May and I joined in, and by the time we reached Aunt Lily's house, we were all covered in splattered white patches.

Aunt Lily lived at the other end of our town on the north side, and to me, it was at the other end of the world. Their house was situated on the outskirts; it was on the last street, and the very end building, next to acres and acres of fields. Daylight was just breaking through when we arrived and we paused on the street, gazing towards the front door.

May was first to move, she walked up to the door and knocked loudly.

Matthew looked surprised when he opened the door to us a few seconds later. For a moment, he didn't speak, and his eyes flickered across us all, before looking down the street, as though he was looking for our mother.

When he did speak, he smiled dearly, 'my goodness, children, come in,' and called out into the house, 'Lily, we have visitors.'

We stepped into the sitting room, wiping our feet on the doormat as we entered and leaving behind bundles of snow as it broke away from our boots. The fire was lit and the heat spilled across the room, embracing us from the cold. I inhaled the familiar smell of burning coal that filled my nostrils with such comfort.

They had a large comfy chair and a settee, both decorated with cushions. There were pictures hanging on the walls and furniture displaying little figurines behind glass doors. I wanted to open the doors and examine each little delicate ornament, painted in beautiful colours and such detail, but my inner self said in my mother's voice 'look, don't touch'.

Through the doorway at the back of the room was the kitchen. The rooms were much bigger and had higher ceilings than our house. The windows in the property were larger than the dingy ones we usually looked out from, making the rooms seem even brighter. Even the stairs that ran off the kitchen were built differently, they were a full flight of stairs with steps; wide and secure, safe for anyone to use and complete with a handrail. Upstairs there were two bedrooms, the smaller of the two Aunt Lily longed to be occupied by a child, but it was not meant to be.

The house previously belonged to Matthew's parents, until his father died earlier that year and, on his death, Matthew inherited the family business and the family home. He owned a grocery store in town that had been in his family since 1863. In the beginning the shop sold only basic goods, but over the years, as things became more available, they were able to sell a much wider range of supplies.

Aunt Lily approached from the kitchen and let out a scream of joy when she realised we were there. She collected our wet coats and boots, urging us to sit by the fire, 'My darlings,' she said, 'you must be freezing, look at you all. We've just had breakfast, are you hungry? I'll make us tea.'

The four of us squeezed onto the settee, absorbing the heat from the fire and defrosting quickly. Matthew sat in his chair, his legs stretched out, his feet crossed as he puffed away on his pipe, eager to know how we celebrated our Christmas day. We bombarded Matthew with different moments of the day and much of the conversation came out as babble, as we all spoke at the same time.

Aunt Lily soon returned with tea and mince pies, which she placed on the table in front of us, and we politely waited for her consent.

'Help yourself,' she said, and we did – four hands diving at the plate quickly, grabbing a mince pie and within several mouthfuls they were gone.

'Does your mother know you are here?' Matthew asked.

'No.' Frank was honest. He was like our father who had taught him to always be an honest man.

'Now, children,' Aunt Lily said, softly, 'I have to say, I am disappointed in you. May – you should know better. That was naughty of you to run off without telling your mother.

Just think how worried she will be when she wakes up and realises you are not home.'

Bert laughed at that statement, and May nudged him to stop it.

'But,' Aunt Lily said, and her face softened to a warm smile, 'I can't send you home on an empty stomach; it is Christmas after all.'

'And,' Matthew clapped his hands, 'it's snowing, I think our yard needs a snowman.'

'Yes,' my face lit up.

'Matthew,' Aunt Lily said, 'they've just come in from the cold.'

We laughed and finished our tea and took another mince pie, feeling cosy and relaxed in their welcoming home.

Afterwards, Matthew took us into the yard. It was small, with a coal shed, the toilet and a washing line hanging across. There was a gate leading to a cobbled passageway which opened onto the fields.

'Plenty of snow in the fields,' he said, opening the gate, urging us to step forth onto the pristinely clean, white blanket of snow that stretched for miles, disappearing into the hills in the distance.

I was first to run through the snow, which was like a fallen cloud that rose above my ankles, untouched and perfectly crisp, glistening like tiny crystals in the sun. I fell on my back, waving my arms and legs up and down, imprinting four snow angels on the ground.

'It's us,' I cried, feeling proud as I stood up and admired my creation.

'That's good, Betsy,' Matthew patted me on the back.

Bert and Frank worked together to roll out a huge ball for the body, leaving a track of green flattened grass behind. When it became too big, Matthew helped push it through into the yard. May and I rolled out a smaller ball for the head. Matthew very carefully lifted the large snowball and placed it on top of the snowman's body.

'Would you look at that,' Aunt Lily said from the doorway,

her arms wrapped around her chest, pulling her shawl across in an attempt to keep warm.

Frank grabbed some coal from the coal shed for the eyes, nose and mouth.

'He's perfect,' I said, standing next to this man of snow, much taller than me.

We stayed at Aunt Lily's until mid-afternoon and she made us sandwiches with left-over meat from Christmas day. We left unwillingly, when the time had come to return home, but Aunt Lily insisted with regret, 'You must make a move, you must get home before it's too cold and the temperature drops even more. Matthew will walk you home.'

'We'll be all right, Aunt Lily,' May said.

'No,' Matthew insisted. 'I will walk you home.'

Matthew walked quickly and we had to jog to keep up with his long stride. The snow had flattened over the course of the day, from the many people that had passed over it. Although still deep in areas, we were able to move through the man-made trail much quicker than we did in the morning.

He told us a few stories on the walk back, we were too out of breath to ask questions and so we listened. Unfortunately, it made the journey end much sooner than we wanted and before long we were standing at the end of our street.

Matthew stood on the corner and waited for us to enter our home safely. Our steps slowed down completely and when we reached the door we delayed entering. We turned to wave goodbye to Matthew and his figure at the end of the street waved back to us.

Bert was the brave one. He opened the door first to an empty living room. Mother could not be seen, but to our surprise, the fire was burning. Laughter came from Mother's bedroom and seconds later she emerged from the room, adjusting her hair and smiling, until she saw us when her face then transformed into the cold, heartless expression we had grown used too.

'Where have you been?' She charged towards us. She looked angry, but she kept her anger under control through clenched fists and gritted teeth.

Before any of us could answer, Mr Irving appeared in the bedroom doorway. On realising we were home, his face grew more serious, he let out a cough and headed over to the door.

'Well,' he paused and coughed again, 'the draft in your window is fixed, Mrs Colborne. Let me know if you need anything else.'

'Thank you, Mr Irving,' she said, 'and I will.'

She touched his arm and with a contented smile on his face, he grabbed his coat and hat. They were on Father's peg covering Father's coat. It was only the day before when Mother was affected by the touch of it.

Father's cap had fallen on the floor and had been left there with the dirt brought in from the outside. Frank seized the cap and placed it gently back in its rightful place.

A cloud of anger hung over Bert's head. It was black, dark, full and ready to let out the downpour of emotion that was building up inside him. Bert managed to keep it under control. He breathed deeply, his nostrils flaring as his eyes squinted, like daggers, at the back of Mr Irving's head as he left through the door.

As soon as the footsteps faded away outside, Mother grabbed May harshly by the arm and with her other hand grabbed the wooden rolling pin off the table. With each word she uttered, she thrashed May hard. With each thrash, May screamed. With each scream, we flinched. Mother said, 'Don't you ever go out again without telling me. Where have you been? *Where have you been?*'

May was almost on the floor by the time her last word was spoken; bruised, beaten and barely able to stand. Tears streamed down her face and she glanced up at Bert. Perhaps she looked to him for help, or to beg him to take Frank and me away. She refused to make eye contact with us. Maybe she was unable to look at us; too devastated that we should see her being beaten.

I could taste my salty tears in my mouth. I could not bring myself to look away. I needed to see. I needed to know that May was all right.

'Aunt Lily's!' Frank blurted out, wanting to end the beating.

'Lily's?' Mother stopped, her arm raised in the air, she was looking down at May. May curled her body into a ball, her arms protecting her head and hidden face. Everything was silent for a few seconds and we were frozen, like Greek statues; a distressing moment carved to tell a tragedy.

Mother slowly turned her head round. She released the rolling pin and it fell to the floor with a clonk, before rolling away. With the back of her hand, she went to smack us all across the face, Frank first and then me. She slapped Bert last and hardest, knocking his face to the side.

He looked back at her. Hate filled his eyes and he expelled his anger, shoving her hard as he yelled, 'don't you *ever* hit May or Betsy, or Frank, or me again. If Father was still alive you would have got more than that.'

Mother stumbled back against the wall and she banged her head on the corner of a shelf. The incident had startled her. She looked flabbergasted by Bert's blow and it took her a moment to register what had happened.

'No Bert,' she eventually said, 'if your father was still alive, he would be disappointed. Your father never laid a finger on me and to see his son push me like you just did, he would have whipped you hard.'

I was frightened. I reached for Frank's hand and I could feel his trembling fingers wrap around mine.

When Mother spoke again, my insides jerked with the sound of her voice and her words hammered hard in my head. With each word she spoke, my whole insides rattled with fear. 'Get upstairs now! Don't come down again until the morning.'

Frank and Bert helped May to stand. Her body was arched, she took quick short breaths and moved with difficulty as she began to climb the stairs.

'Not you, Bert,' Mother ordered.

Bert released his hold on May. He faced Mother and remained where he was, his body still, and his fists clenched. He showed no fear.

May managed to climb the stairs, Frank stayed close behind her ensuring she reached the top safely. Being the last to follow, I glanced back to see Mother open a drawer and pull out a belt. I feared for Bert.

'I'm going to teach you a lesson,' she said, wrapping the belt around her hand. He didn't flinch as she approached him. 'How dare you disrespect me. I am your mother.'

I reached the top step and laid flat on the floor, peering down. Frank grabbed me, he dragged me into the room and closed the door. 'No Betsy, do you want to get a belting as well. You will if she sees you.'

We waited in our bedroom. May didn't speak or make eye contact with us. She lay down on the bed, with her back towards us and sobbed into the pillow. I sat at the foot of our bed and placed a comforting hand on her leg; I felt useless, unsure of what to do. Frank stood by the bedroom door, his ear pressed against it and he listened.

We all heard the sound of whipping from downstairs, and in my head, I counted ten before they stopped, but we didn't hear Bert react. He didn't cry. He didn't scream. He didn't groan. There was only the sound of his footsteps as he climbed the steps and went into his bedroom.

We didn't speak about that part of the afternoon again. That day ended when we waved goodbye to Matthew.

The creepy stories of the Headless Widow and Revengeful Baron had stopped. Whether it reminded Bert and Frank of the night Father died, or whether we all realised that we were now living in our own creepy story, we knew we needed each other. We had to look out for one another now.

Chapter Four

The next months passed by miserably. The snow soon melted and then it was just cold; cold and wet; cold and icy; cold and windy. Spring finally came and the flowers started to bloom, the birds began to sing, the days were getting longer and warmer, and yet our house remained cold.

Mother watched us closely. We had to come home straight away from school, and she watched the clock knowing how long the journey should take. If we went over the expected time home, out came the belt. We made sure we were never late home.

Once we had finished our evening meal we were banished to our room, regardless of the lighter nights and the sound of the other children playing on the street outside. I would listen to the sounds of laughter and play my own game to see if I could guess who the voices belonged to. It was easy to detect Beatrice's squeals, Mark's dictating tone and Stanley's voice, but other children I was unsure about. I often felt isolated as I was no longer part of their fun.

Mother had regular weekly visits from Mr Irving; he was always willing to assist on jobs *only a man can do*. These jobs were often carried out in the evening when we were forbidden to come downstairs. He would stay late into the night and we were usually asleep by the time he left. In the mornings there was no change to the house and no noticeable repair work had been done.

At weekends, Mother sent May and me into town with a shopping list, allowing thirty minutes for us to fulfil her request and it was a race against time. Most of the items were found in Matthew's shop and he was always quick to help us.

Matthew insisted on waiving payments for Mother, regardless of her ungratefulness, 'tell your mother she can pay up, when she can.'

It was when three months had passed and Mother had not paid a single shilling, that Matthew's generosity dwindled off. With regret he had to say 'no, tell your mother, until I see payments made, I am afraid I can't supply her with this food. She has not made an attempt to clear any of her bills since Christmas.'

After Matthew refused the order, that evening Aunt Lily called by the house with a basket full of essentials. She also brought with her a gift for me, knowing the following day was my seventh birthday. Even with her offerings, Mother still refused to let her past the threshold.

May was a spectator, secretly watching it all from the top of the stairs to report back to us later. She witnessed Aunt Lily tell Mother, 'I have spoken to Matthew and we will cover your bill up to the end of March. That leaves you with one week outstanding.'

Mother didn't say thank you, she removed the contents from the basket and placed them on the table in silence as Aunt Lily stood in the doorway and watched her. Mother handed the basket back along with my present.

'No, thank you,' she said.

'Florence, please, she's my niece,' Aunt Lily begged, 'and it's her birthday. Will you not let me see my nieces and nephews?'

'They're in bed.'

'Now? It's early, it's sunny. Why are they not outside with their friends?'

'I'll accept your advice when *you* are a mother, Lily.'

May could tell that the words struck Aunt Lily hard. She looked hurt and stared at the ground, realising her defeat against our mother. May noticed something unusual happen as Aunt Lily lifted her head, her eyes lingered on the middle of Mother's body. She focused on the area for a while, her expression changed from confusion, to a look of disgust and she shook her head, her mouth opened ready to speak.

'Goodbye Lily,' Mother quickly said, closing the door on Aunt Lily before anything else was said.

I woke up the next day to my birthday and another celebration Mother failed to acknowledge. The others gave me a handmade card they had worked on together and on our doorstep, I found some coins wrapped in a handkerchief from Aunt Lily, with a note attached wishing me a happy day, followed by all her love.

I sneaked to their shop after school, running as fast as I could, knowing if I kept to a good speed, I would be home before Mother realised I was late. I bought some chocolate and told Matthew to pass my thanks on to Aunt Lily. That evening in the bedroom after tea, I shared the delicious block of dark, brown chocolate with my siblings. We had several pieces each, allowing it to slowly melt in our mouths; the taste so heavenly. It had been a long time since we last tasted such luxury.

On Monday morning, we were fastening our shoes for school, when Mother walked in from her bedroom. She was dressed in her Sunday best and her hair was tied back neatly.

'Bert, Frank, you're not going to school today,' she spoke firmly to my brothers.

We stopped what we were doing and looked at one another, surprised by her statement. Mother ignored our stares and began to fuss around the kitchen, making sure everything was spotless.

'Why, Mother?' Bert asked.

'Don't question me,' she barked, 'you are coming with me. May, Betsy, you should get going or you'll be late.'

May helped me finish tying my shoes and whispered, 'come on.' As she pulled me to my feet, I glanced at my brothers and smiled before leaving. They did not move, but stood like soldiers, waiting for their next command. We closed the door on them and carried on with our normal Monday school morning.

It was raining – a typical downpour of April showers – and we ran to school, darting and jumping over puddles. May ran ahead. She was much faster than me, and I struggled to keep up. We were joined or overtaken by other children making their way to school. The sound of wooden clogs and metal soles clanking on the cobbles, and the merry scream of laughter from a herd of children, echoed throughout the street.

I was so out of breath and had a stitch from trying to keep up with May. I turned onto the street and could see the unwelcoming gates of the school.

A hand yanked my arm and spun me around. It was Mark and he looked annoyed. Beatrice and another girl were at his side. The other girl, Katy, I recognised from Mark's class; she was tall and towered over me. He pushed me hard and I fell against the wall of the corner house. I looked around, but all the other children seemed to have vanished into the school and May was amongst them, unaware of my incident.

Mark's shove was forceful and he held me in position with his arms. Katy's face was close to mine, her warm breath blew in my face and in my mind, I saw a fierce dragon breathing fire.

'What's your mother doing?' he asked. 'Mum is crying because of that whore.'

'Whore?' I didn't understand.

'My mum says it too,' Katy poked in, 'she calls her a whore too, and that's not good.'

'Since Christmas when you beggars stole our dinner.'

'We didn't,' I said, 'your –'

He squeezed my cheeks together hard with one hand, forcing my mouth to open, and at the same time pressed my head against the wall. It hurt. I felt trapped and suffocated. As much as I tried not to, I began to cry. I so desperately wanted to be brave, but their three faces frightened me.

'Oh look, she's crying!' Mark mocked me, 'and you haven't got your brother to help you this time!' Still grabbing my face, he pulled my head away from the wall and slammed it back again, hard. The impact of my head thudding against the brick caused my vision to blur. He gave me no chance to catch my breath as he shoved my head back against the wall for a second time.

'Don't Mark,' Beatrice pleaded. She was beginning to look worried and looked around anxiously in case anyone was coming.

'I'm talking,' he said, as he spat in my face. I felt queasy from the disgusting spray that landed in my eye, mixed with my own tears and then trickled down my cheeks.

'Why's my dad always at your house?' Mark asked. 'Your dad's dead and now you want ours?'

I tried to shake my head, but his firm hold prevented me from moving.

'That's what my mum thinks,' Katy added, finger flicking my temple hard. 'My mum says your mum needs to get her own man and she needs a good beating.'

'You need kicking out on the street, my mum says,' Beatrice said, she did not sound convincing as she looked about her warily and backed away from me.

They continued to taunt me with the harsh words they had heard their mother say about my family. Katy kicked me hard in the shin, then Mark dragged me by my hair and swung me around like an axe. I fell to the ground and landed face down in a muddy puddle, the water splashed into my mouth and I could taste the dirt on my lips. My dress, socks, knees and hands were muddy, and the plaits May braided that morning had come undone.

The three of them ran off laughing, and I watched on my hands and knees as they disappeared up the school path. I was shaken, terrified and panting. The blood was rushing around my body and everywhere was throbbing. I froze when I heard the sound of approaching footsteps but to my relief, it was a boy dashing to school before the bell.

I pulled myself up and looked down at my dirty clothes.

My knee was grazed and speckles of blood had stained the hem of my dress. As I examined it farther, the rain splashed against the cut, causing watery red streaks to dribble down my leg and stain the top of my white socks. The stinging was minor compared to the throbbing at the back of my head; even the lightest of touches made the pain explode.

As the boy passed, he looked behind at me and when I noticed Stanley's friendly face, I could no longer withhold my tears.

'Betsy, what happened to you?' he asked.

I didn't tell him who did it, that was not something you did – tell on someone else – you just had to fight your own battles and get over it.

We approached the school gates together and Mr Addison, the headmaster, was stood in the doorway holding the bell in his hand. His sharp eyes staring at us through thin slits, the wrinkles on his forehead and around his eyes were apparent. His lips were pressed tightly together, in a thin straight line in the middle of his grey bushy beard. His nostrils broadened as he breathed deeply, he looked as if he was about to explode when he saw us. As we drew nearer to him he appeared to grow, like a giant, and our footsteps slowed down. I wanted the earth to open and swallow me up, or a huge bird to fly down and pick me up, or the rain to cause a waterfall and wash me away.

'You are late!' Mr Addison's deep voice bellowed loud, like the bells that rang out in a church. His eyes lowered and when he caught sight of my poor state, his voice sounded less harsh, 'what happened here, Miss Colborne?'

'I... I...' my mouth opened. I struggled to speak, not knowing how to answer the question. If I told the truth Mark would find himself in trouble and come after me again. If I lied, I'd get into trouble and my mother might find out.

'I fell over,' I eventually lied.

'You fell over?' He questioned me with a deep frown over his eyes and I knew he didn't believe me. 'Must have been quite a fall, to mess up your hair like that.'

'Yes, Mr Addison.'

'What really happened, Mr Rhodes?' He glanced at Stanley.

'I don't know, Mr Addison, I was not there.'

'Very well,' Mr Addison let out a long sigh, and he paused. 'As neither of you are going to tell me the truth, I will have to treat you as liars. We don't tolerate liars in this school and we don't tolerate poor punctuality.'

'Sorry, Mr Addison,' we spoke in unison.

He refused to accept our apologies and we were sent to his office to await our punishment. When he eventually entered, he reached for his cane that rested against the wall of his small office and demanded Stanley's left hand.

'Mr Rhodes, you said to me that you were not there when Miss Colborne fell, which means you came after the incident?'

'Yes, Mr Addison.'

'Which tells me you were already running late?'

'Yes, Mr Addison.'

Stanley's hand was outstretched and his palm exposed, waiting to receive the ten whips Mr Addison had deemed appropriate for his poor punctuality.

I flinched with each sound the cane made; the whistling when it swung through the air and the cracking sound it made when it hit the flesh. Yet Stanley was brave; he concealed the pain by biting down on his back teeth, and his eyes blinked shut when the cane met his skin.

Stanley had lost his father during the war and his older brother, Rupert, took the role as man of the house, providing for their mother. He was eighteen and worked hard at the flax mill for a small wage. Stanley's clothes were worn, with many darned repairs to the torn material that stretched over his body. His trousers sat above his ankles and the holes in his shoes were stuffed with brown paper to prevent the rain from seeping through.

I liked how he always smelt of soap, he was spotless, from his brushed hair to his trimmed fingernails. There was never any dirt on his face, his teeth were white and his clothes were clean. I knew at home he was looked after and very much loved.

My hand was shaking, held out ready for Mr Addison as he stood before me. I held my breath, waiting; then felt the first sting of the cane as it thrashed down. To my surprise, no more followed and I was grateful to have received only that one. It did, however, leave me with an intense burning pain that didn't seem to ease, and I was unable to close my hand without triggering more discomfort. A thin red band was shaped across my palm, but that was nothing compared to Stanley's; his skin was near to breaking, with pinpricks of blood rising near the surface.

At dinner time the rain had eased off and I waited on a bench in the playground for May to join me so we could go home together. Unfortunately, Mark was there. He had collected loose stones from the ground and entertained himself by using me as a target, encouraging a few of his friends to join in. I was struck against my legs and my body, but I tried not to show the humiliation and the pain I felt inside.

I kept my head down, waiting for them to stop and telling myself this was only happening because Bert was not in school. Tomorrow would be a better day.

Stanley was watching from a distance. He knew better than to stand up against Mark, and he waited in the shadows with his back against the wall, his hand tucked inside his pockets. I didn't notice him until he emerged from his hiding place once Mark had left.

'How is your hand?' Stanley asked.

As he sat down beside me, he unravelled a handkerchief, and inside was a thick slice of bread and a wedge of cheese. He noticed I had nothing to eat and tore his bread in half, offering me one of the halves.

I shook my head gratefully, 'I'm not taking your food and I am waiting for May.'

'Will you eat when you get home?'

I ignored his question, 'do you not go home at dinner?'

'Not on a Monday, my mum is never home,' he replied, dropping the bread in my hand, 'I'm not eating if you're not. Besides, May must have gone, I was the last one out.'

'That was strange, May wouldn't go home without me,' and as I troubled myself with possible reasons, he passed me some cheese. We sat in silence and he shared with me the small lunch he had brought into school.

'Where are Bert and Frank?' he asked, when we had finished.

I shrugged, 'our mother has taken them somewhere.'

'A day off school, can't be too bad.' Stanley was smiling, but then the smirk faded, 'it was Mark that made you late, wasn't it? He's been boastful all morning.'

I felt the pressure from Stanley's long stare and I gave in to his curiosity, as I admitted, 'He's angry at my mother. She has done something to upset his family.' There was one word that had been playing on my mind and I asked, 'What's a whore?'

'It's...' he struggled to answer me.

'Is my mother a whore?'

'I don't know. It's not nice I know that much and not a word you should be saying, not unless you want another caning to match your other hand.'

Stanley turned slightly on the bench and looked at me, his smile was warm and friendly. 'My mum always says to me, pay no attention to what you hear, it's what you see that matters.'

I didn't understand what he meant at the time. It was difficult for a seven-year-old to fully comprehend, but I smiled and nodded, pretending I knew, knowing one day I may remember these words and understand. There was one thing I was certain of; he was offering me words of comfort.

At last, it was the end of school. The rain began to fall again as I waited for May. I was so relieved when she appeared this time, and I questioned her over her absence at dinner, bombarding her about my awful encounter in the morning, while I waved my hand underneath her nose.

'Oh, Betsy,' was the first thing she said and she held me tightly, 'I'm so sorry I wasn't there.'

She showed me her hand, marked with a thicker and darker red band, 'Bert and Frank weren't in school and I was punished for it. Apparently, it was a lie when I told Mr Addison the truth and he thought I spoke back to him.'

May was such an obedient girl, who had survived most of her school life without receiving the cane. She would have been ashamed. The punishment was uncalled for and unfair; she had done nothing wrong.

When we got home, the house was empty and Mother arrived an hour later. As soon as she passed the threshold, she threw a loaf of bread on the table and closed the door behind her. We waited for Bert and Frank to follow behind, but they didn't.

'Dinner,' she said, waving her arm at the discarded loaf. We were too frightened to ask about the whereabouts of our brothers.

May sliced the bread, offering to Mother first, when she caught sight of the cane mark on her hand. She grabbed May's wrist, the impact caused her to release the plate and it smashed into several pieces when it hit the floor. My stomach yearned for the food, and it took me all of my strength to stop me falling to my knees and salvaging the bread from the ruins.

My attention was diverted with the sound of Mother's hand smacking against the side of May's face. Fearing that I was in for the same discipline, I folded my arms and tucked my hands inside, hiding my damaged palm.

The rest of the week passed, yet Bert and Frank didn't return, and Mother didn't mention them until the Friday afternoon when we returned home from school. Aunt Lily was stood at the front door, carrying a large bundle tied in a cotton sheet. We approached with caution, trying to catch what they were arguing about. Aunt Lily looked annoyed and her voice was stern.

'How could you do this, Florence?' She said, 'You *disgust* me. If Alfred was still alive...'

'To hell with Alfred, it's because of him, I am here.'

'They're *your* children.'

'I can't stand to look at them without seeing him. I see him all the time.'

Aunt Lily caught sight of us and she quickly wiped away her tears, a second too late – we had already seen.

'Hello, darlings,' she said, dropping the bundle and tightly wrapped her arms around us both.

'Aunt Lily, what is it?' May asked.

'Are you going to tell them?' Aunt Lily looked at Mother.

Mother shook her head and with a vindictive grin said, 'welcome to motherhood. You've always wanted a taste of it, well here's your chance.'

The intentions behind Mother's cruel words succeeded and Aunt Lily's face changed. Her lips pressed together and she shook her head slowly as her eyes laid transfixed on the woman from whose mouth the venom poured.

'Right children,' Aunt Lily said, picking the bundle up from the floor, 'say goodbye to your mother, you are coming home with me.'

'What's happened?' May asked.

'How long for?' I asked.

Our questions were left unanswered, while both women glared at one another, neither one breaking their stare.

'Go!' Mother said, 'I don't want you here.'

What was going on? I looked around at the three faces and May looked just as confused as I was. Aunt Lily let out a disapproving sigh and shook her head at Mother. She perhaps preferred a more subtle approach to the delicate situation, not the cold, honest truth Mother had blurted out.

'No need for a goodbye,' Mother said and slammed the door shut.

Before I began to cry, Aunt Lily gently kissed our foreheads and whispered, 'Come on now, let's get you back to my house. It will be your home for a while, until your mother is better.'

'Is she poorly?' I asked.

'Your father's passing has made her unwell... emotionally,' Aunt Lily picked her words carefully. 'Grief can make people behave in different ways. She will be better soon.'

'Then will we go home?' I asked again, not sounding enthusiastic by the possibility.

'Maybe,' Aunt Lily replied with uncertainty. 'Now, I'm sure I have some of those delicious biscuits left at home too.'

We turned away from our house towards the direction of Aunt Lily's. Until we turned around the corner, May struggled to accept what was happening, and several times she glanced back to see if Mother opened the door, or peered through the window. But she didn't.

The walk was slow. May was quiet and Aunt Lily was crying as she held my hand tightly. I wondered why she was so upset. I thought about how much fun we were going to have, I was eager to taste my biscuits, and to enjoy the time living with Aunt Lily and Matthew. It was going to be like an adventure.

I was delighted about staying with them, looking forward to eating some real food and of course, to be nourished with love. May played the role of mother very well, but she too was only a child, and we both needed someone to depend and rely on.

'Will Bert and Frank join us?' I asked, thinking how pleased they would be when they found out.

'Bert and Frank,' she said with difficulty.

'Where are they?' May asked.

'Will they be with us soon?' I followed, suddenly my happy thoughts were slowly fading.

'No, sweetheart,' Aunt Lily said. 'They have gone away.'

'Away, where?' May sounded alarmed.

'To Canada.'

'Where's Canada?' We both asked, only May's voice was more panicky than mine.

'It's many, many miles, over the big ocean. They've gone to a special home.'

'When will they come back?' May asked, her face turning pale and her eyes wide open.

'Can we go to see them?' I asked, with no concept of distance and lack of knowledge to fully comprehend what she was saying.

'You won't be able to see them,' she paused, 'for a long time. A very long time.'

'So, Christmas?' I asked, hopeful, after all it was a long way off, *for me.*

'I don't understand,' May said.

Aunt Lily explained about the child migration scheme adopted by different charities to provide an opportunity for children whose parents could no longer support them or had passed away. Many children over the years had been sent to Canada to work on farms or as domestics, and receive an education, with the promise of a better life. Aunt Lily assured us they would be well looked after and, with paid work, they would learn new skills. The more she spoke, the more she lost the battle to control her crying, and the roundness of her cheeks glistened in the sun from her fallen tears.

'I am sorry children,' she said when she composed herself.

She dropped the bundle on the floor and reached into her pocket for her handkerchief. After she had blown her nose and dried her tears, she crouched down to my level and took both our hands gently in hers.

'I am so, so sorry,' she said, 'I could have helped your mother. I wanted to help her, but she didn't let me. Bert and Frank would have stayed in England, not travelled halfway across the world to a different country, not knowing anyone, feeling frightened and all alone.'

Her face dropped to the floor and I was worried she was going to cry again. I felt awkward seeing her cry, not knowing how to lessen her distress, after all, how supportive was a cuddle from a seven-year-old? Aunt Lily took two deep breaths and raised her head again, her eyes were coated with a fresh layer of wetness and she said, 'My brother's children, I've let Alfred down.'

'No you haven't, Aunt Lily,' May said.

'You have us,' I said.

Aunt Lily nodded, and the sadness lifted slightly from her face as she smiled. May and I were pushed nearer to one another, and she kissed us both on the cheek. Aunt Lily made a promise that she would keep for the rest of her life and as she spoke, I believed every word she said. 'My house, is your house, treat it like home. I promise I will look after you both as though you are my own and things will be fine. Things always work out *in the end*. I know at the time you don't see it, but in the future, you will.'

Matthew was home when we arrived. He had closed the shop earlier than usual, something he didn't do, but knowing Aunt Lily was visiting our mother he was concerned and worried. When we entered the house, he rose from his chair as if an invisible string was attached to him and the door was pulling him to his feet. A mixture of emotions spread across his face as his eyes darted across the three of us: a look of worry, confusion, surprise and relief as Aunt Lily quickly explained everything in as few words as she could manage.

'I am sorry, darling,' he wrapped his arms around her shoulders and she cried in his arms. May and I stood in the doorway. My eyes explored the room, absorbing the familiarity of my surroundings and, strangely, feeling I was already home. Christmas, when we were last there, felt a long time ago; the four of us sitting cosily on the settee facing the warm blaze of the fire. May thought it too; her eyes were transfixed on the same spot, visualising the ghosts of the past, seeing our brothers happy as we ate mince pies and drank tea. Seeing them then and realising now, we may not have a moment like that ever *again*. The four of us may never be together again.

The realisation hit May, and she howled like a tortured wolf with loud cries I hadn't heard before; her voice had reached a pitch I didn't know was possible. She arched her back and shrieked at the settee, her arms stiff, upright in a defence position, and her fists clenched.

Aunt Lily broke away from Matthew, dropped to her knees and pulled May towards her, cradling her tightly, 'it's all right, sweetheart, it's all right, I am here.'

It took a moment for Aunt Lily's touch to reach through to May and she continued with her bellowing. Eventually, she gave in to the affection, calming down as she collapsed onto Aunt Lily's knees. Her sobs sounding quieter and slowly easing off.

Matthew was stood beside me, his arm, like a heavy weight, resting over my shoulders and he spoke softly to me. At first I didn't hear his words. May's behaviour had shocked me, and I stood, aghast, as I again witnessed this type of pain. My eyes were beginning to sting from not blinking.

'May will be all right, it's a lot to take in, darling,' I gradually heard him say.

When May was feeling better, Aunt Lily helped her into a chair and said, 'never underestimate the power of a cup of tea, I'll make us all a brew.' She picked up the bundle, which we discovered Mother had thrown all our belongings into. Aunt Lily carried it through to the kitchen and beckoned Matthew to follow her.

May and I sat together on the chair, and I held her hand, staring at the dead coal fire, just a hole of black dirt and flakes of coal. We could hear Aunt Lily fumbling about in the kitchen as she spoke to Matthew, but not speaking quietly enough for their conversation not to reach our ears.

'Darling,' we heard Matthew say, 'you don't have to say a thing. They can stay here for as long as they like, forever, if that's what you want.'

'Thank you, love.'

'So, the rumours are true?'

'What did I tell you?' Aunt Lily said, 'I said she's expecting, I knew it. She must have been... when his body was still warm in the ground.'

'And the father?'

'Heaven knows.'

'There've been a few unpleasant accusations made about her recently, Lily, people are talking about her, she's got herself a bad reputation now.'

'She's leaving town.'

'Will she come back for the girls?'

'I don't know. She told me to take them; like they were old rags, poor girls, I couldn't bear the thought of those two being sent away, like their brothers.'

'I know darling, you love them so much.'

'What can we do, Matthew? About Bert and Frank? They'll be heading out there by now. She had it planned for months and goodness knows how she got them onto the ship. She didn't tell them, she just sent them away. The poor boys must be so confused and frightened.'

'Darling, it's out of our hands now.'

'What if they are separated?'

'Lily, darling, we have the girls for now; your priority is them. One day, the boys will come home; they are strong boys, they are like their father, remember that.'

May understood the conversation better than I did and it troubled her. I just wondered what Mother was expecting and the rest flew over my head, as I patiently waited for my drink.

Aunt Lily brought the tea through and the comfort of the warm drink flowed down our throats and settled in our stomachs. True to her words, the drink seemed to have healing powers and we did feel better afterwards.

Later in the evening, Matthew told us stories, and I thought of my brothers and how much I missed them. I missed their ghost stories; I missed the fright I felt from the Headless Widow and Revengeful Baron. I missed the fairies I imagined who brightened my day, and the unicorn that took me to the Secret Wood where they all lived.

I curled up on the floor by Matthew's feet on the soft, fluffy rug, and my fingers fiddled with the wool as he told the story of Gulliver and his adventures in Lilliput. Hearing his deep voice I thought of Father. If I closed my eyes, I could have been back at home, close to him with May, Bert and Frank nearby listening too, and Mother clattering pots at the table in the background. I longed for the past and I began to cry. I tried not to make a sound and my tears flowed in secret, dripping onto the rug.

I kept my eyes shut to prevent further flow and I fell into a deep sleep. I woke up with a start. I had seen my brothers; we were playing, we were fighting, we had argued and, best of all, we had laughed. Father was there too and it was seeing his face that woke me abruptly from my wistful dream.

Matthew must have carried me to bed in the evening and it took a few seconds to adjust to my new surroundings. I was facing the wall, the covers pulled over me and I shuffled round to see May fast asleep by my side. The sun was beginning to rise outside and the room was filled with the light of a new day. I snuggled up to my sister feeling safe, warm and content.

'At least I still have you,' my whispers falling on deaf ears, 'don't leave me.'

Part Two

Chapter Five

Spring and summer became my favourite seasons after moving in with Aunt Lily. The stretch of open fields reaching out for miles gave May and I new-found freedom and adventures. It was during our first summer when we first came across the large lake about two miles away, and with each sunny day that was free to us, our hearts were beckoned there.

To reach the lake we had to cross over two fields and join the narrow country road that bends and winds between open grassland, dipping under avenues of tall trees that arch over the top of the road, shading out the sun before curving along the side of the lake.

The lake glistened, like gems, with the reflection of the sun. A stone wall divided the road from the lake, and a border of wildflowers and thistles thickened the divide further. To enter, we climbed over the wall before the wildflowers began, where only the long wild grass grew, with its yellow, fluffy seed heads poking out above.

It was far easier to trek through and flatten with our feet, than to battle with the thistles. Where the grass stopped, a bed of pebbles began on the ground before the water. The water was clear and clean; the pebbles continued and became the floor of the lake, and they felt smooth on our bare feet as we paddled in it.

It was my favourite place and, when there was no school,

we visited often in spring and summer when the flowers were in bloom, and sometimes in autumn when the leaves were crisp and brown, but the sun still shone.

I absorbed the beautiful, vibrant colours of nature and enjoyed paddling in the fresh water. We could only paddle, as neither of us knew how to swim, and with fear of going in too deep we kept close to the edge where the water came no higher than our knees. It was our secret hiding place. Not many people visited the lake; the long grass in the field and the bushes alongside the road kept it hidden. It was perfect to strip down to your underwear and go for a splash without the worry of a stranger watching.

Unfortunately, for May, her freedom to visit the lake as often as she did almost faded away in 1922, when she left school. She began working at Robinson's Tea Room, which was owned by Mr Robinson and his wife. May was a hard worker, a valued employee and was given plenty of hours' work, which meant less free time with me.

I was not alone for long. Shortly after May left school, I shared the secret of our lake with Stanley and he was curious to see it. He joined me that weekend, and for the two years that followed he was my new lake partner, calling for me whenever the sun shone and admiring it as much as I did. May still came when she could, but as she grew into adulthood, her priorities changed.

It was a sunny Saturday morning in June 1925, and I waited patiently for Stanley to call round, peering out of the window and looking down the street. When at last I saw him running up the road and waving at me, I threw my satchel over my shoulder, filled with an afternoon supply of food, and I ran out of the back door.

I called out my farewells to Aunt Lily and opened the gate onto the open field. Stanley was already there waiting for me, his head down and his hands in his pockets, kicking the tops of the blades of grass. He never entered the field through our property, but leapt over the fence at the end of the road.

'Are you ready?' he asked.

'Ready.'

We ran across the field, laughing and embracing the open air blowing in our faces.

Stanley had recently turned fourteen and finished his last day of school; he was ready to step out into the world and earn a living, whereas I still had another two years left. I tried not to think about school, it was going to be lonely without Stanley; he was my only friend.

Although Mark had left the year before he had made it difficult for me to make friends. When he was a pupil, I was never free of his abusive comments, stone throwing and shoving around.

Over the years, Stanley often stood up to Mark, but despite his courage, he never won the battles and often walked away with a black eye, swollen lip, or kicked ribs. Yet he still attempted to fight him the next time and the next. He felt sure that one day he would defeat Mark.

We walked along the road under the trees. It felt cooler in the shade, a break from the sun. When the lake was in sight, we both looked at one another, a smile spread across our faces as we thought the same thing, but waited for the other one to make the move.

I ran first, climbing over the stone wall and pouncing into the long grass. I picked up speed, the blades brushing against my bare legs as I leapt through them and, with my arms outstretched, feeling the tips tickling the back of my hands.

Stanley gave me a head start before he began to sprint towards me. He jumped over the wall quicker than I did, his hand used for balance as he swung his leg across. I could hear the thud on the ground when he landed, followed by the rustling of the grass behind, the noise grew louder as he closed in on me very quickly.

I let out a squeal of laughter, feeling excited at the anticipation of his pounce. I knew it was coming, I could sense him close. I looked behind and there he was. He slowed down and locked his arms around my waist. The impact made us spin around and tumble to the ground.

We laughed as we laid in a heap on the floor. We rolled on to our backs and gazed up at the sky, as we caught our breath.

'I think I need to give you more of a head start,' he laughed.

'It's the wall,' I panted. 'I can't get over it as fast as you. One day I'll reach the lake before you catch me.'

'I'll always catch you, Betsy.'

He stood up first, offered me his arm and pulled me to my feet. He jogged the short distance to the lake while I decided to walk slowly and snap off grass seeds. I ran my finger and thumb across the stem tightly, pushing the seeds to the top, watching them gather together, like a flower. I admired it for a while before letting the seeds drop to the ground.

'Come on, Betsy,' Stanley called out, he was already in the water, his clothes and shoes left on the pebbles. His legs creating splashes as he trudged through until it was deep enough and he launched into the water. He was a strong swimmer, he didn't seem to get tired, and his long, slender build gave him speed.

I dropped my belongings next to his and slipped my dress over my head; my lemon coloured dress was a loose fit with a low waist and pockets, made by Aunt Lily. Underneath I wore a swimming costume.

I remembered Stanley's past advice to run straight into the water, so as not to give my body the chance to react to the cold. So, I ran into the water. It splashed, spraying drops on my face and bare arms, and it felt so much colder than my legs that were submerged in the water. I sat down and the water reached my chest. I splayed my legs, the movement caused the dirt to lift off the pebbles, clouding the water. After doing this several times and watching the dirt settle, only for me to disturb it again, I remained perfectly still and watched.

Slowly, the tiny, brown grains sank to the bottom and seemed to disappear leaving the grey pebbles clearly visible at the bottom. I could see tiny fish darting about between the rocks, and the occasional, tiny bubble rise to the surface when they breathed.

It was very quiet. The only sound, aside from my breathing, was the birds chirping nearby singing their songs. Stanley was just ahead, gliding through the water; his gentle strokes made no sound.

After a while, Stanley finished his swim, made his way towards me and plonked himself by my side, causing a large splash of water. His dark hair was wet and the drops of water on his skin shone in the sunlight.

'How did you learn to swim?' I asked him.

'My brother taught me, like my father taught him. Sometimes we would go to the seaside.'

'You've been to the seaside? What's it like?'

I hadn't left the town before and could only imagine what places looked like from reading about them in books. Our town was surrounded by large borders of open fields that separated it from other towns and villages, so it was difficult to imagine a world outside. Roads veined out of our town, in various areas, branching out to other places, but I hadn't thought of venturing down them fully and exploring. Perhaps being a child still, I didn't feel the need to, or I feared what was on the other side.

'It's big,' he expressed with his hands, 'you can smell the salt and taste it too. There's a horizon and big waves. I'll take you one day.'

'Really?'

'Yes, it's not far on the train.'

'I've never been on the train.'

'Betsy, you've not lived. When I earn some money, I'll take you.'

My insides felt warm with his promise of taking me out of the town, on my first ever trip to the seaside, and I felt excited by this new dream. Which led me to think of my brothers, who would have travelled through many towns, cities and villages, and sailed for weeks over the sea that parted us.

I still pined for them, but there was nothing Matthew could do, they could be anywhere in Canada, and there was no way of knowing which farm they were sent to and which charity or organisation they belonged to. Mother was the only one who knew, but she had moved away days after we left. Our only hope was that one day they would find their way home.

I had forgotten what they looked like, I struggled to imagine their boyish faces and they became faceless figures in my mind. I feared if I were to see them, I would not recognise them, and the very thought pained me; to know one of my brothers may, one day, pass by me and I would see only a stranger in the street.

'You promise?' I asked, trying to divert my attention away from my troubling thoughts.

'I promise, but if you want to go, you'll have to get swimming, otherwise you won't stand a chance against those waves.'

Stanley was teaching me to swim; he had been wanting to for the previous two years, but I was afraid to go too deep into the water, and it took a long time before I became used to putting my face in the water. He was very patient and wouldn't force me to go farther than I felt comfortable.

He pulled me upright and we moved deeper into the water. We walked until the water reached my ribcage before we stopped. This was as far as I could bear to go. I felt wobbly on my feet even though Stanley was holding my hand.

'How deep is the lake?' I asked, knowing how far Stanley swam out, many times to the other side, with confidence.

'It's quite deep, in the middle,' he replied, 'and there are snakes, crocodiles and large toe nibbling fish in here too.'

'You are lying,' I said, looking around me, 'you wouldn't swim in here if there were.'

'I might cover myself in reptile repellent lotion, so they keep away.'

I really wasn't sure if he was being serious; could there be snakes, crocodiles and large toe nibbling fish deep in the lake? I screamed and attempted to escape back to land, but I slipped all over the place. Stanley held my hand and laughed, 'Betsy, I am fooling around. There's nothing like that in here and you're right, if there were, I wouldn't be in here. Besides, we don't have crocodiles in our country, and the adder is the only venomous snake, and they are too shy, so you won't see them. Oh, and I made up the bit about the toe nibbling fish; I don't think they exist, so you are safe.'

Feeling relieved and annoyed, I scolded Stanley, 'that's not funny.'

A smirk spread across his face, 'come on, let's get you swimming.'

Stanley moved behind me and told me to lie back. I had to keep my back straight and make a starfish in the water. He stood by my side with his hand under the water, supporting the arch of my back. Then he slowly lowered his hand and I sensed him begin to move away from me. I panicked and began to flap my arms, trying to stand.

'Don't panic,' he said, 'we have done this before and you were floating then. Just keep still.'

It took a few attempts before I felt safe enough to remain still and float on my own when the security of his hand had moved away.

'You're floating,' he said, and I whispered, 'Yes.' Once I was used to bobbing around on the water, I began to relax and admire the clear blue skies above me. I had done this before, but only for a few seconds, but this time it felt like minutes had passed until Stanley disturbed me. I was instructed to kick my legs quickly, he mimicked the action with his hands, flapping them up and down simultaneously.

He hooked his arms under mine, still outstretched in my star shape and I copied his movements by kicking my legs. Afterwards, he started moving my arms one by one backwards over my head, brushing past my ears and taking them back to my side. All this time he was moving me along. Then he let go. To my surprise, for the first time in many weekends of trying, I was swimming on my back, on my own.

'There you go,' he said, 'a fair back crawl there.'

I stood up and clapped my hands, feeling proud of myself, 'I did it. I did it.'

'Yes, you did. About time too and it's easier to learn back stroke first.'

The front strokes were more difficult to master and despite my best efforts to perform them as instructed, I failed. He was pleased with my arm flapping and leg kicking, and that I managed to move across the water, although it was more like a doggy paddle. I had made progress, but it wouldn't match Stanley's elegant strokes.

'Your feet are off the ground, that's something,' he teased.

I was still afraid to get my face wet and as I kept curving my back, my feet would sink downwards. With all my waving and kicking I was hardly swimming across that lake.

'Betsy, you need to keep your back straight,' he said.

Time passed quickly and soon hunger took over; we let the rumbling of our stomachs guide us back to land. We sat by the edge, looking out at the water as we raided our satchels for our lunch. We were famished. We emptied our flasks and gobbled most of our food in silence.

'What are you going to do now?' I asked Stanley.

'Finish my sandwich,' he smiled.

'About work, silly, now you're done with school?'

'What? While you play with dollies, what will I do to earn pennies?' He paused for a moment, he was contemplating his choices. 'My brother said he could get me work at the flax mill. I could do that.'

'Do you want to?'

'It's a job.'

'Is that what your dad did?'

'Yes. Everyone starts off in the flax mill.'

'So, you'll follow in your father's footsteps?'

'Yes, but don't you feel like your life is forced on you? Doing what your father did?'

'I don't know.'

He laughed and playfully punched me in the arm, 'you don't have to worry about that, do you? You just have to marry someone, keep the house nice and have babies.'

'Whoopee. Maybe I don't want babies and maybe I don't want to marry. I could work.'

A smile spread across his face and he said, 'you're right, you probably will just work. You will need to get pretty, like your sister, if you want to marry.'

Stanley was only joking, but his words hurt. May and I were the opposite; she had grown in beauty and in confidence. She had inherited Mother's features, had a gentle curved jaw line, high cheek bones and large blue eyes, so noticeable under her long, dark eyelashes that naturally curled. She was rarely without admirers as she developed into a woman, causing more broken hearts than receiving them. I was small for my age with a childlike body, waiting for my breasts to develop and my hips to widen; waiting to become a woman. The roundness of my face and my unmanageably thick, dark hair tied in two plaits only made me look younger. The only resemblance I shared with May were our small rounded noses and smiles.

I looked down at my half-eaten sandwich. I was bothered by what Stanley thought, I didn't want him to see May as pretty like everyone else did. I didn't want him to see me as plain. I wanted him to see *me.*

'Oh, Betsy,' Stanley playfully nudged me, detecting my silence, 'I'm being a fool. I don't mean it.'

I nodded with a forced smile and continued to pick at my sandwich.

'It's difficult being a boy,' he said, 'you work, but what for? You don't have anything and you can't be ill. I'm not ready for that, yet. Rupert had to work to support my mum and me, he still does. He's looked after me and mum since he was sixteen. I'm not ready for that responsibility. I want to come here with you, not work for nothing. Mum says I'm a man, but I'm not ready yet.'

Stanley was close to his mother and looked up to his brother. Rupert was now twenty-three and should be married and supporting a wife with children. But he chose to remain a bachelor, providing for his mother and much younger brother.

'Rupert works long days,' Stanley carried on, 'yet we still struggle to eat. You can't better yourself – you work to live, but if you can't work, you can't live. You know what it was like when your dad died. Your brothers had to be sent away, and you and May sent to your aunt's and your mum...' he paused, 'nothing is guaranteed.'

I studied my food, not knowing what to say.

'It must have been harder for your mother, at least mine had one grown child to help. But your mum had four young children; she had no choice.'

'You don't think she's bad?' I said, feeling surprised at someone showing empathy towards my mother.

'No, Betsy, no one knows what people are thinking, and my mum always says that with rumours you have two choices, either believe them or make your own decisions. I make my own decisions.'

I smiled at Stanley and I reached across quickly placing a kiss on his cheek. He pulled away, rubbing away my kiss like it was contaminated and chortled, 'Betsy, what was that for?'

I shrugged my shoulders and giggled with embarrassment. Heaven knows what possessed me to plant that kiss on his cheek. I could see him blush and he was wearing a fixed smirk on his face as he looked out at the lake.

We enjoyed a few more hours at the lake before we headed home. It was a slow stroll home and we spoke no more about Stanley's future career plans, knowing the near future only meant our regular outings would end. Instead we told jokes, reminisced about the past and laughed, enjoying what could be one of our last days of freedom together.

We were crossing the second field away from home, the border of the town houses visible in the far distance. I could make out Aunt Lily's house at the very end of the town. The grass was overgrown, with thistles and nettles growing in various areas, huddled together waiting to attack, but we had trampled down our own pathway through.

I turned around when I felt something hit the back of my head hard. It felt no bigger than a small stone.

'What's the matter?' Stanley asked.

'Something hit me.'

I was hit again. This time the object landed on my shoulder and Stanley saw it happen. He crouched down and lifted up a stone from the grass, holding it out to me in the palm of his hand. He searched the area, examining our surroundings through squinted eyes and much concentration.

'Oh no,' he said, 'run, Betsy.'

'Why?' I asked, as he grabbed my arm and we ran.

Before we could reach the last field, Oliver, George and Horace, jumped out in front of us; they had been waiting, crouched down behind the long grass. They blocked the entrance to the next field. When I saw the three boys emerge,

I knew who was behind it all, who was targetting me with stones. Over my shoulder, running through the long grass towards me, was Mark, carrying a catapult in his hand and a satisfied look on his face.

'Look who we have here,' Mark said, handing the catapult back to George.

He stood very close to me and his friends circled Stanley. Stanley was looking for an escape route, I could see him weighing up his chances. I knew he could outrun them and make a break for it, but I was too slow to follow and he knew that.

Panic shook through my body. I had nowhere to run, and I was afraid. Mark was a giant compared to me; puberty had graced him with a strong, broad build. His intimidating solidness left him without fear. No one dared to challenge him and when he glared down at me, I felt so vulnerable. He was fearfully threatening.

'What do you want, Mark?' Stanley asked, he was not afraid.

'I thought we would find you here. A birdie told me you two have a love nest here,' Mark said, and his friends laughed.

'Like them young, Stanley?' Oliver asked.

'Shut up, Oliver,' Stanley threatened as he stepped closer to him. George and Horace closed in, standing by their friend with a warning look at Stanley, *you fight him and you fight all three.*

'And what's so special about her?' Mark pushed me, I stumbled back, 'beat me to it, did you, Stanley? Always thought I would have first go at the whore's daughter.'

Stanley went for Mark, broke through his friends' line and charged at him. With a clenched fist and no warning, he landed the first punch across Mark's face that whipped back. Horace and Oliver were quick to grab Stanley's arms, preventing him from making any further attacks, while Mark repaid the punches. His knuckles swung hard in Stanley's face twice, quickly followed by several more punches in the stomach.

I screamed with horror with each blow Stanley received. I saw the grimaced look in his eyes as he took each blow. It was such an unfair fight. Stanley had four of them against him – he had no chance of defending himself. By the time Mark had finished, Stanley looked in pain, defeated and helpless.

Mark stepped towards me, I could feel the warmth of his breath blowing on my face. I swallowed hard, trying not to show my fear, his friend George by his side, waiting for his command.

'You like making my sister look a fool?' he accused.

'I don't.' I stuttered in defence, I was confused, I had never made Beatrice look like a fool, I didn't speak to her at school.

'Are you an idiot?' he asked, whacking my head with the back of his hand several times, 'shall I remind you? You got the answer right, when she got it wrong. Making her look like a fool.'

It look me a moment to realise what he was referring to. A few weeks earlier the teacher had asked a simple algebra question which Beatrice failed to answer correctly. When I was asked next, I gave the right solution. The teacher embarrassed her for not knowing the answer and praised me; it was completely out of my hands.

'I didn't make her look like a fool,' my voice quivered as I spoke.

Mark pulled a knife from his pocket and I held my breath as my eyes followed the shiny, sharp blade. Stanley wriggled and jerked his body in an attempt to break free from Horace and Oliver's hold. George kicked him hard between the legs, he doubled over in pain and fell to his knees. The boys released their hold on him, feeling confident he was too distracted to fight back. Horace kicked him hard between the shoulder blades and Stanley fell face forward onto the ground. Oliver sat on his back, trapping Stanley's hands under his own body and pulled his head back by his hair, his chin pressed into the ground with discomfort as he was forced to watch me.

His eye was swollen and his nose bloody, there was nothing either of us could do to help the other. My focus went back to the silver knife Mark waved in front of me, like the pendulum of a clock. His free hand reached out to me,

I instinctively stepped back, afraid he was going to slice me open. George hurried behind me, grabbed my shoulders and pushed me towards Mark.

Mark snatched one of my plaits with a swift move of his hand, I knew what he was about to do and, with all my strength, I tried to break free.

I failed.

George grabbed my face, keeping it still while Mark sawed away at one of my plaits. All I could do was scream and cry as I felt the tugging of the knife moving back and forth, until eventually the braid flopped over his hand. He triumphantly held it high with a cheer, his friends shared in his joy and hollered when he lobbed it high through the grass. He repeated the same procedure with the other plait.

'Who's a crybaby,' he laughed, tapping my face several times.

'You're a coward,' Stanley managed to say through his teeth, 'you need back up, you can't fight me on your own.'

'I am not a coward!' Mark said to Stanley, but his attention remained on me.

Mark grabbed my legs, George holding my upper body and they carried me a few paces across the field. I could see the thistle bush they were heading towards and I screamed again, kicking my legs and twisting my body, but it was no use. The boys, almost men, had a firm hold on me and I had no chance.

'A leg and a wing to see the king,' the boys chanted as they swayed me back and forth before releasing me into the air.

As soon as their grip on me was released, I shielded my eyes, protecting my face from my sharp landing. I fell into the thistles, the weight of my body sinking into its sharp, claw-like thorns, as they shredded through my flesh. They sliced through my skin and I felt the suffering, as the tiny drops of blood rose to the surface.

I screamed, feeling this excruciating pain that was almost unbearable and knowing more was to come as I tried to escape this thorn tomb. George reached in, taking hold of my arm and yanking me out. My dress caught in the bristles and tore in several places.

They all laughed at me when I rose up from the bush, my skin stained with blood, my cropped hair and my rags that were seconds before, a beautiful summer dress.

They swooped me up again and my body, too weak to fight back, succumbed to my next torture.

'Please, no!' I cried, as the only thing left to do was to beg, 'not again.'

I repeated the same words over and over again, pleading with them.

They moved me away from the thorn bush, but towards a flourishing ball of stinging nettles.

'A leg and a wing to see the king,' they repeated the same chant and I was thrown like before, but this time into a bed of nettles, the leaves' fur embedded into my bare arms, legs and face. The stinging pain throbbed and the cuts burned as I crawled out of the weeds.

I stood up and looked Mark in the eyes. I was crying, tears drenched my cheeks, my body was trembling, my knees were weak and I knew I could take no more.

'That's enough now,' George said, joining the others.

'I hate you,' Mark said.

'Why?' I wept.

'As if you don't know.' There was venom in his voice as he pushed me back into the nettles once more.

'I will always hate you!' he dragged me out with a fist full of my hair, I was on my hands and knees, and he bent over to yell in my ear, 'I hate your family and I will never forget what your whore mother did.'

He pushed me to the ground before he ran over to Stanley, lifting his head up by his hair and said, 'perhaps you need to choose different friends.'

We were left alone as the boys disappeared into the next field laughing and cheering at their success.

I felt sick with fear, every part of my exposed flesh stung, throbbed, tingled and itched; it was unbearable. Stanley was soon by my side. He fell to his knees and wrapped a comforting arm round my shoulder. 'Betsy, look at you, he's a monster. I'm sorry, I couldn't stop him.'

I said nothing.

'We need to get you home quickly to your aunty.'

I didn't notice how badly hurt Stanley was, until he climbed over the fence into the next field. Normally he managed the jump with ease by swinging his legs over in one quick movement, but this time he climbed the planks of woods with difficulty and he let out a groan when he landed on his feet on the other side.

'Stanley, you are hurt,' my voice still quivering.

'I'm fine,' he said through gritted teeth. He held his arms out to help me over, but I refused his offer, concerned about his own pain and I climbed over myself.

'I'm sorry, Stanley,' I began to cry again, 'it's all my fault.'

'Don't be sorry,' he said, 'you have nothing to be sorry about. Mark and his friends are monsters.'

Aunt Lily was in the kitchen when we stepped into the garden. She caught sight of us from the window and came running to the back door.

'What's happened?' With a look of worry on her face, she examined me, lifting my arms to look at my cuts, bending down to inspect my legs and running her hands through my cropped hair.

Stanley explained everything, while I cried when hearing the details of my afternoon said out loud, emphasising what had really happened.

'What a nasty, sick, rotten boy,' she exclaimed. 'If I get my hands on any of the Irvings, heaven knows what I will do to them.'

She sent Stanley into the front room with a damp flannel rinsed in cold water for his swelling whilst he waited for Matthew to come home. She filled a bathtub in the kitchen for me. The warm water doubled the pain of the cuts and made the nettle stings itch more. Aunt Lily handed me the soap, while she poured jugs of water over my head and vigorously washed my hair.

'It'll grow, sweetie,' she said, 'all the young girls are cutting their hair short now. I'll tidy it up and we can put a bow in your hair, you will still be my beautiful Betsy.'

I was not convinced by her kind words, my thick curly hair would resemble a bird's nest on the top of my head, not the neat straight line that sat perfectly under the jaw of the girls with finer and straighter hair than I had.

I rested in the bathtub a while longer, while Aunt Lily scrubbed my dress and swimming costume in the sink. Her hand rubbed the brush so rapidly over the fabric, I was certain she would break through the material. She pulled the dress out of the water and examined the useless rags, no longer fit for its purpose.

Afterwards, she plastered me in a paste made from baking powder and water, slapping it on all over my body before pulling my night gown over my head.

'That'll help with the itching,' she said, 'the cuts are, thankfully, minor and will heal.'

I must have looked a state when Stanley was called into the kitchen. He saw me and tried to conceal the twitching smirk that was spreading across his face. Aunt Lily asked to inspect his bruises and to verify nothing was broken. He raised his shirt, exposing the deep, purple bruise across his left side.

'That looks nasty, but I don't think anything is broken,' she said. 'Sit next to Betsy, I will make you both a drink.'

'I should get going, thank you, Mrs Cooke,' Stanley politely said.

'No, Stanley, Matthew will be home soon; he will take you home and explain everything to your mother. You will not go back like this on your own.'

Stanley obeyed and pulled up a chair by my side while Aunt Lily made a comforting cup of tea with biscuits. We drank and ate slowly, but in silence; our experience was too difficult to speak of.

Matthew arrived shortly after and Aunt Lily closed the door on us. We could hear the mumbling of her voice as she informed him of our dreadful incident.

'He did what?' I heard Matthew yell. 'I'm going to see Mr Irving, the filthy little bastard.'

Matthew charged into the kitchen and crouched down beside me. He took my hands in his and said 'hello darling, our beautiful Betsy. You shouldn't have gone through that... if

I could, I'd make sure Mark and his friends never walk again.'

'I tried, Mr Cooke,' Stanley said quickly.

'I know, Stanley, you were outnumbered and thank you for trying.' He shook Stanley's hand. 'I'll take you home, and then I am going to have a word with Mr Irving, no one treats my niece like that and gets away with it.'

Before leaving, Matthew said to Aunt Lily, 'have tea without me, I may be gone a while.' Stanley looked back at me and our eyes locked for a moment, he looked sorry. I knew he wished he could have done more.

Whatever happened that night, Matthew didn't speak of it again. He came home late in the evening when May and I were in bed, but Aunt Lily waited for his return. I was woken by the sound of them coming up the stairs and the mumbling of their voices as they discussed the incident. I could tell through the walls that Aunt Lily was upset and I listened to her sobbing, but their voices were only murmurs, keeping their conversation private.

Following the incident, Aunt Lily took me out of the school and sent me to a smaller one closer to home. I was settled within a few weeks, and soon felt at ease in the smaller school and classrooms. Aunt Lily often cursed herself for not moving me sooner when I first came to live with her, rather than traipsing two miles across town to my old school.

My only sorrow was that the friendship between Stanley and I didn't strengthen as we grew into adulthood. As children we understood each other and I always felt as if we were soulmates. But the days of us being inseparable were gone and sadly, that dreadful day was the last time I saw Stanley for six years.

Part Three

Chapter Six

It was August 1931, and I had been in service as a maid for Dr Oxley since leaving school in 1927. He had mentioned to Matthew, in passing, that he was looking for a housekeeper to manage his home and Matthew suggested me. Dr Oxley was sceptical at first, due to my age and inexperience, but during my time working for him, I had proved myself capable, efficient and hard working.

He was very much still the miserable, ignorant old man he was when he proclaimed my father was dead twelve years ago. Yet, despite his bad traits, at times I could see the gentleman in him, especially when his loving nephew, Mr William Bradshaw, came to stay. He was the son and only child of Dr Oxley's sister. Since Dr Oxley had no children of his own, he valued his nephew as if he was his own child, and both men had the utmost respect for one another. Mr Bradshaw brought out the best in Dr Oxley and with him he was a completely different man. I found myself looking forward to Mr Bradshaw staying.

Mr Bradshaw was the opposite of his uncle, he was friendlier and very polite. He often found time to talk to me during his visits and genuinely seemed interested in what I had to say. I was unsure of his age, but he looked to be in his late twenties. His eyes were bright blue, like the sky in summer, and they were striking against his dark eyelashes and eyebrows. His hair was dark too, with wisps of silver running through making him look more distinguished and intelligent. His skin was smooth and he always looked fresh faced, with a slight show of ageing around his eyes.

He was a solicitor, following in his father's footsteps. He lived in the city and he would escape the busy life as often as he could, finding the town ran at a slower and more relaxing pace. He was unmarried and never mentioned that he had a woman in mind. It surprised me that a handsome, middle-class gentleman who was wealthy, as well as kind and sincere, chose to be on his own.

Every morning I began my work at half past six, carrying out the same routine. I would walk through the town centre, cut through the graveyard, normally past Father's grave to wish him a good morning, before reaching Dr Oxley's street.

The street was not far from my first home and I often considered walking down to see the house, but the memories attached to it kept me away. His house was in the middle of a row of terraced properties, installed with electricity and an inside bathroom. It felt so modern and comfortable compared to the houses I was used to. We still used a tin bath filled with kettle water, kept warm by the fire in winter and our toilet facilities were outside, in a wooden shed.

I had my own key to the house, enabling me to enter every morning without disturbing Dr Oxley. The house was big for a man on his own. The hallway was long and the floor was covered with small beautiful square tiles, decorated in a red, burgundy, green and blue detailed pattern. There was a staircase directly in front of the door, with a dark wooden banister and a thick chunky handrail that curved at the bottom.

'Good morning, Betsy,' Mr Bradshaw greeted me, when I passed the open door of the first room.

The sitting room was big and square with patterned wallpaper. A picture rail in dark wood ran around the top and several pictures hung from it. There was a large fireplace framed with a green and cream marbled mantelpiece. Either side in the alcoves were matching bookcases packed with various books, and in the centre of the room was a comfy settee and two armchairs with high backs. A large rug filled the whole room, except for a border of dark polished floorboards around the edges.

Mr Bradshaw was sitting in an armchair. He was reading a book with his back to the window letting in the morning sun, which created a golden aura around him. When he did visit, I often found him already awake when I arrived and enjoying one of the many books available to read.

'Good morning, Mr Bradshaw,' I said, 'would you like a cup of tea now?'

'I'll have one with my breakfast, thank you, Betsy,' he returned to his book.

The room at the end of the hallway was the dining room, which I needed to pass through to reach the kitchen. This room had a fireplace and a marble mantelpiece matching the other rooms. In the centre of the room was a dark wooden table and six chairs. Each chair had arm rests and was cushioned in a cream fabric. Hanging above the table was a large, ornate chandelier.

I walked over to the two tall cabinets that stood in the alcoves by the fire and removed the lace cloth from a drawer to cover the table. I returned for the silver cutlery needed for breakfast and I prepared the table for Dr Oxley and Mr Bradshaw. I removed the gold-plated dinner plates and tea service from the upper shelves to carry through into the kitchen.

This was the only room without a fireplace and, being at the back of the house, it was shaded from the sun even in the summer. It had a range stove for cooking that used coal to fire it. It was running constantly, so whatever the month it was the warmest place to be. It also had a sink with running hot and cold water, which was so practical; Aunt Lily's sink still only had cold water.

I began to prepare the men's breakfast. The whistling of the kettle on the stove, when the water was boiling, and the sizzling food in the pan, were the usual sounds to fill the kitchen in the mornings. The delicious smell of bacon, eggs and sausages cooking made my mouth water and my taste buds tingle.

Breakfast needed to be ready for seven o'clock on the dot. As he was a man of strict routine and needed things done by the letter, Dr Oxley would already be sat at the table waiting. Once breakfast was ready, I carried it through to the dining room on a tray and, as expected, he was there, sat at the head of the table. Mr Bradshaw was seated at the opposite end of the table.

Both men sat in silence. Dr Oxley was leaning back in the chair reading the paper, with his elbows resting on the curved wooden arms, and Mr Bradshaw continued to read his book. On hearing me enter, Mr Bradshaw placed the book on the table and flipped open his napkin, which fell neatly over his knee. Dr Oxley waited, he didn't break away from his reading until I had placed his plate in front of him and poured his tea. I served Mr Bradshaw second and left the tea pot on the sideboard ready for top ups.

'Dr Oxley,' I began nervously, 'I wonder, if it's not too much trouble, if I could finish earlier?'

There was a dance being held that evening at the local hall, which was quite a popular event in the town. I was eighteen, perhaps a little old to be going to my first dance; May was sixteen when she first went and had been many times since over the years.

'Early finish?' Dr Oxley was abrupt, he didn't make eye contact with me, but concentrated on slicing into his bacon and taking a mouthful. 'How early?'

'Five?'

'Five? That would mean dinner before five?'

'I could finish at half past five?' I quickly responded.

He shook his head in disbelief, 'that will cause complications to my stomach.'

'Oh come on now, Uncle,' Mr Bradshaw joined in, a cheery smile across his face, 'how often does Betsy make a request to finish early?'

'That's how it starts, William, I allow it this once and she will expect it every week.'

I nervously clutched on to the empty tray, my hands were shaking and I held it close to my chest like a shield, as the two men discussed my proposal.

'Anything nice planned?' Mr Bradshaw asked me.

'There's a dance on and my sister would very much like me to go.'

'Betsy,' he said with a smirk, 'I grant you an early finish, you work hard, and my uncle and I will dine out tonight, my treat.'

'I can make your dinner.'

'William!' Dr Oxley scolded.

'It will be my pleasure, Uncle,' Mr Bradshaw raised his cup of tea as a toast, 'see it as my gratitude to your good hospitality over the years. Go on, let the girl have an early finish and enjoy herself, enjoy her adolescence.'

'Those places only cause trouble,' Dr Oxley spluttered, but he hesitated for a moment and finally said in defeat, 'very well Betsy, you can finish at five.'

'Thank you, Dr Oxley,' I said and smiled gratefully at Mr Bradshaw for his aid.

Feeling pleased with Dr Oxley's agreement, I left the men in peace and busied myself in the kitchen feeling excited and looking forward to my night ahead.

I'd bought a new dress a few months before and I thought it would be suitable for the dance. It was lavender with a floral print, it had a folded down collar, a matching belt brought it in at the waist and it hung loosely to finish at my calves. Fashion had changed a great deal over the past fifteen years, especially for women; clothing was less restricting with less coverage. There were now factories mass producing clothing, and we were able to buy dresses off the peg rather than hand make them, although most of my clothing was still handmade.

May wore a dark blue dress with white spots on, similar in style to mine, which suited her, complementing her pale blue eyes and fair skin.

She was on tenterhooks, nervous about meeting Roger at the dance hall, as she fluttered around the bedroom, her fingers shaking uncontrollably and her breathing quickening with anticipation. They had seen each other many times, but only while May worked and where he had become a regular customer. This was to be the first time she would meet him outside her work; free from the restriction of a quick greeting, secret smiles from across the tea room and the brief conversations they were used to.

To divert her mind from focusing too much on her meeting, she hummed to herself as she finished getting ready, and I knew from the effect he had on her and the glow in her cheeks, that she was falling for him. She was twenty-three and ready to fall in love, marry and have children – that was all she ever wanted. In the past, she'd had many close acquaintances, but none of the men matched up to her expectations.

'I'll do your hair,' May suggested.

I thanked her, taking the stool in front of the dresser and she began to unravel the rollers from my hair. They had only been in an hour and a half, not long enough to create any tight curls, but long enough to work with the natural wave of my hair. May pinned several curls on top of my head and twisted the rest of my hair to sit in a bun at the back, a similar style to her own.

'I'm looking forward to being introduced to Roger,' I said, 'it will be nice to put a face to the name.'

The very mention of his name provoked a wide smile to spread across May's face and a blush in her cheeks. 'Yes, Betsy, he's wonderful and such a gentleman. He says the sweetest of things to me; makes me feel special.'

'He does sound wonderful, I really hope things work out, you deserve to be happy.'

'Thank you, Betsy. I've not told Aunt Lily and Matthew that I'm meeting a man tonight.'

I laughed, 'you did right, Aunt Lily will only get excited and start planning a wedding.'

'What would you do, Betsy,' May stopped styling my hair, her hands rested on my shoulders and, as she looked at my reflection in the mirror, her smile faded. 'If I married? Would you be all right here?'

I rolled my eyes at her and grinned, 'May, I would be absolutely fine. Please don't think about me, you deserve to be happy. Besides, you're not properly courting yet, let alone marrying.'

May exhaled deeply and slowly, not so much a sigh, more

a release of a deep breath she had held on to for too long, 'I just worry about you, you're my little sister, I've always taken care of you.'

I cupped my hands over the top of hers, 'stop worrying and think of yourself. You need to live your life, not worry about mine.'

May wrapped her arms around my neck and kissed my cheek. She was everything to me, not only a sister, but a true friend and many times a mother. It was because of her unimaginable strength when we were growing up that I was strong enough, in adulthood, to face the world alone, to fight my own battles and take my own path, just like she should take her own.

Before she pulled away, she teased, 'maybe you will meet someone tonight? A few of Roger's friends will be there.'

I shook my head and rolled my eyes at May, feeling very doubtful. With little experience talking to men, I was unsure if I was ready to love. From a young age I knew what was expected of me; to learn to cook, to clean, to be a loyal and obedient woman, marry and have many children. Even my line of work meant I was preparing myself for my known future, but at least with my job, I was not vowed forever to someone, I could change my mind.

May and I linked arms as we walked towards the town hall; a fifteen-minute trek, our heels making a clonking sound on the cobbles and echoing against the houses. The town hall was a suitable venue, with a stage for the band and a makeshift bar selling refreshments in the corner.

The hall was simple, with white walls, wooden beams and high ceilings. The atmosphere it generated was truly magical and I saw a room full of elegance and grace. The hall was full of people drinking and dancing; everyone seemed genuinely happy and full of energy. I watched in envy as people danced the waltz, the foxtrot, the quickstep and the charleston, women in the arms of gentlemen, gracefully gliding and sweeping across the dance floor. I was a poor dancer. I'd not had the chance to learn anything more than the few simple steps May had taught me, and I was not confident enough in myself to remember them.

Jazz was becoming very popular; everyone adored the uplifting sound; the rhythm and the beat were so infectious you just had to dance. Even Matthew had become partial to the new music phenomenon. Whenever it played on the wireless at home, his feet or hands would tap along and his head would be bobbing along, merrily.

'There he is,' May said, pointing to the tall dark-haired man slipping through the crowd towards us.

Roger was exactly as May had described. He was friendly, charming and sincere. He kissed her cheek first, then introduced himself to me. He politely took my hand and raised it to his lips, planting a quick kiss. 'A pleasure to meet you, Betsy, at long last.'

'Likewise,' I smiled back at him.

'Follow me, we are sat over here.' He waved us to follow him.

He avoided passing through the dance floor and we walked the long way round to where the tables were situated. The loud music thrilled me most of all, the different instruments played by talented men – the sound they created filled the room and reached deep inside, touching the soul. It amazed me how they could play for so long and not seem short of breath or show any signs of tiredness; they didn't seem to falter.

Roger led us to a table which was occupied by a man and a woman, the man sat with his back to us. Another man was leaning over the table talking to them. When he caught sight of us approaching, he straightened to standing. He was tall, strong looking and when he stood he looked perfectly symmetrical, his legs evenly apart and his shoulders perfectly aligned. From a distance he looked handsome, with a strong jawline and short mousy brown hair.

It was when I was close enough to see his face clearly, that I recognised the man and by that time it was too late. He had seen me too, with a smile at first, that gradually faded.

My face mirrored the same disappointment, my chest became tight and I felt an explosion inside my stomach, releasing a hot liquid that poured down my inner walls, the same feeling you get when you swallow a hot drink on an empty stomach, but reaching much lower down. I was frightened. My body pounded with the increased flow of blood and I could feel the thudding pulse in my head, echoing in my ears.

Mark's blue eyes met mine and he knew who I was. There was no need for introductions, before Roger could speak, Mark stepped forward and greeted us both, falsely polite. 'May,' he said first, kissing her hand, 'I have not seen you in years, I hope you are well.'

'Very well, thank you, Mark,' she replied. May was a true Christian with a forgiving nature, she wouldn't ever hold a grudge and genuinely believed people changed. *'Could I be the same?'*

'Betsy, such a pleasure to see you again,' he smiled, his fingers felt limp, barely touching mine, as he rose my hand to meet his lips. I pulled away fast, I was expressionless, *'how could I speak to this monster?'* Our tension was discreet; Roger didn't notice and his introductions moved to the seated couple.

I was snapped out of my stare when a woman's voice called out my name, 'Betsy Colborne? Is that really you?' Beatrice rose to her feet and threw her arms around my neck. I stood still, my arms pinned to my side, feeling as though I had entered a different world.

Beatrice was taller than I remembered, she no longer looked like the plain child I'd last seen six years ago; she had blossomed into a pretty woman, with blonde hair. She now wore make up which accentuated her beauty and made her blue eyes stand out against the carefully applied colours.

She dropped her arms, looking pleased to see me and pulled me down to sit at the table. Next to me sat the man she was talking to and when I looked into his green eyes, the colour of olives, my heart missed a beat. He still looked the same, with a warm, friendly face and chocolate brown hair. The only difference was that he was now a man, filled out with maturity and not as slender as he once was.

'Stanley?' I said his name in disbelief.

Roger was thrilled that we all knew each other, clapping his hands together, before pulling out a chair for May. Whereas

I looked upon my childhood friends and felt confused, desperately trying to digest what had happened.

'My goodness,' Beatrice said, her face wide with excitement as she sat between May and I. 'We all wondered what happened to you two. It feels like such a long time since I last saw you.'

May broke into conversation with Beatrice while I nervously looked at the other three guests. Mark and Roger remained standing, Roger was talking and Mark listened, his eyes dropped to look at me. It felt like daggers, and I looked away in the direction of Stanley. *'What happened?'* I thought, *'for Stanley and Mark to be friends?'*

'It's good to see you again, Betsy, you've not changed,' Stanley remarked.

'Really?' I raised my eyebrows and chortled, 'I hope I don't still look like a child?'

'No, no,' he laughed, 'you don't look like a child.'

'You and Mark friends now?'

Stanley with his elbows resting on the table leant closer to me, 'I work for Mr Irving?' I frowned, rolling my eyes in the direction of Beatrice and Mark wondering if he meant their father. 'Yes, Betsy.'

'Doing what?'

'Mending shoes, of course.' His head twitched and he looked puzzled that I would need to ask that question.

'With Mark?'

'No, no, Mark joined the army when he was old enough.'

I opened my mouth to ask a question, but Roger's voice spoke out and distracted my attention when he asked May, 'shall we dance?'

She accepted his offer and as she stood up to leave, Beatrice threw a glance at Stanley, and our brief conversation came to an end as the four of them left the table and joined the dance floor.

I was left alone with Mark.

I shuffled in my chair, turning to face the dancers, telling myself to remain calm. I watched Stanley take Beatrice's hand and spin her around to face him. He wrapped one arm around her waist and with his other hand firmly grasped her hand, pulling it close to his chest.

They moved well together, the music was a much slower pace, and the movements were more intimate, their bodies pressed close together, their legs entwined and occasionally they separated for Beatrice to gracefully pivot under his arm.

Mark pulled out the chair next to me, I could feel the vibrations of the legs drag across the floor, but I did not look at him. I could smell the cigarette he lit and felt a breeze on my arm as he waved the match out.

'Do you smoke, Betsy?' he asked.

I slowly turned to face him, my eyes met his and the look of shock would have been so clear on my face. I was completely horrified by his question, expecting something more from Mark, whether it was an insult or an apology.

'Do you smoke?' he asked again, offering me a cigarette.

'No,' I replied and he slipped the cigarette back into his top pocket.

'What was I supposed to do?' I wanted to walk away from him, but I was too afraid to stand in case my legs gave way. I wanted to look away, but I feared what he would do when my back was turned. I felt defensive, the past had left scars on my very existence thanks to this man, and scars never go away; they are always there as a reminder.

He leant forward his elbows pressed on the table and his fingers locked together with the cigarette resting in between. 'I've not seen you for a while?'

'No,' was all I wanted to say.

He inhaled deeply on his cigarette, the tip lighting up and burning down the paper. He flicked his thumb at the end and ash fell off into the tray. I watched his every move.

He looked at me again, his eyes no longer filled with hate, *'was he being amicable?'* 'Did Stanley tell you I am in the army?'

I nodded.

'Four years now.'

I made an 'oh,' sound.

'Small world isn't it?' he said, nodding his head in the direction of the dance floor, 'when Roger said he had met a woman called May, I never assumed it was May Colborne.'

My smile was weak, a twitch of my lips was all I could manage.

'Have you seen anything of your brothers?'

I shook my head.

'They were good boys.'

'Thank you,' I said, I was not convinced his words were genuine, there was no expression when he spoke, like he had raised a brick wall as a barrier to his true self.

He finished his cigarette and he began to tap on the table to the beat of the music. My eyes were busy, searching around the room, looking at people, looking at the band and looking at his fingers drumming. It was awkward sitting there, beside him.

'A cobbler was not me,' he broke the long silence and laughed, 'I was too heavy handed.'

'I can believe that.'

He removed the cigarette he had previously offered me and took a match to it, and continued talking, 'Stanley took to it like a duck to water, he will do all right, I reckon he will take over one day.' His thumb flicked the end of the cigarette, 'I'm not bothered, I didn't want it anyway, being a soldier is more for me.'

I nodded.

'I owe you an apology,' Mark said, his blue eyes met mine and the sincerity of his voice stole my breath for a second, and I felt suffocated with a wave of emotions, overwhelmed that after all this time he had shown remorse. 'I was horrible to you and I am sorry. What I did, was horrid. It was inexcusable. I have realised that there are far greater enemies out there.'

'Thank you,' I smiled, accepting his apology, feeling grateful for his acknowledgement, perhaps he had changed though something in my heart warned me and cried out to be careful, there was something else.

The others returned to the table. May touched my arm as she sat down, making sure everything was fine and I smiled reassuringly. Beatrice was soon in her ear, talking again and as I watched on, I noticed how much she spoke, and May politely nodded, listened and reacted accordingly.

Stanley's hand touched my shoulder and he leant forward to whisper in my ear, 'may I have this dance?'

He offered me his hand and my mouth opened as I glanced down at it. I stumbled over my words as his question took me by surprise. 'I've never danced before,' I said honestly and feeling embarrassed at my confession.

'Don't worry, I'll show you,' and he took my hand to lead me on to the dance floor, 'just copy what I do and I'll take the lead.'

Stanley held me firmly, one hand on my waist and the other wrapped around mine, I was trembling when I placed my hand in his. He left a distance between us, enough for me to look down and watch his feet as we glided across the dance floor. Then, his arm moved around my back, drawing me nearer to him and closing the gap between us. My body stiffened and I held my breath. Unable and too afraid to breathe, I peered over his shoulder and watched the other dancers. Overwhelmed with nervousness, my whole body was shuddering under his arms and I was certain he could feel me shaking. His leg, in between mine seemed to stay there as our sequenced steps meant our feet moved together and our bodies stayed close.

'Don't be nervous, Betsy,' Stanley whispered in my ear, 'it's me.'

My heart thudded in my chest and pulsed in my ears. I felt dizzy and I thought, *'but it's not you, not how I remember you.'*

The music changed and the pace quickened, I struggled to keep up with his faster steps. Other couples on the floor danced so well. They looked so graceful, their arm and leg movements perfectly coordinated as the music took them across the floor. I'm sure I looked as though I was dancing on hot coals. It helped to imagine those hot coals as at least I was able to keep up with the music.

As the songs played out, I enjoyed dancing with Stanley, he made me seem half decent. I felt comfortable and at ease in his arms, and he was not bothered if I made a mistake or stood on his foot. He always held me tightly, ignoring my errors, preventing me from falling and making light of it. I could not have imagined the night would unfold as it did. I had not expected to see Stanley Rhodes let alone dance with him.

'I have a wonderful idea,' Beatrice said, when the end of the night came and we were ready to go home, 'shall we all do something tomorrow afternoon?'

'All of us?' Mark said surprised.

'It will be like old times,' Beatrice insisted, 'why don't we go to the lake that you are so fond of?'

It was addressed to Stanley. I smiled at him, *'he still goes to the lake,'* I thought to myself, *'our special place, he still goes there.'* Whereas I had never wanted to go back.

'We don't have to go there,' Stanley said.

'You like to,' Beatrice continued, 'that's settled, we'll go there.'

Stanley glanced at me, I presumed to make sure I was fine with the arrangements and I flashed him a smile.

'Just no games of hide and seek,' Stanley teased, his eyes still on me and he winked, remembering our old childhood favourite, *'or blind man's bluff,'* I thought.

May and Roger had already made plans for the following afternoon, but without an excuse in mind, I accepted the invitation.

Chapter Seven

It was noon the following day when we met at the start of the country lanes; the lanes that I was very familiar with that led towards the lake that I knew all too well; both were long since forgotten. The lake hadn't meant the same to me after that dreadful day and without the company of Stanley, it was just another lake.

I borrowed May's bike to travel with the others. I wore a cream dress that kept rising up my leg as I rode the bike, exposing my slip underneath. I pinned my dress down whenever the wind caught underneath it in a desperate attempt to keep my dignity, but often failed and the only thing I could do, was to drop behind everyone to save my embarrassment. Mark took the lead, Beatrice and Stanley rode side-by-side and I tagged along behind.

'What's May doing?' Stanley asked, slowing down until I caught up with him.

'Roger has taken her to the pictures,' I replied.

May would have loved to come; she enjoyed the countryside, especially the lake where we spent our childhood.

'How do you know Roger?' I asked.

'Friends in common, small town, all that,' he laughed, 'he works at the flax mill, knows my brother.'

'My goodness, Rupert, how is he?'

'Married at long last.'

'That's wonderful, and your mum is well?'

'Absolutely, all is well with the Rhodes. What about you?' he asked. 'What have you been up to over the last, how many years?'

'Too many years, Stanley, we were children when I saw you last.'

In a matter of seconds I briefly filled Stanley in on the missing years of my life, and I realised how dull it must have sounded. I had no adventures to tell or interesting facts to unfold, I was a book with only a couple of pages. Despite how boring I may have seemed, he listened and appeared to show an interest.

'No gentleman after your hand in marriage?' he chortled.

'No,' I laughed, and mimicked his voice, remembering his words the last time we visited the lake. 'What was it you said, I'd better be pretty like my sister if I want to marry?'

'Who said that?'

'You did, or words to that effect.'

'I would not say such a thing,' he laughed and added, 'well, you proved me wrong.'

Feeling embarrassed I changed the subject, diverting the conversation back to him and drawing conclusions, 'what about you and Beatrice?'

'Not exactly –' before he could finish his sentence, Beatrice had slowed down and interrupted him. 'What are you saying about me, I heard my name?'

'Just about you two,' I was quick to reply, but the 'two' was drowned out by Stanley.

'As children,' he added.

'Oh Betsy,' Beatrice scorned, 'why can't you just forget about it? Mark said he was sorry; we were children for goodness sake.'

'Beatrice,' I was taken aback, 'we were talking about you and Stanley.'

'Oh,' she laughed nervously.

Stanley, not sure what was going on, peddled ahead. I noticed an edge in Beatrice's voice. She was a feisty one and could get on her high horse over the slightest misunderstanding. I made a mental note to myself to be careful what I said in front of her.

'He just needs to build up the courage,' she whispered, 'and ask me.'

'Ask you what?' I thought.

Mark was far ahead in the distance and he had stopped, unmounted his bike and waited for us to catch up. The men lifted the bikes over the stile into the field and we pushed them through the long grass. The stile was new, and there was a more pronounced pathway than there used to be; the grass had completely worn away. It was not a path to someone's special place now, but a walkway for many.

The lake was calm and still, perfectly reflecting the blue sky above. It was warm, with the sun shining brightly and not a cloud in sight. On this day, it could still be my special place, there was not another soul around other than the four of us.

'How perfect,' Beatrice said.

We dropped our bikes. Beatrice sat down on the pebbles. She leant back with her arms outstretched behind her supporting her weight, her eyes closed facing the sky to absorb the sun. With a contented smile on her face, she stayed like that for a while until her arms ached, when she then sat up to gaze at the lake.

Stanley removed his shoes and socks, rolled up his trousers and made his way to the edge of the water. He picked up a handful of flat pebbles and skimmed them across the lake. I slipped off my heels and rolled down my stockings, carefully folding them to fit inside my shoes. I walked over to his side. The pebbles were large enough and smooth enough to not cause discomfort as I crept over them. They were cold and wet beneath my feet, and when I reached the edge, the water pooled around my toes. It felt cooling in the heat.

I watched the pebbles skim through the air perfectly, they bounced five times across the water, delicately leaving behind a beautiful pattern of ripples as they disturbed the still water. He repeated the same throw again and another five times the pebble skimmed across.

'How do you do that?' I asked. I picked up a pebble myself and tried to mimic Stanley, but as soon as it hit the water, it made a loud plopping sound and sank to the bottom.

'Make sure your pebble is nice and flat,' Stanley explained, showing me one of his, 'you need to get the right angle and flick your wrist as you do it.'

'Is there anything you don't know?' I commented, rummaging through the pebbles by my feet and searching for a flat one.

'What do you mean?' He threw the last pebble in his hand and faced me.

'You always have something to teach me,' I smiled at him, as I stepped closer and held out my hand revealing a flat, oval shaped pebble sitting in the centre of my palm. 'What about this one?'

'Let's see.' Before Stanley had chance to examine the pebble, Mark had joined us and gently took my wrist to judge the pebble, 'perfect. How many are you on, Stan?'

'Five?'

'Right,' Mark whispered in my ear, 'I have to beat five.'

'Still the competitive sort,' I thought to myself.

'Watch,' Mark said and winked at me. He took the pebble from my hand and in a swift movement, released it across the lake. To his disappointment it only skimmed three times.

'Better luck next time,' Stanley teased.

Mark attempted to beat Stanley's record a second time, but when the rock skimmed across the water another three times, he was defeated and walked back to his sister, his head low. I could not help but smile at his loss, feeling a strange sense of justice.

'Try this one,' Stanley said, handing me a grey stone.

He stood behind me, placing a hand on my waist, the other held my hand with the pebble tucked inside. His fingers stroked mine and his touch was electric making the hairs on my arm stand on end. He buried his chin in my neck, our cheeks touched as we glanced out at the lake. He positioned my fingers around the stone and pulled my arm back, while he demonstrated the flicking movement with my wrist, I kept my joint relaxed, allowing his actions to control my body.

'When I say let go, you let go,' he said, and I nodded. He pulled my hand back, and thrust it forward, 'let go.'

I released the stone, and we watched with anticipation, neither of us taking a breath as my first attempt soared through the air above the lake and skimmed across the water once, before breaking the surface and sinking to its new-found bed.

'Well done,' Stanley said, sounding impressed and I felt pride.

I laughed. Stanley released his hold on me to find another pebble which he placed gently in my hand.

'You don't change,' I said, 'you are still the same fun character.'

'No, I'm not, Betsy,' he smiled.

He waved his arms in the direction of the lake as a signal for me to go ahead on my own. I re-enacted the motions Stanley had demonstrated seconds before, but the stone fell with another loud plop.

'That's a shame, try again,' Stanley encouraged.

After many attempts and much laughter, I finally did it. One successful skim and a plop, which was met with an applause from Stanley. He looked impressed and pleased at what his student had accomplished, 'You did it.'

'All thanks to you.'

We joined Beatrice and Mark, and as we approached, Beatrice jumped up and grabbed the basket that was strapped to the back of her bike. She seemed very theatrical, as she waved her arms around, fussing over the food and making sure everyone had something to eat.

'Do you want a hand, Beatrice?' I asked.

'No, thank you, Betsy.'

I sat down next to Stanley, and he returned my smile; he had such a warm and friendly smile. Mark removed his top and made a pillow across the ground in front of us. He laid down on his back, one arm behind his head, the other on his chest, and he pulled one knee up, looking relaxed as he sunbathed.

We enjoyed our lunch and chatted away. I noticed Stanley was particularly quiet, I knew something was on his mind, I recognised it from when he was a child – he often became withdrawn. He caught sight of me watching and smiled widely, looking like his jolly self again. *'I just wished I knew what was bothering him.'*

'We should have brought our swimming costumes,' Beatrice said.

I laughed nervously; I would not have felt comfortable in a bathing suit in front of men.

'Did you keep up your swimming, Betsy?' Stanley asked.

'No, not since you tried to teach me,' my voice faded out towards the end and I shook my head, saying louder, 'I can't swim.'

'You must practice,' he insisted, 'it's a good skill; a lifesaving skill.'

'Oh yes, I forgot,' Beatrice chuckled. 'You two used to come here all the time. Your secret place.'

There was a condescending tone in her laughter.

'Do you know, Betsy, he only brought me here this summer, after he had gone on about what a pleasant place it is. I don't see it myself, it's just a lake,' Beatrice paused, 'but it's quiet and that is something. I prefer the park, myself. How often do you come here, Betsy?'

'I don't anymore,' I said, feeling uncomfortable.

'Well you should,' Beatrice laughed, mockingly, 'after all you said you can't swim. I haven't had the pleasure of Stanley teaching me how.'

'You have never asked,' Stanley said in his defence.

'Oh, Stanley, I *can* swim.'

As she said the words, she looked at me.

After we had eaten, we went for a splash in the water, the coldness felt so inviting in the heat. I hitched my dress up, tucked the hem in my undergarment and walked until the water came to my knees. I could see the bottom clearly, the pebbles that made the bed and the dirt that lifted and clouded the water as I moved. Beatrice had managed to roll her dress up and tie it at the front, it was short, but it kept her hands free to gracefully move through the water.

Stanley had stripped down to his swimming trunks and swam close by. I watched him discreetly, taking sneaky peeks in his direction and feeling how some things don't ever change. It was so familiar; it could still have been six years ago.

My daydream was soon interrupted when Mark took huge strides towards me creating large splashes as his legs trudged through the water. I started to scream playfully as I was sprayed with the water. I laughed and tried to run away, but I failed miserably, my foot slipped on the rock, and I fell face first into the water. I knelt up, with the laughter of Beatrice and Mark surrounding me. Something felt strange in my stomach – memories came flooding back of when they would laugh after they taunted me, and in my head that is what I heard.

I tried to shake away the thoughts.

Stanley was quick to reach me and his arm aided me to stand, while I steadied myself on the slippery rocks. My dress was soaked and felt heavy as it clung against my skin. The bottom of the dress rested on the top of the water, waving and moving to the flow.

I glanced across at the other two; Mark was looking at me, his expression was more amused and friendly, than mocking, instantly melting my concerns. I didn't see Beatrice's face; she had turned around and was heading back to land.

'Did you hurt yourself?' Stanley asked, he was still supporting me and I clung on to his arms.

'I am fine,' I smiled, 'I'll dry.'

We looked at each other for a while, not moving, not talking, just looking. I could hear Mark splashing through the water, as he left the lake to join Beatrice.

I released my hold on Stanley and wrapped my arms around my chest, feeling exposed and paranoid my dress had become see through. Stanley didn't notice, his eyes were on mine the whole time and he whispered, 'if you are ever passing by you must call in the shop; don't be a stranger.'

'I will do,' I promised.

Chapter Eight

On Monday, I began my normal early start at work and I noticed Mr Bradshaw's car was still parked on the road. I had expected him to return to the city over the weekend as he normally only stayed a few days to a week at the most.

With this in mind, I prepared breakfast for both Dr Oxley and Mr Bradshaw.

Dr Oxley was his normal punctual self, sat at the table for seven o'clock, waiting. I took a deep breath before I entered the dining room carrying the breakfast, knowing I would be greeted by his not so cheery self.

As I anticipated, he was seated at the table with his glasses perched on the end of his nose. His thick grey eyebrows sat like caterpillars above his eyes making them look small and piggy. The deep-set wrinkles across his forehead painted him with a permanent frown. I imagined even if he smiled, he would still look displeased, *'I suppose the pressure of being a doctor takes its toll.'*

'Good morning, Dr Oxley,' I said cheerfully, 'No Mr Bradshaw this morning, I'm sure I saw his car outside?'

He didn't answer.

He leant back on his chair allowing space for me to place his breakfast before him and continued to flick through the pages of his newspaper. I poured tea into his half empty cup and picked up the tray with Mr Bradshaw's breakfast still on.

I could hear him breathing heavily and I sighed under my breath at how ignorant he was.

He must have sensed my frustration and finally spoke to me in a monotonous tone, 'My nephew is quite unwell at present.'

'Oh, I am sorry to hear it,' I said clinging to the tray, I was sincerely concerned.

'He will need to eat, so take his breakfast up to him.'

'What is the matter with him?'

Dr Oxley looked at me through his eyebrows and seeing his scowling eyes, I felt awkward. *'Perhaps I should not have asked the question?'*

He folded the newspaper twice and placed it on the table. He continued to look at me with a disapproving stare as he removed the glasses and placed them on top of the paper. He flicked open the napkin, allowing it to fall over his knee and he brushed the creases flat.

'My apologies, Dr Oxley, I should not have asked that,' My voice quivered.

'He is suffering with a chest infection, it will soon clear.' He said in a very matter of fact tone and he was not going to say anything more about it. 'Betsy, once you have delivered his breakfast, please report back to me.'

'Yes, Dr Oxley,' and I left the dining room.

I carried Mr Bradshaw's breakfast upstairs and knocked gently on the door. The tray was shaking and the cup rattled as I balanced the tray on one arm to knock harder.

'Yes!' A weak voice spluttered and coughed from inside.

I opened the door; a thick, strong, musty smell immediately assaulted my nose making me feel sick. The room was dark and stuffy, and the lack of fresh air was suffocating. I took a deep breath before stepping over the threshold.

I walked towards Mr Bradshaw lying in his bed; the covers pulled up to his neck and his hand over his mouth, shielding his cough. He looked awfully unwell and weak. I placed the tray on the table next to him.

'Good morning, Mr Bradshaw, how are you feeling?'

'Just a cough,' he said, his voice was croaky, and his eyes were dark and heavy.

'Would you like me to open your window and curtains, I think the fresh air will do you good?'

'No.'

'Will you let me help you to sit more upright?'

Mr Bradshaw resisted at first, his illness had left him feeling grumpy and miserable. I ignored his out-of-character behaviour and I attempted to hook my arm underneath his, trusting my instincts that lying flat was not helping his cough, 'you'll be more comfortable if you sit up more.'

'Leave me!' His voice was still bitter and his body stiff, but he was too weak to fight me off.

He had no energy to resist, and I managed to drag Mr Bradshaw up into a vertical position. He supported most of his weight, while I, with my free hand, quickly fluffed up his pillow and reached for the two spare pillows lying next to him. When the pillows were piled up, I gently eased him back against them and he looked more comfortable.

'I may not be a nurse, but I have common sense, Mr Bradshaw,' I said in delayed defence.

Ignoring his earlier refusal, I tugged open the heavy curtains; the material was thick, and the velvet felt so soft and fluffy. A streak of sunlight filled the room and fell across the foot of the bed, Mr Bradshaw groaned and turned his head away from the brightness.

I opened the window. The fresh air whooshed through the gap, it was freshening, and I inhaled the outdoor summer smell of flowers and wet grass from the early morning dew, drying in the sun. I turned to face Mr Bradshaw and said triumphantly, 'like I said, the fresh air will do you good.'

Mr Bradshaw looked weak, his eyes partly shut, his face pale and sweat formed on his brow. I walked over to his bedside and pressed my hand against his forehead, feeling the heat of his skin beneath my palm. He groaned at my cold touch.

'You have a temperature,' I said softly.

I lowered his bed covers to his waist, his night shirt was drenched against his skin and I could have wrung out a bucket of sweat from his clothes. The breeze through the window blew gently across him and I felt sure it would cool him down.

'Mr Bradshaw, maybe if you change your pyjamas you will feel better, you're soaking,' I said. As dismissive as he was about my advice, I ignored him and I removed clean pyjamas from his drawers. I left them at the bottom of his bed, while I went to the bathroom and returned with a basin of cool water and a flannel.

I unbuttoned his pyjama top, peeling it from his back and, with a grumble, he slipped his arms out of the sleeves. I sensed he ached and found my fussing unbearable when I moved him as often as I did, but I was gentle and assured him it would be over shortly.

I wrung out the flannel and gently mopped his brow and around his neck. He welcomed the coolness of the cloth against his head and closed his eyes. I pressed it against his forehead and left it there for a moment.

I lost myself for a moment as my eyes glanced down at his well-defined bare chest and curiously flickered to where the sheet began at his hips. I could feel my blood pulsing in my veins and the curiosity of my youth urged me to touch. I managed to resist, of course I did, but my cheeks were burning as I drew my attention back to his face and I removed the cloth from his forehead.

'Shall we leave your top off?' I said, it was not intended as a question. 'Until your temperature is lower?'

I rinsed the flannel in the water and he opened his eyes slightly. I could make out his blue eyes peering at me and he started to splutter again, with the crackling sound of phlegm moving in his chest.

'I know you won't feel like eating, but at least drink the tea.' I poured the milk from the jug into a cup and added the tea. 'You need to drink plenty.'

Mr Bradshaw said nothing, but I felt his glare on me as I offered him his tea. He shook his head at first, but I persisted, waving the cup under his nose until he took it from my hand and began to sip.

He looked at me through tired eyes and opened his mouth to speak, but then closed it again. It took him a while to sip through the beverage and I waited patiently for him to finish. He handed me his empty cup and I offered him another, but he held up his hand to refuse.

I left him alone to sleep. I gently brought the door to a close and I smiled to myself; there I was, untrained in nursing of any sort, taking care of a patient in a doctor's house!

Dr Oxley showed no concern or displayed any notion of worry on his face when he waited at the foot of the stairs for me.

'He's still unwell, Dr Oxley, he has a temperature. I've opened the window and tried to make him as comfortable as possible.'

'He will get better,' he replied and handed me a piece of paper that was curled up in his hand. 'I have been called out, and I need you to call into town and purchase a few items. I want them before I return.'

I folded the paper in my pocket, 'yes, Dr Oxley, I'll go now.'

It was a short walk to town and before I even reached the street, I could hear the hollering of the town folk making a living, the sound of a tram rattling down the road and a few honking car horns. The town was filled with people, darting around, all walking in different directions and all careful not to collide with someone else.

My attention was drawn to the cobblers shop by a young boy stood outside, yelling at the top of his voice, encouraging people to buy a newspaper. He waved one, rolled up like a telescope in his hand, and carried many more in a bundle in his bag.

The cobblers was a small shop with paned glass windows, making it appear dark inside. Above the door the family name, 'Irving's,' was displayed and I asked myself, *'Why was Mark not taking over the family business?'*

Before I realised, I had subconsciously opened the door and the ringing out of the bell, that hung over the door, brought me back to reality. I was standing in the middle of the store, asking myself, *'What have I done? Why have I entered the shop?'*

The familiar voice of Stanley called out, 'I'll be with you in a minute.'

I stood on the spot and watched him for a while, his back hunched over as he belted a sole into place. From a distance I observed how hard he worked and admired his attention to detail. He soon finished and turned around to assist his customer; a look of surprise spread across his face when he saw it was me.

'Betsy?' he asked and walked around the counter to greet me.

'Morning, Stanley. I have never been in here, you don't get much light, do you?'

I looked around the small, dark room.

'Depends on the time of day, in the afternoon the light comes through until early evening.'

'Where's Mr Irving?'

'Oh, did you want to see Mr Irving? I'm afraid he comes and goes now; you will probably get him in this afternoon. He tends to stay in the afternoon. Is there anything I can help you with?'

'No, I –,' I looked around the room, feeling silly; perhaps it was too soon to call by after he suggested it only the day before. I chortled and looked up at Stanley through my eyelashes, 'I was just passing.'

Stanley nodded once and mouthed 'Oh,' with a smile, his hands rested on his hips. We stood silently for a moment. His white apron fell below his knees, stained with black and brown marks. There was something attractive in his casual workwear; he was wearing a tie that was poking out at the top of his overall and his shirt sleeves were rolled up revealing his tanned forearms.

'Are you busy on Wednesday afternoon?' Stanley broke the silence.

'No,' I responded too quickly, I normally finished work around noon on a Wednesday for Dr Oxley.

'Can I take you out for something to eat and to the pictures afterwards?' he asked, he looked nervous when he spoke, but his question made me burst with happiness.

'Yes, I would like that.'

We had just made plans for our date as a man entered the shop; he removed his hat and politely greeted us with a 'Good morning.' Stanley knowing the gentleman, greeted him by name, whilst holding out his hand for a welcoming handshake. I was glad of the interruption as I was in danger of losing my composure. I took the opportunity to leave, raised my hand to signal goodbye and slipped out of the door, Stanley acknowledged my departure with a nod, a smile and a wink.

I stepped out onto the street, closing the door behind me and hearing the sound of the latch clicking as it dropped down into place. I needed to take a deep breath before I could continue with my errands.

Wednesday afternoon was soon upon me and I became increasingly anxious as the time drew nearer. The morning at work went by in a daze. I finished at noon, allowing plenty of time to go home, change and return to town for half past four when I was due to meet with Stanley.

I struggled to choose a dress to wear. The only one suitable was the dress I had worn the previous Sunday, but I preferred to wear something different. May had offered to lend me her pale blue dress the night before and when I failed to make a decision from my own clothing, I selected her dress from the wardrobe.

Being shorter than May, the dress fell below my calf, but with the floaty style of the outfit, I was able to get away with the different length. The sleeves were loose and hung by my elbows, the neckline curved revealing a modest amount of skin, and I borrowed Aunt Lily's gold chain with a cross on to complete the outfit. I wore cream, closed shoes, with a slight heel and a buttoned buckle that went over the top of the foot.

It was a pleasant walk into town, although being cooler than it was at midday, I wrapped a shawl over my shoulders. Stanley was already waiting at the planned location outside the church gates. His back was pressed against the railings and he was looking down at the ground. I could see the top of his hat and the outline of his jaw, and the sight of him caused butterflies to flutter quickly in my stomach.

I took a deep breath and said, 'Good afternoon.'

His head lifted and my cheeks turned scarlet, I could feel the heat burning in my flesh, and when his eyes met mine, and he smiled, my insides melted.

'Are you hungry?' he asked and I nodded. His hand touched my shoulder, only for a moment, to guide me in the direction he wanted to go. 'I know where we can go.'

Stanley led me to Robinson's Tea Room at the end of the square where May worked. He held the door open for me as I stepped inside and looked around for May, but she was nowhere to be seen. It was busy, but we found a vacant table next to the window and Stanley pulled out a chair for me.

'Have you ever tried their steak and kidney pie?' he asked, taking the seat opposite.

'No, I haven't, but May recommends it,' I replied.

He insisted I try it, and ordered two steak and kidney pies and a pot of tea. It was a while before the waitress served our food and, as soon as she walked away, Stanley with a hand gesture signalled me to tuck in. He had already picked up his fork and was looking ravenously at his pie.

I cut into the crisp pastry, steam rose from the middle and the savoury meaty smell that rose with it was divine. Stanley had paused from eating to have a drink, he leant back in his chair, his whole hand engulfed the delicate china cup, and he watched me take my first mouthful.

'Good?' he asked.

'Very good,' I agreed, enjoying the sensation of the meats and the gravy tucked under a layer of light pastry.

'They are the best in here. Is May not working today?'

'She's supposed to be,' I said after I had cleared my mouthful. 'You've been here a few times before?'

'Not that often. Roger comes here all the time, but I think we both know why.'

I smiled to show my understanding and went on to say, 'Mark has changed.'

'I think people grow up,' Stanley returned his cup to the saucer and picked up his fork. 'I am pleased he apologised to you, that's the least he could do.'

'We were children and like you just said, people grow up. You seem close to the family.'

'Mr Irving is a good man,' Stanley swallowed his mouthful, 'I did work at the flax mill for two months after school, but one day Mr Irving made me an offer. I think he always knew Mark was not cut out for this type of work and saw me as an ideal apprentice.'

'Do you enjoy it?'

'Absolutely,' his face lit up when he spoke, 'I do enjoy it, but it wasn't easy in the beginning, Mark and I would find ourselves in heated debates and close to –,'

'*Close to fighting,*' I finished the sentence in my head.

'Well, anyway,' he continued, 'things happen for a reason.'

Stanley finished his meal and he sat back and waited for me to finish. His continued gaze didn't make me feel awkward or uneasy, he looked to be thinking over something in his mind.

'So, you've not seen your mum since?' he eventually asked.

I shook my head, taking a sip of my tea.

'And your brothers? Betsy, I am sorry, that must have been awful for you. Do you know where they are? Have you been in touch?'

'No, I don't know where either of them are. My mother hasn't been in touch and my brothers haven't come back. I wish I knew, but I don't.'

'Betsy, we don't have to talk about this now.'

'Thank you, Stanley, it's nice to know they are still remembered,' I took a deep breath and said, 'it would be easier to deal with if I was in touch with them, but I don't know if they are still alive or well.'

I looked down at my plate, my eyelids pressed together knowing if the air touched my eyes I may cry and I hoped to prevent the embarrassment. Stanley's warm hand rested on top of mine, and I managed to gaze across into his sympathetic eyes, so full of understanding and he repeated softly, 'we don't need to speak about this now.'

I smiled feeling thankful.

Stanley stood up and walked over to the counter to pay while I finished my drink, looking out of the window. All the shops were closed on a Wednesday afternoon, but the town was still busy with people strolling about and children playing. I watched them playing games I knew too well, running freely and happily without a care in the world. The gathering of children could easily have been my siblings and I, and a tear rolled down my cheek. I quickly wiped it away; Bert and Frank were always in my thoughts and prayers.

At times I wanted to see my mother and ask her '*why? Why she sent them away? Why did she not ask Aunt Lily for help?*

Why did she hate us when Father died? Why? Why? Why?'
I felt angry with her, things could have been different, *'why
did she do what she did?'* I still remember Mark calling her
a 'whore.' I remembered learning for the first time what a
whore meant and being shocked, disgusted and horrified. I
spent several days pondering over the meaning and asking
myself, *'did she become a whore? What really happened?'*

'Fancy seeing you here.' May was clearing the plates from
our table and the sound of her voice snapped me from my
daydream.

'I wondered where you were.'

'Betsy,' she looked concerned and her voice dropped to a
whisper, 'are you all right? Have you been crying?'

I touched May's arm to reassure her, 'I was just thinking of
Bert and Frank.'

May followed my glance to the children playing outside. She
froze for a second, I knew she saw it too, but she continued
to wash down the table, her other hand carrying the empty
plates, 'I see. Enjoy your day Betsy and you must tell me all
about it tonight. I will see you back home, this evening,' and
before she left the table she added, 'you suit my dress.'

May disappeared into the kitchen and as I watched her go it
dawned on me how long it had taken Stanley to pay the bill.
He was not stood at the counter, but standing across the room
leaning over a table talking to Mark; my stomach sank at the
sight of him. Seeing him by surprise still had that effect on
me, even though I knew things were different, I could not shift
the unsettling worry and fear.

Stanley straightened his back and I could see his face. He
looked annoyed, his arms were folded and he said something
to Mark before walking away. Mark's face shared the same
expression and didn't alter when his eyes fell on mine. I
looked away.

'Betsy, are you upset?' Stanley asked when he approached
me, his face had returned to its pleasant self.

'No, no,' I quickly responded.

He studied my face for a moment as I rose to my feet and
stood close to him. He searched my eyes, trying to understand

something, perhaps considering whether to ask more questions, but decided against prying and reached for my shawl instead. He wrapped it over my shoulders and handed me my bag. My emotional moment had passed and I returned to enjoying his company once again.

We left the tea room and made our way to the pictures. There was a long queue outside the ticket office and we waited patiently as it slowly reduced. We passed the time discussing films we had seen, the first time we went and our favourite film. We laughed when we realised how much we had in common. Stanley visited often, it was his favourite pastime. He was fascinated by the technical side of it all and I sensed the excitement in his voice.

I remembered the first time Aunt Lily took May and me to the cinema; that motion picture telling a story on the huge screen. It was a moving story, breathtaking and wonderful, an experience I would treasure forever. I felt so privileged to live in a time to experience such an invention.

We were soon seated in the crowded theatre and when the film rolled, Stanley laughed out loud joining in with the rest of the auditorium. He had such a contagious laugh when he found something amusing, a sound which came from the pit of his stomach that I didn't find too loud or annoying – it made me feel happy. The film was funny and I was laughing, but it was Stanley's chortling that had me in stitches; tears streamed from my eyes and I felt wonderful.

The room was dark, but our faces glowed by the bright lights of the screen and Stanley looked at me to ask, 'are you having a good time?'

His words blew from his mouth on my neck causing goose pimples to rise on my arm.

'Yes,' I whispered back.

His face was close to mine, but our bodies didn't touch, although I was *fully* aware of him. The blood pumped quickly through my veins, and I desperately wanted to hold him, to feel his hands, but they remained resting on top of his knee.

The light was blinding when we left the dark theatre. The sun was starting to set, and the temperature had dropped slightly, enough for me to shiver when a breeze passed through the holes in my shawl. My arms cradled my body in attempt to keep warm as we embraced the evening.

'I had best take you home, you look freezing,' he said, and removed his jacket to wrap around my shoulders. The inside of the jacket was warm from his body heat and, like a hot water bottle, I instantly felt the benefits.

'Thank you,' I said, no longer shivering.

It was only eight o'clock, and the night still felt young, I was not ready for home, but Stanley headed in that direction. The journey was slow as we took small steps trying to steal as much time together as possible.

'It's been nice seeing you again, Betsy, I have thought about you a lot over the years.'

'Really?' I was surprised, my eyes wide and a large, impressed smile on my face.

'Yes, I always wondered what you were doing and I did think about visiting you.'

'Why didn't you?'

He paused for a moment, his head bowed, as he concentrated on the ground in front of him. 'I felt guilty that I didn't stop Mark and I was angry with myself. I couldn't face you after that; I was weak.'

'You weren't weak, you always stood up to Mark.'

'I still do,' he laughed.

Disappointment hung over me when I saw the entrance to my street and I, half-heartedly, started to edge across the road preparing for our goodbyes.

'Can I show you something first?' Stanley asked, 'it will only take a minute. It's there.'

Stanley pointed to the bridge that the train crossed over, which was only a few paces in the distance. The road that travelled underneath the bridge eventually ran alongside the lake.

I agreed and he pulled my hand. We started to run, and I clonked along in my heels, trying to keep up with Stanley who was behaving like a schoolboy, eager to show me something. We slowed down when we approached the bridge and stopped when we were underneath. Everything echoed; from our voices to the sound of my feet.

'When I worked at the flax mill, before Mr Irving offered me the job, I thought about working for the railway. They had just built this bridge at the time and I knew it would be the link to the rest of the country. I thought about where I could go and what I could do. I would feel like a free man.'

'Sounds wonderful.'

'Yes, it did.'

'Do you regret it?'

'Things happen for a reason,' Stanley said, shrugging it off and his tone changed to sounding more excited, 'right, it's time. Lean against the wall and wait.'

In the distance, I could hear the rattling of a train at speed chuntering along the tracks overhead. We both pressed our backs against the wall and waited, looking at each other and smiling.

The train was coming nearer, I could feel the vibrations of it passing through the wall, it gradually increased and became louder, as it roared above. We laughed as it passed over.

The sound of the train faded away and everything was still once more.

Stanley moved first and stood in front of me, while my back was still pressed against the cool bricks. Both his hands rested against the wall, either side of my shoulders; I was trapped, but I didn't mind.

For a moment he didn't move, and his closeness made me feel nervous, *a little*, enough for me to be aware that my heart rate had increased, but also, to be aware that I had a sense of wanting him. I thought he was going to kiss me. I hoped he would and it felt as though he wanted to, but instead, he placed a gentle kiss on my forehead.

He took a small step back, dropping his hands by his side, as he did so, 'do you have any plans on Sunday?'

'No,' I whispered, trying to conceal my disappointment.

'Can I take you to the seaside?' He broke away from me, taking a step back. 'I made a promise to you when we were children, do you remember?'

'Yes,' I said, feeling disappointed he had moved away.

'Yes, you remember or yes, to coming?'

'Both,' I chortled.

'Great.'

Stanley took my hand, pulling me away from the wall and walked me home. After we made arrangements for the following Sunday, he said goodbye, leaving me with a gentle kiss on the cheek before we parted.

Chapter Nine

Mr Bradshaw's health began to improve to the point that, much to my disappointment, by the following weekend he was well enough and getting ready to return home. I had enjoyed his extended stay and nursing him over the course of the week. He was a breath of fresh air from his uncle and it was a change from my usual duties. It gave me a feeling of importance – a purpose; I was needed.

'Good morning, Dr Oxley,' I greeted him, feeling surprised to see him already sat at the table as I passed through to the kitchen. I didn't expect a pleasant response, just his usual, yet this particular morning I was shocked when he replied, 'Good morning, Miss Colborne.'

Completely shocked by his kind gesture, I froze in my tracks, and gawked at him in disbelief, convincing myself that he too was now coming down with something. Sure enough, he was sat there looking perfectly well in his grand chair, fully dressed, with the newspaper in his hand and his glasses perched at the end of his nose. He was looking at me, and his mouth twitched into a smirk, 'I trust you are well?'

'Yes, Dr Oxley,' my voice was shaky.

'My nephew said he was impressed with the level of care you have shown him this week and how attentive you have been. Well done, Betsy, you have really proved yourself.' He looked back down at his newspaper.

As I carried on towards the kitchen, I felt a sense of pride that Dr Oxley, after four years, had finally acknowledged and complimented me.

Lost and distracted in my thoughts, I didn't notice Mr Bradshaw appear in the entrance of the kitchen, leaning against the doorway with his arms folded. I jumped out of my skin when I saw him.

'I am many things, Betsy, but invisible I am not.'

'Mr Bradshaw, I'm sorry I didn't see you there.' *How could I have missed him? How long was he stood there for?*'

'When you have finished, can you call into the study?'

'Yes, Mr Bradshaw,' I responded and he left me alone.

Once I had cleared the breakfast pots, I made my way to the study to meet Mr Bradshaw. Normally Dr Oxley kept this room locked and I was only allowed access on those rare times he wanted the room cleaned. Of course, Mr Bradshaw was allowed to use the room whenever he pleased.

I knocked on the door and waited for his command to enter. I found the room unsettling compared to the other rooms in the rest of the house. The walls displayed many frightening medical instruments and, locked behind the glass doors of a cabinet, there were different medicine bottles on show. I was always glad when I left that room.

Mr Bradshaw waved his arm for me to sit on the chair opposite him. It felt very formal and took me back to the day when I applied for the job with his uncle. Mr Bradshaw was sat where Dr Oxley sat all those years ago, his arms leaning on the table and his hands clutched together.

'You look well, Mr Bradshaw,' I remarked.

'And I thank you for that, Betsy. We are both grateful for all that you have done.'

'Thank you, Mr Bradshaw, it was nothing, I was glad I could help.'

He shuffled through some papers in front of him and I watched him carefully. He tapped the papers on the desk, checking all the sheets were in line, before placing them down on the table. He cupped his hands and looked at me. While he paused, his expression grew serious, not what I was used to from Mr Bradshaw and I felt anxious by this change.

'Have you ever left the town?' he asked.

I shook my head and replied, 'I've only been as far as the next village.'

'You've never seen a city? Never been on a train? Never been farther than the closest village?'

I shook my head and he continued, 'as you know I live in a city and Miss Sharp has been my housekeeper for many years and provides an excellent service. I am needing to take on another housekeeper to assist her and my uncle suggested you.'

'Me?'

'I am extremely pleased with your work and I am confident you will understand my ways, so I wish to make you an offer. You are not obliged to answer today, I expect you need time to consider, but I very much wish for you to come and work for me. I will pay you well and I think it will bring you opportunity, more opportunity than here.'

My jaw could have hit the floor; my mouth was open so wide that a locomotive could have steamed through it. I had been given an opportunity to go with Mr Bradshaw, to experience a different style of life. My world had solely been the town, even when I learnt that Bert and Frank were in Canada, I had truly never wanted to know how far that was. I preferred my bubble and beyond that didn't matter.

'Oh, Mr Bradshaw,' I said, feeling overwhelmed by his offer. 'I don't know what to say, I am speechless. What about Dr Oxley?'

'He wants you to go, you've really proved yourself this week and he feels it will give you a chance in life. Besides, he said he always wanted someone older working here,' and he laughed at his statement.

I thought for a moment and considered Mr Bradshaw's offer. I was tempted at the prospect of a new experience, but the thought of moving away from the place I had spent my whole life terrified me. Was it foolish for a working-class girl to think, *there was more to life than this?* I was lucky to work in a household that treated me so well, but there again was I foolish to let him leave without taking a chance on the opportunity he laid before me?

'Mr Bradshaw, I am really unsure,' I hesitated.

'Betsy, I don't need your answer today.' He stood up and placed some papers into his bag, 'I'm travelling back this morning and I'll return sometime in September. That gives you a month to come to your decision. If you wish to take the opportunity, you can come back with me then.'

'Yes, Mr Bradshaw, and thank you so much for thinking of me.'

'Betsy, my uncle has given you permission to finish at five tonight.' He raised his eyebrows and smiled.

'But I finished early last Saturday,' I reminded him.

'I know what it is like to be young and I think you should enjoy yourself. Not too much mind, I still want you to come and work for me. I am only showing you what a good boss I will be.'

I thanked him gratefully.

When I finished early that evening and told May of Mr Bradshaw's offer, she saw it as a reason to go to the dance, 'to celebrate a new beginning,' even though I had not completely made my decision. For now, going to the dance was the only thing I was certain of.

'Are you going to go?' May asked, once we had found a table.

We both scanned our eyes around the room. I knew May was searching for Roger; I was looking for him too, but hoping that Stanley would be with him.

'I would do it even if it's just for a year,' May said, when I didn't answer her. 'Just think of the experience – you could enjoy a new world before you marry and have a family.'

I laughed, 'that's all we have to look forward to – marriage and babies.'

'Yes,' May's face beamed, 'and I can't wait to have a husband who loves me. I would cook his favourite meals and teach our children to be good, honest people. Can you remember what life was like when Father was still alive?' Then May shook her head answering her own question. 'I don't suppose you do, you were only young. I remember how much Father loved our mother and I want that. That's all I have ever wanted, to find love, real love and have a family.'

'You will,' I promised her.

'I hope so.'

We sat in silence, enjoying the music and my mind wandered to Mr Bradshaw. I thought about his offer and remembered once asking myself, perhaps as a child, 'is there more to life than to live and to die?' Perhaps this was my opportunity to live?

May was the first to recognise someone, her back straightened, her chin lifted, and her head rocked slightly as she desperately looked at someone through the crowd. She was frowning and she looked concerned, 'Betsy, Mark's over there and –'

I followed her glance, unsure why Mark's presence had caused this worry in May. I spotted the back of his head, bobbing around in the middle of the dance floor with a woman in his arms and nothing struck me as alarming. The dance led them nearer to us and I lowered my eyes, not wanting to pry, but May continued to stare, looking horrified.

'Oh my goodness,' May exclaimed and raised her hand to cover her gaping mouth, 'he looks in a bad way.'

'Who does?'

'Mark,' she scorned, 'he's just danced past us, who do you think? His face is a mess.'

I peered over my shoulder trying to catch sight of Mark, but whenever I saw him, someone else danced in our path.

I shrugged at May.

'I wonder what happened?' May was still staring at the dance floor, wanting to know more, 'Roger will probably know. Where is he?'

She searched the dance floor for Roger and when she failed to spot him let out a deep sigh. She rose to her feet, 'Come on, let's dance, we may find out more if we are nearer to Mark,' and she dragged me on to the dance floor.

The floor was rammed with people so May and I followed everyone else, dancing around in circles. I laughed at how ridiculous we both looked, not completely sure who was leading who, but May was distracted, her attention was everywhere else but on me.

Her distraction caused me to lose my balance and stumble over her feet. I fell backwards in slow motion, closing my eyes and bracing myself for the hard landing. I could see the people continue to dance around me and heads slowly turning, all eyes were on me watching me fall. Yet I didn't reach the floor – an arm caught me just in time. My rescuer pulled me to my feet and swung me out of the way of the other dancers. The show was over.

It all happened so quickly and before I knew what was happening, I was stood on the outskirts of the dance floor, my head spinning slightly, clinging on to the arms that had rescued me.

I was unable to support my own weight, my mind taking time to adjust to the unexpected outcome, while those arms continued to support me. I looked up into familiar green eyes that were looking down into mine. Stanley. My insides fluttered; butterflies dancing a quickstep inside me and, although the world around me continued, within my moment with him time stood still. Perhaps only a few seconds passed, but to me it was longer and I felt the words come to my mind so clearly as my soul said to me, 'I'm going to marry you.'

Stanley spoke first, 'Betsy, you should sit down, you've gone white.'

'I am so sorry, Betsy, it was my fault,' May said at the same time.

'What happened?' Roger had come over and I could see the relieved look on May's face that he was finally here.

May said a few words to him, but I paid no attention to their conversation, I was too busy looking at Stanley and his battered lip. A painful looking split sliced his top lip and the area around was swollen, becoming more obvious when he smiled.

'Stanley, your lip,' I exclaimed. I reached up and cupped the side of his face, careful not to touch his recent wound.

He placed his hand over the top of mine and I saw that his knuckles were grazed too. 'What have you been doing?'

'I should really see to Betsy,' I heard May say.

'I will look after her,' Stanley said.

May smiled at Stanley, then looked at me and her expression read, 'would you mind?' Assuming Roger had asked her to dance, I smiled back at her and then watched them dance away.

'Let's sit you down,' Stanley said, with one arm still around my waist and with the other he took my hand, guiding me to the table where I had previously sat. He pulled out a chair and I lowered myself down slowly. I felt his arm slip away from me.

'What happened, Stanley?' I asked, as I examined his face.

He didn't answer and instead, stared down at his hands that were cupped together on the table.

'Stanley,' I leant closer to him and said what I feared in my stomach, 'have you been fighting with Mark?'

He looked at me, his head didn't move and his eyes peered from below his eyebrows. I could see my prediction was accurate.

'Stanley, why?'

'It doesn't matter, Betsy,' Stanley shook his head and I rested my hand on top of his. His thumb slipped around mine to gently stroke my hand.

'We had a disagreement,' he explained, 'we do from time to time.'

'But to physically fight with one another? What state is Mark in?'

'All he got from me was a black eye and a headache.'

'And you?'

'I can't feel a thing,' he licked the wound and smiled.

'Has this not complicated things, you hitting your boss' son?'

'No, it was a disagreement between Mark and me. No one knows what happened, they think it was a drunk that turned on us both.'

The band played a slower song and the dancers changed their pace in time with the music.

'What about now?' I asked, 'have you two sorted your disagreement?'

Stanley shrugged, 'perhaps, for now.'

'For now?'

'Yes, for now. Besides, he goes back to the army tomorrow.'

He looked behind at the band playing. I made a sound, I had something to say, but before I managed to speak, Stanley interrupted me, 'shall we dance?'

I decided to leave the dispute between Mark and Stanley for the time being and give in to my inner desire. I smiled and held out my hand, which he gently received and guided me onto the dance floor.

We danced the foxtrot; the simple steps he had shown me previously. As during our first dance, our bodies touched as his arm curled around my waist and my hand rested on his shoulder. This time I felt less nervous and more relaxed in his hold.

'Have you impressed Dr Oxley?' Stanley asked in a whisper in my ear, 'I don't normally see you here.'

'Have I disappointed you?' I tested him.

'No,' he laughed, 'the opposite. I'm pleasantly surprised.'

We spent the rest of the evening together. Mark crossed our path a few times and the thick tension between them both was suffocating. Mark held his stare with Stanley, his look was chilling, but I felt more uncomfortable than Stanley did. *'What had happened to cause this trouble between the two of them, when the week before they were friends?'*

Unfortunately, the band stopped playing, announcing that the evening had come to an end. Stanley stood with his arm still around me and we continued to face one another. People around us began to leave the dance floor.

'I will walk you home,' Stanley said, his voice seemed much louder now the music had stopped.

'There's no need, I will find May and walk back with her.'

'In that case I will walk you both home,' he proclaimed.

I didn't have chance to respond before Mark approached

us. His straight back made him appear even taller and more intimidating, with his chin slightly raised, as he looked down his nose at Stanley. Stanley was not fazed by his presence and stepped closer to him.

Mark's new flame stood back a few paces, looking around the room, waving goodbye and smiling at the people she knew. She was completely oblivious to the tension between Mark and Stanley, but I saw the anger in Mark's eyes. I had seen it many times before and his sharp tone made the hairs on the back of my neck stand on end.

'Don't forget where your loyalties lie,' Mark warned.

'I am fully aware of where my loyalties lie,' Stanley said.

He positioned himself ready for a fight, legs slightly apart, fists clenched and arms in. Fearful that a fight would break out, I placed a comforting hand on Stanley's chest, reminding him that I was there and urging him not to get into trouble. The adrenaline must have been pounding through his veins, I could feel his thudding heartbeat beneath my palm.

There was a silence. Both men stared at one another; both looked annoyed. I quickly looked around to see if anyone else had noticed, or if there was anyone close by to step in should something happen, but no one seemed to notice – only me.

Mark eventually backed down and walked away. I let out a sigh of relief as I watched him leave. Stanley, however, remained rigid, his jaw pulsed from biting down on his back teeth, and his eyes were fixed on the back of Mark's head. He did not drop his guard until Mark had left the building.

'Stanley, forget it,' I reiterated.

'Come on let's get you home,' his voice still sounded uneasy and he was not completely relaxed. When we stepped outside into the dark and cooler evening, his eyes darted around, making sure Mark was not waiting.

He continued to survey the surroundings until we had moved away from the town centre. The people around us slowly dispersed and it was just the four of us strolling down the empty street. I could hear the gentle murmur of May and Roger talking happily ahead, their arms linked, while Stanley and I followed, keeping a small distance between us.

Stanley's hands were tucked inside his pocket, and I contemplated slipping my arm underneath his, but my nerves prevented me from doing so and instead my arms swung loosely by my side.

It was a while before Stanley removed his hand from his jacket and his knuckles brushed past my arm. I twitched and spanned my fingers, hoping to touch him again, but as I searched, my chance was disturbed with the thudding sound of footsteps fast approaching from behind. At the same time, we broke away from one another and spun around to see who was charging towards us.

Before Stanley could prepare himself, Mark was on top of him, dragging him to the ground and landing hard punches. I screamed in fear, my hands covering my mouth, my eyes wide open, feeling useless, as I witnessed the fight.

Stanley blocked the punches the best he could, while he tried to push Mark away in between the constant beating.

The commotion was heard by May and Roger, and they were quick to reach us. May was by my side, her arm around me and guiding me backwards to a safe distance.

'What are you doing? Stop it!' she yelled.

Roger grasped the back of Mark's jacket and pulled him to his feet, 'enough!' he said, standing between them.

He remained calm and assertive, trying to keep the peace as his head moved from side to side, cautiously watching both men closely. Stanley climbed to his feet. To my relief, he looked unharmed, only his clothing looked scruffy and his hair was ruffled.

'I don't know what this is about,' Roger spoke sternly, 'but there are women present, and this behaviour is not acceptable.'

His words had no impact on Mark, he was full of rage and eager to strike again. Roger was ready and when Mark charged towards Stanley, he forcefully pushed him back and pinned him up against the wall, his arm pressed underneath his neck.

It was May's turn to panic, her whole body became rigid and her fingers pressed into my shoulder.

'I said enough,' Roger warned. 'I think you need to go home and sleep it off.'

If it had not been because of respect for his friend, Mark

could have broken away from Roger, but he was not going to fight him, we could see that. His body showed no resistance to Roger's barrier, and Mark's arms dropped loosely to his side as he lowered his defence, but Roger held on to his.

'Have you finished?' Roger asked.

'Yes,' Mark eventually said.

Roger took a moment to assess him, to be certain his battle was over, before he stepped down and moved away. May let out a sigh of relief, her arm dropped from mine, but neither of us moved closer to the men.

Mark pointed his finger at Stanley, 'I'm watching you.'

'Mark, it's over,' Roger said, 'go home, fella.'

Mark shook Roger's hand to show no hard feelings, and touched his hat and nodded in mine and May's direction, 'my apologies, ladies. Goodnight.' Nothing more was said, and he left in the direction he came.

Roger turned to Stanley and patted him on the back, 'are you all right, fella? What was all that about?'

Stanley shrugged, 'he just has anger issues.'

Roger, not wanting to pry any more on matters that were not his concern, went over to May, wrapped his arm around her and placed a kiss on her cheek, 'Sorry you had to see that. It's all over now.'

I approached Stanley, 'are you hurt?'

'I am sorry, Betsy.'

He didn't lower his eyes to look at me – he continued to stare after Mark. 'You shouldn't have seen that.'

'What's going on?'

'Nothing for you to worry about and no, I'm not hurt.'

Chapter Ten

The following morning, I went to church, as I did every Sunday, with Aunt Lily and Matthew. I was eager for the service to finish, looking forward to meeting Stanley at the train station as arranged, and when the service came to an end, I darted away quickly.

The train was crowded and, because the day was so hot, it was stuffy and uncomfortable. The musty smell of sweat reeked in the confined space and the window nearest to us was jammed shut giving us no relief.

The train screeched as it battled up the steeper inclines and I clutched my seat, afraid it would admit defeat and roll backwards, or even worse, our carriage would break away leaving us hurtling back down the hill. I felt relieved when we reached the top and I was certain I heard a triumphant 'ahh!' from the engine.

It was worth the struggle, for at the top I could see so far into the distance and was able to admire the breathtakingly beautiful scenery below. I let out a cry of excitement and bewilderment, when, beyond the flat countryside, I could see the sea. There it met with the sky in a medley of different shades of blue; a perfectly straight line dividing heaven from earth.

'Can you see the horizon?' Stanley asked, noting my curiosity.

'Yes, it's absolutely beautiful,' I remarked.

The train travelled down the other side of the hill and headed in the direction of the coast. We soon arrived at our station and from there it was a short walk to the sea front.

'My goodness, there it is,' I screamed out. My insides ready to burst when I saw the sea.

Stanley laughed and watched me behave like a child, exploring and discovering something for the first time. The new experience awoke all of my senses. The unusual feeling of my feet sinking into the sand and a difference in balance when walking across it. I slipped my shoes off and felt the warmth of the light brown sand on my bare feet for the first time. I wore no stockings, even though it was Sunday, and I could feel the sand slip between my toes, which I wriggled with every step, before taking the next one.

I crouched down and scooped up a handful to examine the tiny grains, studying the different colours of white, grey, brown and gold from the crushed down ancient stones and shells from the sea. The sun shining on it made it sparkle; I was holding a newly discovered treasure in my hand. The grains slipped through my fingers when I spanned my hand, I rubbed the remainder with my fingers, feeling the gritty texture grate against my skin.

The salty smell of the sea filled my nostrils, and the crashing of the waves roared in my ears, accompanied by the screeching song of the gulls, as they soared in the skies overhead. The sea became golden brown as it washed over the sand, and the waves lapped, frothing gently along the shoreline.

The texture of the ground changed the closer to the sea I walked. As my feet sank into the wet sand I could feel it getting much cooler. The temperature of the sea took me by surprise when it quickly pooled around my feet; it was icy cold, and I let out a shrill cry. I didn't back away as the water crept away and returned to lap around my feet again. I watched it repeat the same rhythmic movement a few times over, sometimes it didn't reach my toes and other times it would engulf my feet up to my ankles.

After I'd had enough of exploring the sea, I returned to Stanley. He was perched in a quiet place not far behind me, watching and looking amused at my first experience of the ocean. Most of the beach was packed with people, making the most of this sunny day, yet we were away from the crowd.

'Well, is it how you imagined?' Stanley asked, as I dropped on the sand beside him.

'Even better than I imagined,' I beamed at him, and I played with the sand, gathering handfuls and patting them together.

'I've not been here since I was a child.'

'I still remember the day we planned to come here,' I reminisced.

'I remember.'

'And how it ended.'

'Do you see those rocks over there?' Stanley quickly asked.

I followed his hand which pointed to a gathering of rocks further along the beach that formed where the sand ended. It was not too far away and a more isolated part of the beach.

I nodded.

'I will race you to it,' he challenged me.

'Oh come on, Stanley,' I half smiled and sighed, 'there's no way I could outrun you, and we've not done this since we were children. Besides, I'm at a disadvantage... I've not run on sand before.'

'I'll give you a head start,' he insisted.

I stood up, rolled my eyes and began to run. I could feel my dress rising from the pick-up in speed and I soon gave up tugging on the hem. I charged forwards, my feet sank into the soft ground, and I felt the spray of sand fall against the back of my legs. As my lungs filled with the salty sea air and the wind blew gently against my face, I felt a new sense of freedom.

The rocks were nearly within my reach and even with all my determination to get there before Stanley, it was no use, the stomping of his feet was gaining on me, fast. Just like when we were children, he was behind me, ready to grab me, but I dodged his reach and moved in zigzags in different directions, while we laughed and relived a childhood game of tig.

Two girls were close by and watched with amazement at the two adults before them playing. The older of the two ran over and her younger sister followed, 'can we play?' she asked.

'Of course,' Stanley said and started chasing after them. While I caught my breath, I watched Stanley, so full of stamina he kept going, chasing the two girls around in circles, while they screamed with laughter at this game. He was very good with children, *'a natural father,'* I thought.

The fun with the girls was soon over when their mother cried out, 'Lucy and Rosemary, come back and stop pestering the people.'

The girls sighed as they walked back to their mother, dragging their heels behind them. Stanley waved his arm in the air and reassured their mother, 'it's no problem.'

He was too distracted to see me slip away and run the short distance to the rocks. When he turned to me, I had reached our final destination, my arms folded and I stood triumphantly, looking smug. 'I do believe I won.'

'I do believe that's cheating,' he tutted, when he reached me.

Stanley climbed on top of the rocks and held out his hand for me to follow. Holding his hand, we carefully crossed the jagged rocks, balancing on various heights until it came to the edge where it met the water, and we sat down.

Our bare feet dangled over the edge allowing our toes to skim across the top of the water, feeling the occasional spray when the waves bounced back from the rocks. Until one large wave crashed underneath our legs covering us with icy cold water. After that we were on the lookout, watching the waves creep towards us and anticipating the next big one.

With the raised rocks behind us, our location gave us privacy from the people on the beach; I felt like we were in our own cocoon, sheltered from the world behind us.

I shuffled back from the edge and Stanley swung his legs round at the same time. He took me by surprise when he leant back and rested his head on my knee. A contented smile spread across his face as he closed his eyes and crossed his fingers over his chest.

'Are you comfy there, Mr Rhodes?' I asked laughing.

'Very, thank you, Miss Colborne.'

I began to run my hands through his hair, feeling the strands slip through my fingers and watching it fall back into place.

He didn't react to my touch and I carried on, revelling in the thickness and the silky softness. *'It was as though the missing six years, hadn't happened.'*

'Betsy,' Stanley said, after a long silence, 'how far away does Mr Bradshaw live?'

'About eighty miles.'

'Quite a distance!'

He knew of Mr Bradshaw's offer, as I had mentioned it to him briefly the night before, but he hadn't responded, he just listened and said at the end, 'I see.' I didn't know his thoughts on the matter, as his reaction was unreadable; he gave no indication to his feelings.

'I think you should go, take the chance,' Stanley's tone was serious.

'That's what May thinks,' I replied, feeling disappointed.

'It pays, it puts a roof over your head and it's a job. These are worrying times, Betsy.' Stanley was not about to dampen the conversation by discussing the ripple effect the Wall Street crash in America had caused on the world, but he was keen to discuss the possibilities of the right opportunity, especially when his initial dream was to move away.

For a few minutes neither of us spoke; neither of us wanted to discuss the chaos of the world. I glanced out to sea, the refreshing sea breeze brushing against my face, listening to the music the waves played – a gentle roaring that purred in my ears.

I was the first to break the silence, 'are you going to tell me now, what is going on between you and Mark?'

Stanley sat up, tucked his legs in and wrapped his arms around his knees, as he looked out at the sea. From time-to-time he glanced behind at me as he spoke. 'When I first worked for Mr Irving, business was expanding and he was grateful for the extra hands. Mark didn't want to be there, and he always took liberties, coming into work late and taking unauthorised time off. When he did work, he was useless, damaging soles and bending nails; he was too heavy handed. In the end, Mr Irving lost his temper and that's when Mark said he wanted to join the army. And he did. Mr Irving didn't try to stop him;

he was happy to see him go, but I think he always thought he would eventually come back and work for him.

'This time, when Mark came home, he openly discussed his concerns in front of me, but Mark was adamant he doesn't want the business. Then, Mr Irving made me an offer.'

Stanley paused and I just waited. I knew there was more; he had not answered my question, but I assumed it was over the offer, remembering Mark saying that Stanley would one day take over the business.

'Mr Irving has had enough of working now, he wants to take a step back from the business and pass it on to someone else. He's disappointed that Mark doesn't want to come back, but he likes me, how hard I work; I have proved myself, and I work harder than Mark ever did. He said the business is mine.'

'That's brilliant,' I blurted out, feeling genuinely pleased for him.

'On one condition,' Stanley was quick to add. 'It is mine, providing I marry Beatrice. His way of keeping it in the family.'

'*I was not expecting that.*' Suddenly, my insides tugged and I felt broken. 'And what did you say?' I asked, not sure I wanted to hear the answer.

'I said 'yes,' Betsy. Things are hard at the moment, unemployment is rising and with everything going on at the moment in America, not to mention Germany, I am lucky to have this job. I have no choice.'

'Do you love Beatrice?'

'She's a nice enough girl,' he paused, 'but no, I don't.'

'Then why marry her? Why is Mr Irving asking you to do that, when you don't love her?'

'Apparently, although he cares for his wife, he doesn't love her. He married her because his parents wanted him to. He said, you get used to it, and Beatrice has always loved me, so at least he can make his daughter happy.'

Perhaps I should have felt bitter that anything between us had ended before it had even begun. That those recent, new-found feelings for him had been quashed before they had chance to fully develop. Perhaps I should have felt annoyed that he hadn't told me sooner, and perhaps I should have been angry that he made me feel there was something there by spending time with me. But I didn't feel anything other than sorry for him; he looked trapped; with no choice during our world's crisis, but to accept the offer.

'At least I have a choice.'

'Was it because of me that you and Mark fought?' I asked.

'It was always because of me.'

'Betsy,' he faced me when he spoke, 'I am sorry I wasn't honest with you sooner. If this had happened a few weeks ago, things would have been different. I had made my promise and Mark just wanted to remind me of that.'

I believed him.

We parted that day with a bittersweet farewell, not knowing when we would see each other again and wondering what could have been.

Chapter Eleven

In September, I left my home with just a single suitcase and welcomed in my new future working for Mr Bradshaw. He collected me in his car in the middle of the afternoon. It was my first experience of riding in a motor car. It was a bumpy ride along the cobbled roads; the car rattled and juddered as the engine hummed.

I watched the passing scenery, taking in the views of miles and miles of fields; an ocean of green, yellow and orange. It looked so peaceful with the clear, blue sky and nothing in between. Here nature was free; flowers grew wild, creating beautiful colours; horses galloped in fields, livestock grazed, and birds swooped and flew off at the sound of us approaching.

We drove through many small villages and towns. I took it all in, the buildings, the rooftops, the gardens, yards and streets. There were tall buildings and church steeples that stood high above everything. In those few hours I saw more of the country I lived in than I had in my entire life. I realised just how big it was; bigger than I ever imagined it would be and certainly more beautiful. I had read about the country from books, but the experience was much more personal.

'City life is very different to the town life you are used to,' Mr Bradshaw spoke, as we continued down a long country road, 'so much busier and so much more going on.'

'I'm looking forward to it.'

'Glad to see you so positive. I feel as though I know you quite well, Betsy, we have spoken many times, but I'm not sure you really know me. Would you like to ask me any questions?'

'I know all I need to know,' I replied.

He laughed, 'Surely, you have some questions? – I shall give you three to ask me.'

I looked across at Mr Bradshaw. His eyes were transfixed on the road, but the corner of his mouth turned upwards. He was smiling, enjoying the game he was playing with me.

'Three questions it is,' I said and pondered carefully on what to ask him. 'Question one, why are you not married?'

He twitched his head slightly to glance across at me, looking amused by my question. With his left hand on the wheel, the other supported his head, as his elbow rested on the door.

'I could say, I have not met the right woman, but that would be lying,' he answered and thought for a moment, before adding, 'I suppose I haven't ever felt the need to settle down with one particular person, the added responsibility of supporting a wife and children.'

'Do you not get lonely?'

'Question two,' he pointed out, holding up two fingers on the steering wheel. 'No, I don't. I can focus on work. To employ a housekeeper is cheaper than a wife,' he chortled, 'I have friends that I socialise with.'

'You said you would be lying, if you said you haven't ever met the right woman?' I asked.

'When I said you had three questions, I did not expect them to be this invasive.' He laughed, but the smile dropped slightly, as he thought about my question and to stall from answering he added, 'Is that question three?'

He glanced over his shoulder to briefly take in the scenery. It was not a difficult question, just personal, and I could see from his twitching, it was difficult to answer.

'You don't have to answer that one, Mr Bradshaw,' I said after a long silence, in an attempt to dispel the awkwardness.

'There is someone,' he eventually said, 'but we are very different.'

I made a 'hum um,' sound, acknowledging what he was saying and not wanting to pry any further. A few minutes passed and neither of us spoke. I rattled my brains trying to recall a name of a woman he may have mentioned in the past, but I could not recall one.

Eventually, I asked, 'how old are you?'

'How old am I?' he laughed, 'you have known me for four years and you have not worked it out? How old do you think I am?'

'I couldn't possibly guess.'

'Of course you can. I won't be offended.'

'You would if I said fifty,' I joked.

He made an 'ooh,' sound and threw me an animated annoyed expression, 'seriously?'

'No,' I said and for a moment I thought about his age, he kept glancing over at me, waiting for my answer and eventually I guessed, 'thirty-five?'

'Do I look that old?' His voice shrieked in surprise, but the side of his mouth twitched again.

'I'm sorry,' I apologised and scorned, 'you said I wouldn't offend you.'

'I'm thirty-one, but thank you for pointing out that I am looking old, and you are sneaky, Miss Colborne. I said three questions and I do believe that was four questions.'

'Indeed it was,' I smirked, glancing out of the window.

We arrived late afternoon, as Mr Bradshaw had anticipated. We drove down the main road, past rows of terraced houses made from sand coloured bricks. A castle sat high in the distance, positioned to watch over the city and we could see the top of a church steeple close by. He turned down a road which ran parallel to a canal and halfway down he pulled up outside a house.

The nets on the window twitched and a few seconds later the door opened. A slight woman stood in the doorway, I imagined her to be older than she was, but she appeared to be a similar age to Mr Bradshaw. She gracefully waltzed down the stone steps to greet him and smiled, looking pleased with his safe arrival. 'Good evening, Mr Bradshaw, I trust the journey went well. Supper is on the stove, ready to be served,' and then her attention was diverted to me, as I stepped out of the car, 'hello dear, I'm Miss Sharp and you are?'

'Hello, Miss Sharp, pleasure to meet you. I am Betsy Colborne.' I introduced myself.

'Supper sounds delightful, Miss Sharp,' Mr Bradshaw said, removing the suitcases from the back of the car.

'Pass them to me, Mr Bradshaw, I'll take them to your room.' She picked up Mr Bradshaw's suitcase and said to me, 'if you follow, I will show you around.'

I nodded and picked up my own suitcase.

Miss Sharp led the way, Mr Bradshaw close behind and I followed, taking in the surroundings, looking at the properties and admiring how the street curved, as it followed the bend of the canal. Miss Sharp said in a low voice, only meant for Mr Bradshaw's ears, 'good heavens, Mr Bradshaw, she's so young.'

'She is more than capable, Miss Sharp, you will see.'

Miss Sharp showed me around the house, it was modern looking, with honey oak floorboards and nicely decorated with subtle floral wallpaper. There were three rooms downstairs, the sitting room, dining room and kitchen. On the first floor, there were three bedrooms; two larger rooms, a box room and bathroom.

On the second floor were two further bedrooms and a small bathroom; one bedroom was Miss Sharp's and the other would be mine. I was thrilled to discover the bathroom had hot running water and a flushable toilet. The rooms were plain, compared to the rest of the house, but they were well equipped, with a single bed, a set of drawers and a wardrobe. The window in my room overlooked the garden. There was a small area of grass in the middle, surrounded by a beautiful flower bed, and a bricked path curved around the edge and extended to a seating area at the back of the garden, where a cast iron table and two chairs waited.

'This is wonderful,' I said to Miss Sharp.

My role in the house was simple and perhaps less involved

than I was used to with Dr Oxley. I worked hard, keeping the delicate ornaments, chinaware, silverware, glassware, brassware, practically any kind of ware, spotless and gleaming, following orders from Miss Sharp.

She had so many orders to give. I wondered what was left for her to do.

She took full charge of the food, preferring to cook, and I became her skivvy, always left to do the more difficult jobs.

I hardly saw Mr Bradshaw, he occupied his day working, and by the time he came home, I had retired to bed. Mr Bradshaw's main client, Mr Jenkins, was mentioned often and his was a name I became accustomed to. I soon learnt he was a wealthy man who owned a great deal of land. Mr Bradshaw oversaw the legal side of everything, and his advice was valued and trusted by Mr Jenkins.

Chapter Twelve

A month had passed and it was a pleasant Saturday afternoon. The sun shone through the window, casting a golden path on the floor in the sitting room and highlighting the dust motes that twirled around in the air. I gazed outside at the beautiful autumn day as I straightened the curtains and fluffed up the cushions. I could see the canal ahead enjoyed by a few people making the most of the good weather. There was a young couple, arm in arm, walking slowly and in the opposite direction to an older man briskly walking past. The sky was blue and although the cold months were ahead, the last bit of summer was holding out.

Mr Bradshaw would host dinner parties at his house. Mr Whittle would be hired for the evening to prepare the splendid feast, and Miss Sharp would assist him in the kitchen while I was left to thoroughly clean the main areas. Tonight was one such night. There would be twenty guests and although Miss Sharp mentioned their names, there was only one that stood out, Miss Jenkins, the only child of Mr Jenkins.

'Don't forget the chandelier,' Miss Sharp mentioned from the doorway.

'Oh yes, Miss Sharp,' I responded.

I used a chair from the kitchen to reach the chandelier. I carefully ran the cloth around each of the eight lights and removed the dust from the curved frames. Afterwards, I switched the lights on to check and not entirely satisfied with the result, I cleaned them again.

'It looked fine the first time.' The voice caused me to jump and I lost my balance. I held on to the back of the chair to steady myself and Mr Bradshaw grabbed my waist in case I fell. He immediately let go once I had steadied myself and stepped down.

'Mr Bradshaw, this is not the first time you have crept up on me,' I said.

'Betsy, you have done a marvellous job, the place looks spotless. The guests will be arriving soon, take a break and get cleaned up ready to assist Miss Sharp.'

I felt nervous, Miss Sharp had already given me the rundown of events earlier that day; I would be responsible for taking the coats on arrival, offering welcome drinks and then serving the meal.

As the minutes drew nearer, I felt nervously sick. My heart was in my mouth and I took deep breaths to steady my nerves. I used the half an hour I had spare to clear away my cleaning equipment, get washed and change into an outfit Miss Sharp had left out for me.

It was an old-fashioned, long, black and dismal dress, made of thick, heavy material, covering my arms and falling to my ankles, with buttons that fastened at the front of the body. I felt miserable and looking at myself in the mirror I could see that the colour had drained from my face. The only flesh on show was my hands and face. I looked like the Headless Widow from the stories my brothers had told me when I was young. If they could only see me now. I smiled as I thought about those stories and how scared they had made me.

I wandered downstairs feeling uncomfortable in my drab garment. Mr Bradshaw caught sight of me, he was smartly dressed in a modern three-piece suit and a burgundy cravat. He laughed when he saw me, 'Oh Betsy, what do you look like? It's only for one night. Though I do think we need to update your formal attire, you look like a Victorian maid.'

As much as he found joy in my occasion wear, I did not. I gave him a look that told him I was feeling suffocated and restricted. This only increased when the guests began to arrive and I saw the beautiful outfits the ladies were wearing.

They were very glamorous with their hair worn in the styles of the latest stars of the silver screen, adorned with beautiful jewelled hats and combs. They wore the most elegant of gowns, with matching shoes and long gloves fitting to the elbows. They all wore spectacular jewellery filled with diamonds that sparkled in the light of the elegant chandelier.

I was handed fur shawls and scarves from the ladies. They looked me up and down as they inspected Mr Bradshaw's new maid. I was certain they were laughing at me.

Once they had all arrived within a short period of time, I wandered around the sitting room offering the guests flutes, filled with sparkling wine, from a silver tray. I waited in the corner, hiding in the shadows close to the door; I could have been part of the wallpaper. For a while, no one noticed me.

Yet I noticed everyone.

The guests were a mixture of various ages and I wondered how they were connected? What created this large circle of friends, or was it purely business? I presumed Mr Bradshaw had studied with the men who were a similar age to him, whilst the older gentlemen could be friends of his late father. Most of the women were the gentlemen's wives, but a few were single. Out of those few, I was intrigued to know who Miss Jenkins was.

The men laughed with big, deep, booming laughs and the women giggled. Everyone seemed happy – the room filled with noise. Smoke from the cigars and cigarettes rose, creating a cloud in the room. All the glistening and sparkling from my morning's deep cleaning soon disappeared in the grey fog, stealing away the smell of freshness with it.

My attention was drawn to two women, who I presumed were single, and a gentleman hovering around Mr Bradshaw.

'Oh, William, you do like your skivvy young,' one of the women said to Mr Bradshaw. I didn't react, remaining perfectly still and pretending not to hear.

'Young enough to work harder and cost less,' the man next to Mr Bradshaw added.

'Miss Colborne served my uncle for four years, she's highly

experienced.' Mr Bradshaw formally addressed me, and I felt a sense of pride as he defended me amongst his friends – he hadn't addressed me by my surname before.

The woman who had spoken, I soon realised, was Miss Jenkins. She was a beautiful woman, dressed in an emerald green satin gown. The colour emphasised her dark eyes, like pools of chocolate, and her dark hair curled around her face in tight locks. The satin gown clung to her hourglass figure, limiting her movement as she glided across the room, hips swaying, purposely drawing the attention of all the men as she passed by them.

I noted how her presence filled the room. She was the honey pot and the rest of the guests were the bees. She made people laugh; women found her powerful, independent and amusing, while the men found her beautiful and desirable – all were blinded by her womanly, provocative charms.

I could feel her scrutinising eyes judging me and I remained ignorant to her words as she continued to mock me. 'I always feel sorry for the poor, they always look so pale and dull, malnourished and thin.'

'You do feed your staff don't you, fellow?' The gentleman, a Mr Formby, said, who was a similar age to Mr Bradshaw. He stood straight and held his head high, with an overabundance of arrogance that was equally matched by all the other men in the room. They all placed themselves on a pedestal, ranking themselves above everyone else with grand discussions of wealth, property and future prospects.

The women were equally as competitive with discussions of clothes, expenses and styles, and those who had children were boastful about their child's achievements. The verbal war between the guests remained harmless and civil, but it was amusing enough for me to find entertaining, with a realisation of how trivial their rich lives were. I thought to myself, *'surely health is their wealth, to not know hunger, to be warm and comfortable, to have enough money to pay for medicine and treatment if any of them fell ill; surely that was enough?'*

The meal consisted of a splendid seven courses of small delights; crepes, soup, stuffed fish, chicken, lemon mousse, cheese and coffee served with mints. Mr Whittle ensured each delicate course was presented perfectly to convey his craftsmanship; nothing was out of place.

Together, Miss Sharp and I served each course; I remembered the rules of serving to the left and making a minimum fuss. Miss Sharp and I waited at opposite ends of the room, her earlier instruction ringing in my ears, 'do not look at the guests, they do not require an audience whilst eating.' I was to flutter by them, not to be seen.

Mr Bradshaw sat at the head of the table and close to him sat Miss Harris. She was young, not as beautiful as Miss Jenkins, but she was full of grace and kept Mr Bradshaw's interest during the whole meal. He was happily engaged in their conversation.

Miss Jenkins was used to being the centre of attention. Her voice rose above the others and she controlled the topics discussed. She was very entertaining in the way she expressed herself, her actions were so dramatic, extending her arms and telling stories in such detail. She gave an elaborate account of her walk in the park, describing the flowers she passed, naming the birds she heard and whom she encountered there. Whenever she spoke about someone, her comments were demeaning and cruel; about their age, a gain of weight, an unhappy marriage, or their poor quality of clothing. While the others laughed and seemed to adore her, I disliked the woman all the more.

'Oh, Mr Bradshaw,' Miss Jenkins attention was drawn to the head of the room, I watched Miss Harris' face lower to focus on her coffee, disappointed at her disrupted conversation, 'I intend to throw a celebratory party in spring, it is after all my birthday. Shall I put you down for one or this time will you arrive with a guest?'

'Miss Jenkins,' he replied, 'you must know me by now, I prefer to arrive alone.'

'Well, Mr Bradshaw,' she smiled, charmingly at him, 'it's not healthy to be alone, those who are alone, die alone. Perhaps one day you will turn up with a woman attached to your arm.'

'I would like to see that,' Mr Formby laughed and raised his glass to Mr Bradshaw.

'Well, if all else fails,' she chortled, with her teacup in her hand, 'you could always bring the skivvy.'

A few laughed, and Mr Bradshaw sipped his wine as he stared intensely at Miss Jenkins, but she was not fazed by his warning look and dismissed him with a playful smile.

The conversation moved swiftly on and it was a relief when the guests retired to the other room. As the last guest left the dining room, Miss Sharp approached me, 'you are not the first maid to be taunted by Miss Jenkins. She's a jealous woman and feels threatened by any woman younger than herself being so close to Mr Bradshaw. I suppose she fears their duties go beyond the domestic ones, if you understand me, Betsy?'

My cheeks burned, and my eyebrows rose in shock by what she implied. I quickly looked away from Miss Sharp, too embarrassed to meet her eyes.

'Now,' she continued, 'you have two choices. You could be a coward and clean up in here while I attend to the guests, or you could go in there with a tray of drinks, head held high, and show that woman you are not troubled by her.'

I agreed to face the guests and left the comfort of the empty dining room to enter the crowded front room. I wandered amongst the guests and offered the drinks – brandy to the men and sherry to the women, and all, apart from one, selected the correct drink. Miss Jenkins, with a devious smile, took a brandy from the tray and her dark eyes looked through me waiting for a response. She watched my every move as I continued to serve the last of the drinks, knowing perfectly well, one man would be left with a sherry.

I could feel my hands shake, and the tray began to rattle as I watched each glass, one by one, be removed from the tray. I was frightened that the action of Miss Jenkins would humiliate Mr Bradshaw and ruin the dinner party that was running perfectly well. I wondered whether to serve Mr Bradshaw last and hope he would realise the error and take the sherry without anyone noticing. It was too late to sneak out of the room and fetch another brandy.

The last brandy was taken from the tray, and two glasses of sherry remained, but what baffled me as I scanned the guests, was that everyone had the correct drink. I stood befuddled, my back close to the wall and I searched again the hands of everyone. Sure enough, everyone had a glass and I felt a huge release from worry drain from me, as I breathed out.

Miss Jenkins sipped her brandy; if she was annoyed about her failure to humiliate me, she disguised it well. As I waited for a moment by the door, to be sure the guests were content, my eyes discreetly flickered to Mr Bradshaw and Miss Jenkins.

Miss Jenkins was seated on a comfy chair by the window and Mr Bradshaw stood beside her. His arm rested on the back of her chair with his drink grasped in the other hand, as they engaged in conversation. Her eyelids fluttered, as she gazed up at him through her long eyelashes, and when he spoke, she would smile widely, hanging onto his every word with such fascination.

Her attention was diverted when Mr Formby called her name and she turned away from Mr Bradshaw. My ears seemed to home in on their voices, past the pleasant chatter of the other guests, and I began to wonder *'why was I bothered by Miss Jenkins?'* Their words didn't reach my ears, but the mumbling of their voices I could identify, being more pronounced than the others.

I blinked slowly and when my eyes opened again, they met the gaze of Mr Bradshaw. His head was turned to the side and he watched me. His blue eyes locked on mine, like the powerful force from a magnet; I was unable to look away. The temperature in my cheeks rose and I could feel them burning. I could barely breathe, feeling suffocated, as though an invisible hand had covered my mouth preventing me from taking in any air, and I slowly inhaled, allowing small amounts to filter to my lungs.

For those moments, I saw only him. Until one of the guests crossed our path and broke our stare.

I quickly escaped from the room. My heart thudded so hard against my rib cage I was certain it would break through. I could barely keep the tray still and the amber liquid swayed inside the glasses.

I hurriedly carried it through to the dining room where

Miss Sharp was brushing down the chairs and I placed it on the table. I took several deep breaths to calm myself down.

'Ah, Betsy,' she said, walking over and taking a glass of sherry, 'I see Miss Jenkins took a brandy. I know that woman's trick, I always pour an extra one of each just in case. Have one, dear.'

She tipped her head back and swallowed the sherry in one gulp. I followed her cue and picked up the second glass. The liquid burned my insides and settled my nerves, as my pulse gradually returned to normal.

'Thank you,' I said.

'I just need to wipe down the table and sweep the floor, then I'm done in here,' she said, 'but you go on into the kitchen, have something to eat and you can wash up after. You look like you need a good meal. There's some leftovers on a plate in the oven.'

'Thank you, Miss Sharp,' I said. Miss Sharp had piled all the dirty plates onto a trolley, which I pushed through into the kitchen. Mr Whittle was no longer there, he went home once the last course was served, and my heart sank when I saw the rest of the plates from every course piled up on the side, along with the pans he had used.

I let out a groan at the volume of work left to be done and, feeling exhausted, I turned my back on the dirty crockery, cutlery, cups, glasses, pots and pans, and opened the oven. I welcomed the smell of my warm dinner of chicken, steamed vegetables and roast potatoes that blew from the oven.

The meal was satisfying and boosted my energy to embrace the washing up. Over an hour had passed by the time I had finished and everything was returned to its rightful place. The dining room and the kitchen were clean and tidy once more; like a party had never taken place.

The rest of the house grew quiet as the guests dwindled away, and when I was certain the last guest had left, I entered the living room to clear away the dirty glasses. I was expecting the room to be empty, presuming Mr Bradshaw would retire to bed early after an exhausting evening entertaining. However, there he was, sat in his chair, the same chair Miss

Jenkins was sitting in earlier, with his legs crossed and a book perched on his knee. His finger and thumb gripped a page ready to flick it over, as his eyes zigzagged over the last few lines, while his other hand held his unfinished drink.

The air was thick with the foul stench of smoke, and fresh dust had settled on the floor and pieces of furniture. There were many dirty glasses scattered around the room to be collected, and I hesitated for a moment, my head peering around the door, unsure whether to enter or return again later.

'Come in, Betsy,' Mr Bradshaw said over the sound of the page turning, as his eyes shot up to address me.

I did so quickly, parking the trolley in the centre of the room and gathered all the dirty glasses.

'I won't be long, Mr Bradshaw,' I said, 'I just want to get these glasses out of your way.'

I was quick to gather all the glasses, setting them on the trolley and being careful not to crack any of them. Within a few moments, I was ready to leave the room.

There was the sound of the book being slammed shut and Mr Bradshaw said my name. When I glanced at him, his head was lowered and he focused on the front cover of his novel.

'Yes, Mr Bradshaw?' I replied.

He rose from the chair and stood before me. I focused on his shoulders, too afraid to look into his eyes, too afraid that if he saw mine, he would see into my soul, and he would see my desire. My forbidden desire, my new desire for him. It was like a thick cloud that had covered my eyes had been lifted and hidden feelings had surfaced to the top; my unknown feelings for Mr Bradshaw. *'When did they start? I had been fooled by my feelings before.'*

'I've poured you a drink,' he said, handing me the glass he was holding, 'sit down for a moment, you deserve it.'

With a shaky hand, I accepted the glass and unconsciously took a large gulp. The strength of the brandy burnt the inside of my nose and the back of my throat, causing my eyes to sting and begin to water. I closed my eyes tightly waiting for the moment to pass, and the heat from the liquid trickled down my throat until it settled in my stomach.

Mr Bradshaw laughed at my reaction and placed a supportive hand on my shoulder, 'take it easy, that stuff will blow your socks off.'

Feeling embarrassed, my lips curved into a smile and I sat down in one of the other chairs while Mr Bradshaw returned to his previous seat. I sipped the brandy the second time, and although I still felt a warming sensation, it didn't burn as much.

'You took me by surprise today. I am very impressed,' Mr Bradshaw praised me. 'I thought you remained calm and handled everything well.'

I shook my head in disagreement.

'You must excuse Miss Jenkins, her bark is worse than her bite,' he said, 'She's a strong-minded woman, with strong views. Her father is extremely wealthy, and her mother was a suffragette, it's no wonder she's the way she is. I've known the family all my life, our fathers were good friends, and I have worked for Mr Jenkins since I was qualified. We go back a long way, Miss Jenkins and I.'

I remained quiet, though the mention of her name caused the brandy inside my stomach to bubble. I sipped the drink, keeping my true feelings of his friends trapped in my thoughts. 'How often do you throw these dinner parties, Mr Bradshaw?' I asked, wanting to change the subject.

'Not that often, three times a year, if that,' he replied.

He leant forward, he was closer to me, his elbows rested on his knees and his eyes looked deeply into mine. I felt vulnerable, this new hold he had on me frightened me and made me feel weak.

'I apologise for tonight, Betsy. I didn't expect my guests to be so rude to you.'

He spoke with such sincerity; I believed him.

'Please, Mr Bradshaw, enough said.' I quickly finished the drink and stood up, 'if you will excuse me, I am tired, and I have these glasses to clean.'

I prayed he would say no more and allow me to leave, I needed to find sanctuary in my room, and I needed to process my feelings, but his voice stopped me as I pushed the trolley a couple of paces towards the door, 'Betsy, before you go.'

I paused and thought, *'let me go.'*

'Do you miss home?'

'I've only been away a short while, not long enough to truly miss home,' I replied.

'You had more freedom back home, you liked dancing, more opportunity to meet a suitable husband.'

'There's plenty of time for that.'

'You lost your father at a young age?' I looked back at him and frowned, *'why was he asking these questions?'*

'Please, Betsy, I don't mean to pry, I just want to understand you.'

'Yes, it was just a cold at first that developed into pneumonia,' I continued to speak with broken sentences, as I recalled that winter in 1919. 'I didn't notice at the time – he was always my father – always doing what he was expected to do – but I can see, now I've grown, just how poorly he was. I can't remember how long he was like that for; struggling each day, but it must have been going on for a while – each day he was growing weaker – but we, us children, didn't notice his struggling. It was only at the very end, when he had fought enough did we see it. I don't think our mother really knew, he kept saying it was just a cold, but I think the pneumonia was quick to take him *in the end.'*

The room was silent and my eyes slowly lifted to meet Mr Bradshaw's, and I felt touched, as though I could see into his kind, gentle soul. He had not moved, his soft eyes resting on me, filled with sympathy and understanding. *He cared about me.*

'You must miss your brothers?' His voice soft, as he broke the silence.

'I do,' I admitted, 'but I feel guilty that I don't think about them as often as I should. I suppose they have been gone for so long now; they are men, their memories of home would be vague, why would they come back? They would have returned by now, if they were going to.'

'Life has a way of working out *in the end*, Betsy, I am sure.' I paused.

'That's what my father would say,' I said with a heavy heart, looking at Mr Bradshaw, *just like him.*

Part Four

Chapter Thirteen

Two years passed by and it was summer in 1933. Miss Sharp had finished her employment with Mr Bradshaw back in spring 1932, leaving me to maintain the house on my own. This new responsibility was an incentive for me to stay longer than the one year I had previously planned. Mr Bradshaw was a wonderful employer, he was fair and kind, and I knew our relationship was unusual for a master and servant, as he at no time made me feel like a housemaid. Nothing felt like work and I enjoyed all that I did; keeping his house and looking after him.

We had our own routine. I had normally finished my daily work by the time Mr Bradshaw had returned home from his, which meant most evenings we could enjoy supper together. Afterwards we would retire into the living room, where we would either read our own books, or pass the time talking to one another. Mr Bradshaw seemed to welcome my company. I think Miss Sharp kept herself to herself and he often felt lonely.

I didn't work weekends; Mr Bradshaw often made other arrangements and he would be away for most of the day. I took full advantage of my free time. I would go to the pictures, take long walks in the park, or spend time browsing in the shops. There was plenty to do in the city I had grown to love, but everything I did, I did alone.

Mr Bradshaw's visits to his uncle were not as often as they once were, his workload had increased, preventing him from taking extended breaks away. When he did make the journey, I usually went with him to spend time with my family for a few days. I often thought about them and missed them a great deal, especially May, but our lives had changed. I was as content with my employment with Mr Bradshaw, as she was fulfilled at home with Roger.

It was the morning of May and Roger's wedding. Mr Bradshaw generously rescheduled his work and offered to drive me home to attend May's big day. He saw it as an opportunity to spend a few days with his uncle.

Every time that I returned home, I was hit with an overwhelming sense of homesickness. I was able to repress this emotion while I was away, but as soon as the familiar surroundings of my hometown came into sight, my true feelings came flooding out. It was made worse when I saw the comfort of Aunt Lily's house, my childhood haven, looking like it always did – my loving home.

It rained in intervals that day. The unpredictable weather did not cast a dull moment on the beaming bride. She was bursting with happiness the entire morning. By the afternoon there were long breaks of blue skies and sunshine, and Aunt Lily saw it as a sign of a successful marriage.

May looked blissful and beautiful in her simple white dress that was handmade by Aunt Lily. To complete the outfit, she wore a white satin hat with a veil that covered her face. I wore a lavender bridesmaid dress that flowed elegantly to the floor. The thick ribbon around my waist was tied into a large bow at the back and the sleeves, although long, were loose fitting, making it ideal for a summer wedding.

Matthew was thrilled to walk May down the aisle; he was almost skipping with pride. I followed behind, feeling equally proud that she now had what she always wanted – to be a wife.

The church seemed different that day, even though nothing noticeable had changed. There were the same dark walls, high windows, cold stone floors and wooden benches. The only difference was that the church felt warm and radiant from the bright colours worn by the wedding guests. Everyone's faces were filled with so much happiness and the melodic sound from the organ brought a true sense of hope.

Many times I had sat in the pews listening, watching and praying, as I remembered those I had lost and being thankful for those I still had. Although the church always filled me with hope, it also reminded me of my sadness, but I didn't feel it on that day.

The congregation shared in the celebratory union of May and Roger, and the sun broke through the high windows, casting a warm glow of orange and yellow, like a blessing to the newlyweds. May looked nervous and her bottom lip quivered when reciting her vows, but the whole time she wore a large smile, so hopeful and filled with love.

It was official, and the bride and groom were free to set foot into the world as husband and wife. The married couple slowly made their way down the aisle, passing through the cheering guests and I followed behind, peering through the gaps their bodies left.

My wandering eyes caught sight of a figure stood still at the back of the church and I shuddered. His age, his face, his identity, all hidden underneath the cap he wore, casting a veil like shadow to shield his face. He wore a long brown coat that was too thick to be worn at that time of year. How still he stood and how rigid his body looked sent cold shivers shooting down my spine, causing the hairs on my arms to stand on end. I stared at this chilling being, feeling a dreadful sense of familiarity.

He quickly left, escaping through the doors and disappearing into the daylight. No one else noticed him, but me.

As we stood in the grounds the bells were ringing merrily, announcing the marriage to the town folk. I was distracted as I searched for the man, but he was long gone, lost in the crowds of people in the busy town below. A terrifying thought crossed my mind, 'was he real?'

'You look like you've seen a ghost?' May broke me from my trance.

'Congratulations, May,' I said, ignoring her question. 'You are a beautiful bride and I couldn't be happier for you. I wish you and Roger a long, happy future together.'

'Thank you. Is anything the matter?' She held me tightly, not being fooled by my diversion.

'I am fine, stop fussing about me. Today is your big day.'

'I am so glad you are home; I have missed you so much.'

The celebrations continued back at the house with a buffet of sandwiches and cold meats spread out across the kitchen. The small gathering of guests managed to squeeze inside, milling between the living room, kitchen and outside.

The Monday was my last full day and I was home with Aunt Lily. It was just after midday when I was in the yard hanging out the washing and I overheard Aunt Lily say, 'she's outside.'

I was not expecting anyone. I quickly threw the last sheet over the line, straightening the ends and sliding the pegs into place. I turned around as my visitor approached the back door.

We neither spoke nor moved and just looked at one another. I, in disbelief, and Stanley, in hesitation. It had been two years since I last saw him and my insides jolted, just like it did once before.

Stanley took a few steps down into the yard, 'I heard you were back.'

'Only until tomorrow,' I perched my hands on my hips and glanced down at my clothing, aware of the dirty apron I was wearing. I was quick to remove the item and discard it in the laundry basket.

'How's the city life?'

'Much noisier than here. It's nice to have some quiet time, where you can hear the birds.' I nodded my head in the direction of the fields, where the birds were chirping merrily in the distance.

Stanley smirked, 'if you miss the freedom of the countryside that much, do you have time to come for a walk with me?'

I agreed to the stroll and we found ourselves walking through the two fields towards the lake.

'My favourite place in the world,' Stanley said, perching down on the pebbles. 'I still come here you know.'

'Really?' I smiled, sitting down beside him with a feeling of flattery, knowing I was the one to show him the lake. 'The last time I was here was with you, Beatrice and Mark.'

Stanley removed an envelope from inside his jacket and just held it for a while, before he handed it to me. I saw my name scrolled in the centre, *just my name*, Miss Colborne, in beautiful handwriting and I realised what it was.

'We have a date,' Stanley said.

'Congratulations,' I tried to sound genuine as I stared down at the unopened invitation.

I was expecting it to happen; I knew it was bound to happen one day and yet I perceived it as bad news. It bothered me more than I thought it would and I could not bring myself to break the seal on the envelope.

'When is the wedding?' I asked.

'October.'

'Only two months away.'

'I would have posted the invitation, but as you are here I wanted to hand deliver it.' Stanley paused, 'I hope you can come.'

I was unsure how to answer, confused by my own feelings. I had hoped the years apart would have altered that, but I still had such strong feelings for him. I still felt complete in his company. I understood him and everything about him, *'this should be our Wedding Day.'* 'I wish you all the happiness with Beatrice, but I don't think I can attend.'

'Because of work?' He made his own assumptions.

'Yes,' I lied.

'Well, you have the date if you change your mind.'

I slipped the unopened invitation into the pocket of my dress and we spoke no more about his wedding.

'What's Mr Bradshaw like? Is he a good man?'

'Very,' I was quick to answer. 'He's a wonderful man, very kind and fair. He treats me like an equal.'

'How does he treat you, Betsy?'

I was taken aback by Stanley's sharp tone, emphasised by a worrying frown. I stared back at him with confusion and searched his eyes for an understanding. I hesitated to answer straight away, but I eventually replied, 'like I said, he's fair.'

'Please, explain.'

'He's rearranged his plans to bring me here. He's always happy with my work and he's kind to me, makes me feel more like a friend than an employee. He's very good to me.'

'What does he expect in return?'

'Nothing,' I was defensive, 'nothing, Stanley, he's a gentleman, a *real* gentleman.'

'And you live on your own with him?'

'Stanley, where has this come from?' I said, rising to my feet, 'if you're going to be like this I am going home.'

'I'm sorry, Betsy,' Stanley was quick to stand and he held onto my shoulders to stop me from moving, 'I worry about you, I just need to know you are safe.'

'I am, Stanley.'

'Do you love him?'

'No, Stanley, I love you.' I thought to myself.

His green eyes were staring hard into mine and I looked away from his questioning glare.

He repeated the same four words and I took a deep breath, 'I care a great deal for him, Stanley. I have worked for him for two years and I see him every day.'

Again, he asked me.

'Well, I –' I paused.

'Do I love him? Mr Bradshaw?'

'Oh, Betsy,' Stanley shook his head, 'you silly, silly girl. What are you doing falling in love with your boss? You shouldn't go back there, you should stay here, you'll only get hurt.'

'I'll get hurt here too.' 'I don't think you have a right to ask that, but I'm not falling in love with him, Stanley. I am well used to protecting my feelings.' *'I'm stronger than you think.'*

The glare in his eyes softened, 'just take care of yourself.'

It was peaceful by the lake; the only sounds came from the wind gently rustling the nearby trees and our lowered voices. He made me laugh, and I felt happiness in his company, but also sorrow, knowing it was nothing more than two old friends reminiscing in their special childhood spot.

'Do you ever bring Beatrice here?' I had to ask. *'Of course, he brought her here.'*

'No, she's not keen on me coming.'

'Oh, why not?'

'She knows I used to come here with you.'

'Oh,' I mouthed the words.

Stanley didn't mention Beatrice again, and although I was glad of it, I did find it unusual that an extended conversation could be had without mentioning his future wife. After all, she was to be a huge part of his life and had been over the past two years – surely most of his time was spent with her.

We spoke about May's wedding, and I was talking about the service when Stanley noticed something and said, 'did something happen? You don't sound as happy about the day as you should?'

I shrugged it off, 'ah it was nothing, really.'

'No, tell me.'

'I saw someone at the back of the church.'

'Who?'

'I don't know. He looked familiar, but looked like he didn't belong – he looked out of place.'

'Did you see his face?'

'No, he wore a large coat and a cap, everything was well hidden. Perhaps my mind was playing tricks on me.'

'Who do you think it was?'

I shook my head, 'I can't say, I am being stupid.'

Stanley placed a comforting hand on my back, 'Betsy, you can tell me, I won't ever think you are stupid.'

'I thought it was my father,' after a long pause, I added, 'I told you it was stupid. I was up early that morning; I was tired and my mind was playing tricks on me.'

'Could it have been one of your brothers?'

I shook my head. I was certain my brothers would have spoken to me at some point if it were one of them.

Later in the afternoon Stanley walked me back to Aunt Lily's house. My hand rested on the latch of the gate ready to tug it open, but I hesitated and looked up at Stanley. I knew the next time I would see him he would be a married man. I wrapped my arms around his neck and held him tightly.

'All the best of luck for the future,' I whispered in his ear, 'please, just be happy.'

His arms slipped around my back, his chin nested in my neck and we held onto our embrace for as long as possible.

Beatrice's big day in October soon came and passed, but I didn't attend the wedding. Part of me wanted to go and many times leading up to that day, I stared at the invitation, at the neatly scrolled letters of their names written side by side, and the request for my company. I kept trying to convince myself to go until I was certain it was too late to accept and I declined the invitation.

Chapter Fourteen

Over the months I received several letters from home. May never mentioned Beatrice and Stanley, and in my replies I didn't ask. Her letters were often brief, but she always kept me well informed about our family, and in January the news arrived that they were expecting their first baby in July, a month before their first wedding anniversary. The thought of becoming an aunt gave me a new sense of life.

I was glad for spring, I found winter very lonely. The nights seemed to last forever and the days were so cold. I suffered with chilblains and avoided leaving the house if I could as the icy weather only irritated them all the more. I saw Mr Bradshaw less in the evenings, as he had important deadlines to meet, and most of the time I felt so isolated.

The chilblains passed with the first sign of spring and with it, my depression diminished. The flowers were starting to bud and the leaves were growing back on the trees. The world felt alive once more and soon it was warm enough to sit outside when I had time to myself to enjoy the signs of summer coming.

Mr Bradshaw was not due back until late afternoon and I must have been outside for an hour lost in a book I had selected from his collection. It was an unusual book to choose at this time of year, but it was my father's favourite story and it brought back fond memories of my childhood.

'Mr Bradshaw,' I said in surprise when I noticed his figure cast a shadow over the page of my book, 'I didn't realise you were home; would you like a cup of tea?'

'No, thank you, Betsy,' he said, sitting down on the cast iron chair next to me, 'what book have you got there?'

'A Christmas Carol.'

'How wonderful,' he took the book out of my hands and examined the back cover, 'I've not read this book for years. Charles Dickens is one of my favourite authors, alongside James Joyce and Rudyard Kipling. Are you enjoying the story? Though it's the wrong time of year to enjoy a Christmas tale. You must read the rest of his books – I'm sure I have them stored somewhere if they're not on the shelves.'

'Thank you, Mr Bradshaw.'

He spent a few minutes flicking through the pages, quoting sentences from the book. He passed it back to me left open at the page I was on. He leant back in the chair, rested his foot on his knee, 'do you still enjoy working here?'

'Yes, I do, Mr Bradshaw,' I replied, making a mental note of the page number and closing the book. 'Very much so. I couldn't ask for better working conditions and the experience of being here goes without saying.'

'I've not been around as much lately and I worry that you get lonely. You're coming up to the end of your third year here. You're away from home and you have no friends here. All you do is work for me.'

His statement worried me and I wondered what he was building up to, fearing he may want me to return home. I thought for a moment and I carefully answered, 'Mr Bradshaw, I've not had many friends. Everything I did, I did with May. I have always preferred my own company.'

Mr Bradshaw nodded to show he understood and his eyes darted around the garden. He was thinking about something, 'when did you last go to a dance?'

I paused and thought back to my last dance, 'before I came here.'

'That's what I thought. You need an evening where you can enjoy yourself, wear a gown, go to a dance and be young.'

I chortled at his suggestion, 'who with? A woman doesn't go to these things on her own.'

'With me?'

My mouth gaped open in surprise, my eyes widened in disbelief and his words repeated again in my head. I looked at him and he seemed serious, but I needed to hear him say it before I would believe it. His eyes remained on me and nothing in his expression suggested he was joking.

'You've recently had a birthday, your twenty-first I believe, which passed by uncelebrated, let this be my birthday present to you.'

I didn't know what to say. It was very nice of him to offer to take me to the dance and I wanted to accept his offer. The thought of doing something different and going somewhere I could hear live music again thrilled me, but it was the thought of going with Mr Bradshaw that frightened me. It made me anxious, *'would we dance together? Could I dance with him?'*

'You don't need to worry about a dress, I think you can have a new one, my present to you,' he added when I failed to answer.

'Mr Bradshaw, you have taken me by surprise,' my head was spinning for the right answer and I found myself saying, 'yes.'

We made a decision to go the following Saturday. Mr Bradshaw requested the assistance of his trusted friend, Mrs Cropper, to help me find a suitable gown. Even though I insisted the dress I wore to May's wedding would be appropriate, he was not convinced.

I warmed to Mrs Cropper, she was an older woman, but very stylish and glamorous. She had a natural instinct on what would suit people from the colour of their eyes and hair. 'Burgundy is the colour for you,' she said, 'it will bring out the darkness of your eyes and add colour to your cheeks. I know just the thing.'

The evening soon arrived, and Mrs Cropper styled my hair with big curls and applied make up to my pale face – more than I would usually wear, so much so, that when I caught my reflection in the mirror, I barely recognised the woman looking back at me.

The gown was a long, simple, but elegant style. The satin material had a round neck and flowed from the shoulders down my back in a deep v shape exposing a lot of skin. It loosely shaped my figure and moved gracefully with me when I walked, as though it was made for me. The sleeves hung like wings, ending at my elbows and the colour, as Mrs Cropper predicted, suited my complexion. She left me with a pair of diamond clip-on earrings to wear, to complete the outfit.

I stood alone in my room and stared at my reflection; feeling a fraud, feeling pretentious, as if I didn't belong in my own skin.

Mrs Cropper and Mr Bradshaw were talking in the doorway of the living room, when I emerged at the top of the stairs and overheard her say, 'Mr Bradshaw, I can't say I agree with you taking a maid to a dance. Everyone there will disapprove and think of poor Betsy and what you are doing to her.'

My presence was noticed when my heels clicked on the tiles on the hallway floor and their conversation ceased. The way Mr Bradshaw looked at me, his mouth slightly parted and the rise of his eyebrows, made me feel elegant. My transformation had taken him by surprise. He took my hand gently in his and planted a kiss on top, 'Miss Colborne, you look beautiful.'

His compliment flashed colour to my cheeks.

Mrs Cropper spoke, 'She's a true lady, this one.'

Mr Bradshaw thanked her as she gathered her bags to leave and she left with a whisper in his ear, that I clearly heard her say, 'be warned.'

He didn't respond to her words, but smiled confidently and reassuringly back at her. I stood behind wondering, *'what does she mean? Are her words aimed at me?'*

It was a short walk to the Plaza, but our pace was slower than normal, and as I adjusted to balance in my new shoes, Mr Bradshaw offered me his arm. I slipped my arm through his, feeling grateful for the support as the heels were higher than I was used to.

We walked in silence and I searched for things to say, but I felt so very nervous. It was bad enough that my legs felt shaky, but my heart was beating faster than it had ever done before. I just hoped Mr Bradshaw could not sense my fear as he walked so naturally and calm.

As much as I was nervous, I also felt the part. I had never felt so beautiful and worthy before in my life. Even if it was just for one night, I felt wonderful and found something to say, 'Mr Bradshaw, thank you so very much for this gown. I haven't owned anything so beautiful before.'

'Miss Colborne, you are very welcome.'

The Plaza was very different to the dance hall I had been to. Several stone steps led up to the large double wooden doors and above them was a lit-up sign. As we climbed the steps I hitched my dress up, careful not to catch my shoe on the hem and stumble. A smartly dressed doorman held open the door and touched his top hat as we passed through, 'Good evening sir, good evening madam.'

The room was grand, set out in different levels with high ceilings and it was twice the size of the hall back home. The dance floor was set lower than the seating area and was already filled with people dancing. The couples looked so glamorous – the men in their smart, black dinner suits and the ladies in beautiful gowns. A band played on a stage at the back of the room and the whole scene was highlighted by the soft lights shining down from the walls and ceiling.

I'd not seen anything like this before, *'How the other half live,'* I thought. As much as I felt privileged to be there, to experience something so different, I felt out of place, like I did not belong. My grip tightened around Mr Bradshaw's arm.

Mr Bradshaw continued moving deeper into the room, greeting the people he knew, and he was unfazed by the curious eyes that fell on him and me.

'Relax,' he whispered in my ear, 'it's me they are surprised by, not you. Would you like to dance?'

I shook my head, 'I am a terrible dancer, I would fall over and make a fool of myself.'

'Nonsense, we will just have to take it slow,' he smirked at me.

'It's too crowded.'

As much as I tried to find excuses, Mr Bradshaw ignored each one and guided me onto the dance floor. We faced one another, our chests inches away from touching and I could feel the gentle blow of his breathing against my forehead. I concentrated on the trimmed stubble around his chin and his neck, unable to meet his eyes.

I swallowed hard. I had forgotten how to dance; I had forgotten what Stanley had shown me.

His hand cupped mine, while the other one curved around my waist and I tensed as I felt the warmth of his hand against my bare skin; our bodies close and our feet moving together as we danced the foxtrot. My nerves didn't completely settle throughout the several dances – fully aware I was in the arms of Mr Bradshaw; I felt as though I was floating. I took a few deep breaths in an attempt to regain control.

'Shall we have a rest and a drink?' Mr Bradshaw asked me.

I agreed and he took my hand, excusing himself as we dodged the other dancers to the edge of the dance floor. Mr Bradshaw led me to a free table, but immediately turned around to walk back in the opposite direction. His action was sudden and I had a hunch he was avoiding someone.

We found a table next to the railings that looked down on the dance floor. He pulled out a chair for me to sit down and as I lowered myself into the seat, I recognised the female voice that was approaching.

'Mr Bradshaw, I thought that was you,' Miss Jenkins' arms outstretched and she tightly clung on to Mr Bradshaw's shoulders, she turned her head from one side to the other to receive a kiss on both cheeks. 'My goodness, this is a pleasant surprise.' Her voice seemed to drift away as she noticed me, 'pleasure to meet you, Miss –?' She held her hand out for me to shake.

She looked at me with unfamiliarity, and I anticipated for a moment as to whether I should lie about my name, but I responded proudly, 'Miss Colborne, Miss Jenkins.' I shook her hand firmly.

'What a coincidence, she has the same name as your skivvy maid.' Then, she realised and placed a hand over her mouth, laughing out loud, 'Oh Mr Bradshaw, you do surprise me.'

'Tonight, Miss Colborne is my equal.'

'Don't be so absurd William dear, she will never be your equal.' Addressing Mr Bradshaw by his christening name was relevant – as a signal to me that *she* was his equal.

Miss Jenkins stepped closer to Mr Bradshaw and whispered in his ear, but loud enough for me to hear her say, 'don't forget, I expect you to still have one dance with me.'

'I am here with Miss Colborne, what type of gentleman would I be if I left her alone?'

'Nonsense. She's a big girl, she's used to being on her own and besides, all this is above her don't you think?'

'Miss Jenkins, you are spoilt and pure poison.'

Miss Jenkins tilted her head back and laughed, 'do you think I am wrong, Mr Bradshaw? Look around you – who and what do you see? Everyone is the same here, but not her.'

Mr Bradshaw's eyes fell on me and I smiled, a reassuring smile that I would be fine on my own. *'Let the spoilt child have her way,'* I thought to myself.

'Miss Jenkins I shall have one dance with you, but first I must ensure Miss Colborne has a drink.'

Mr Bradshaw attracted the attention of a waiter and Miss Jenkins leant closer to me, her hands pressed flat on the table, 'all this reminds me of a fairy tale. It must be wonderful for you to play Cinderella, though you mustn't forget what happens at midnight. Remember your place, scullery.'

Once my drink arrived, Mr Bradshaw fulfilled his promise and danced with Miss Jenkins. From where I sat, I could see them perfectly well. They moved naturally together; a different dance to the simple movements he kept for me. They were made for each other and I saw their mutual desire for one another, *'she was the woman he once loved but could not have.'*

I felt more a fool and humiliated than hurt or disappointed as they waltzed through two dances together. *'After all, what was I expecting?'* I wouldn't ever be anything more than what I was; underneath the nice clothes, the layer of make up and fancy jewellery, I was still only a maid. A valuable lesson was learnt as I watched Mr Bradshaw and Miss Jenkins, *'if*

I expect nothing, then I would never be disappointed,' and I vowed to myself to remember that.

'I must apologise, I didn't expect to see Miss Jenkins here today,' Mr Bradshaw said, when he eventually rejoined me, 'and she would continue to persist if I didn't dance with her.'

'Apology not necessary, Mr Bradshaw.'

'I trust you are still enjoying yourself?'

'Yes, thank you.' *'Now, I am.'*

Once again we danced and this time I felt more relaxed in his arms – perhaps it was the gin and tonic I'd had. I was disappointed in myself for not knowing how to dance properly and wishing I could move like Miss Jenkins. In my mind I could still see the two of them together and I hoped Mr Bradshaw was not disappointed in me.

Over his shoulder, I caught the disapproving gaze of Miss Jenkins – a cold stare shot at me from across the room and when I looked into her sharp eyes, if only for a moment, a dreadful shudder swept down my back. I lowered my eyes and focused on Mr Bradshaw. I tried to block out everyone around me and imagine I was alone with him, somewhere else far away from Miss Jenkins. I was lost in the moment feeling a warm sensation inside me. The question Stanley asked me, 'do you love him?' came to mind, *'do I love him?'* My fingers pressed into his shoulders; he was real, he had invited me, he wanted me there.

I wanted him.

Something in my body language must have changed. Mr Bradshaw pulled back a bit to look at me. His eyes searched mine and his expression changed to one of concern, 'Betsy, please don't look at me like that.'

'Like what?' I questioned with confusion. I was looking at him, like I always did.

'Like you love me, Betsy. I'm not who you think I am. This will not have a romantic ending.'

My eyes widened in horror as the words repeated again in my mind. I stepped back from him, placing my hand over my cheeks to shield my embarrassment.

I suddenly felt very hot.

I felt humiliated.

'How did he know?'

I was glad when Miss Jenkins approached Mr Bradshaw – she must have sensed something while she was watching. *'When they were alone before, had she said something to Mr Bradshaw? Did she know something and warn him?'* After all, she was quick to spot the tension between us.

Mr Bradshaw's mouth parted, he had something to say to me, but Miss Jenkins didn't give him chance to speak, 'it looks as though you have exhausted your maid. She's not made for dancing.'

She continued to speak to him and like a barrier, she stepped between us. I chose this time to escape and hastily manoeuvred through the people. I didn't stop and I didn't turn around until I was through the wooden doors and outside.

My pulse raced and I felt suffocated – as if an invisible hand had grasped my throat and was restricting my breathing.

I was the fool, and I ran the best I could, back to his home. *'How could I face him now? How could I continue to live here?'*

Chapter Fifteen

I was grateful that the following day was Sunday and being my usual day off I could pass through most of it without seeing Mr Bradshaw.

I was not expected to work that day, but to keep my mind distracted from replaying the night before I was in the dining room cleaning the chair legs. I had hoped the long walk in the morning would have cleared my head but, unfortunately, it only encouraged my mind to wander all the more.

I washed away the dust, being more attentive than usual and paying closer attention to every minute detail of the frame. This seemed to work; the more I concentrated, the less I thought about Mr Bradshaw and only snippets of the evening seeped through.

Then, I heard the front door close and my heart sank. I felt sick at the familiar voice of the female he had returned with. If I could have hidden in time, I would have, I even contemplated lying under the table, but it was too late as just as I was about to crawl underneath, Mr Bradshaw was peering around the door.

He said in his calm and normal mannerism, 'Betsy, I know you don't normally work today, but would you be so kind and fetch a pot of tea for two?'

'Yes, Mr Bradshaw,' I said, looking down at my hands clutching the damp cloth.

I left the cloth on the side of the bucket and went into the kitchen to heat the water on the stove. I was anxious, wandering around the kitchen throwing the necessary crockery on the tray with my trembling hands. I was making more noise than usual, items were clanking and clinking together and my feet shuffling along the hard floor.

The loud whistle of the boiling kettle rang out like an alarm warning me it was time and I carried the tray through into the living room. I had no choice, I had to face her and she would see that my Cinderella moment was over.

Miss Jenkins sat at an angle, her back to me and her body pointed in the direction of Mr Bradshaw. He mirrored her body language and their knees were almost touching.

I didn't make eye contact and placed the tray on the table. My cheeks were flushed, but thankfully my hands were steady as I carefully stirred the tea leaves inside the tea pot before returning the lid. I felt her scornful eyes on me as I dropped a splash of milk into each cup and poured the tea through a strainer.

Miss Jenkins took the teacup and examined the contents. She slurped and made a sound of disgust as she pulled her face away, 'My goodness, that is awful.' She returned the cup to the tray, 'you have not brewed the tea long enough.'

'I am sorry, Miss Jenkins, I will get you a clean cup.' I picked up the cup and saucer. Unable to look at Mr Bradshaw, I spoke to his untouched brew, 'would you like a fresh cup?'

'Mine looks fine, thank you, Betsy,' he replied.

'Nonsense, it looks like dishwater,' Miss Jenkins scolded and I thought, *'do you know what dishwater looks like?'*

'Take it all away,' she ordered.

I quickly left the living room. My heart banged fiercely in my chest and, feeling too hot, I took a moment to step outside the back door. I welcomed the fresh air as I bent over, my hands pushed into my knees and I concentrated on my breathing. It slowly released the tension that had built up across my chest, but my heart continued to thump sending jolts through my body.

I returned in a matter of minutes with two clean cups and

a refilled tea pot. I placed the tray back down and waited, allowing enough time for the tea leaves to brew. I poured the tea in exactly the same way I did before.

'What are you doing?' the condescending voice of Miss Jenkins startled me. 'You never add the milk first.'

I stared blankly at Miss Jenkins. *'What game was she playing?'* In my opinion her tea was perfectly strong the first time and my second attempt was brewed to the same strength. Her quarrels over the milk being poured first was due to her pickiness and wanting to ridicule me. I sensed she felt great pleasure in belittling me and reminding me of my place.

'You always pour the tea first, otherwise how you can tell the strength?' she spat at me and directed her next statement to Mr Bradshaw, 'that's what separates us from the working class. It looks to me like the milk has spoilt too, maybe you need to sort your staff out.'

If I had the strength in me, I would have spoken out against Miss Jenkins and told her what I thought about her obnoxious and snobbish attitude. Instead, I quivered inside and took her shameful comments with me as I left the room.

For the rest of the afternoon I busied myself in the garden, taking my anger and upset out on the weeds as I yanked them from the ground and threw them into the bucket. Each weed I saw as people that had wronged me and I found great satisfaction in naming them as I ripped their roots from the ground and held them tightly. How limp and pathetic they looked in my clenched fist.

'There you are,' I heard Mr Bradshaw say as he stepped down from the kitchen door and walked across the path towards me, 'I wondered where you were.'

'Did Miss Jenkins enjoy her tea in the end?' My voice was bitter as I poked the ground with my trowel, flicking over the soil to get to the weed I imagined her face was attached to.

Mr Bradshaw laughed at my comment and took in a deep breath, 'so good to have summer on its way.'

I didn't respond. I continued to attack the ground as though it was fighting back. It felt good to release all my anguish as I turned the soil over.

'I wanted to talk to you, if I may?' Mr Bradshaw crouched down next to me, balancing on the balls of his feet, his elbows resting on his knees and his hands cupped in front of him.

I placed the trowel on the ground to show I was listening and with the back of my hand wiped the sweat from my forehead. I focused on the ground, waiting for him to continue; I could not bring myself to look up at him.

'I hope there are no hard feelings from last night, it was not my intention to upset you. I value you as a worker and I value you as a person. If I have ever given you the wrong signal, then I am sorry. Last night I just wanted to show my appreciation, nothing else.'

'There are no hard feelings,' I said.

'Thank you,' Mr Bradshaw seemed content with my response and rose to his feet, taking a few steps across the path towards the house.

'It's Miss Jenkins, isn't it?' I blurted out. I didn't intend to be so direct, I wanted it to come across more as a matter of fact.

'Pardon?' he stopped, but he didn't turn around, only his head moved slightly and I could see the side of his cheek.

'The woman you love. When I first came here, you said you loved someone, but you couldn't ever be together – it's Miss Jenkins.'

Mr Bradshaw paused for a moment, 'Betsy, I know you don't see it, but she is a remarkable woman.'

'What makes her so remarkable? All I can see is that she is rude and vile.'

'Vile?' he raised his eyebrows at me and chuckled to himself. 'She fascinates me. Don't get me wrong, there are times I despise her and find her rude.'

'Why have you not married her? It is obvious she feels the same way. It was obvious last night when you two were dancing.'

'I could never marry her, Betsy, she is a higher class than me and her parents would not approve. Besides, all that I admire about her, I would not want in a wife.'

I rose to my feet, wiping my hands on my apron, but they were still dirty. A loose strand of hair fell over my face and I knew I looked a dreadful sight, dressed in my filthy apron and rags. Very different to the elaborate dress I had worn less than twenty-four hours ago, and very different to Miss Jenkins.

'If you love her, that shouldn't matter,' I said.

'Should you always marry for love?' He took a step closer to me.

'Should you always marry for money?' I challenged. 'Surely money would only make someone happy for a while, but to spend your life with someone and wishing they were someone else is a lifetime of misery.'

'I don't want her money. If I asked Miss Jenkins to marry me she would say no. If she said yes her parents would disinherit her, she would live the rest of her life miserable because I would not be able to give her that same quality of life.'

'What does it matter, as long as you are happy? So, will you two just wait for the day her parents have died to marry, or will she give everything up to be with you?'

'Neither of them. We accepted that a long time ago; it will never be.'

From that day on we kept a more professional relationship. We dined alone and those evenings once spent together, had now all stopped.

Chapter Sixteen

Mr Bradshaw took me back home in July to be with May when the baby was due. He intended to stay with his uncle for a fortnight and it was my choice if I returned with him to the city or stayed longer.

Aunt Lily and May were waiting for me when I arrived. I dropped my suitcase and ran into their outstretched and welcoming arms. Tears filled my eyes, *'I was home.'*

'Betsy, you look so well,' Aunt Lily complemented, but I didn't feel it.

'So do you, both of you,' I replied, looking at May and her perfectly round bump. She was glowing and her skin was radiant, her face had filled out and her nose broadened slightly, but she was a picture of good health. 'How are you May, are you taking good care of your precious bundle?'

She laughed, 'the bundle is taking care of me, always moving, always kicking and making sure I am all right.'

I gathered my case and followed them inside the house. May waddled from side to side at a slower pace to Aunt Lily, the way she carried her body, she seemed uncomfortable, but her face looked so happy.

'She's not the only one expecting,' Aunt Lily was quick to say, like a secret she could no longer keep and blurted out. 'Beatrice is pregnant too.'

'She is?' My voice squeaked.

'Only three months gone, her mother is overjoyed.'

'He's only gone and done it,' I thought to myself. *'Married and a family. It was bound to happen sooner or later.'*

'That's nice,' I struggled to say.

'No need to talk about that now,' May spoke over me and I caught sight of her throwing Aunt Lily a warning glance. 'Not now,' May echoed the words.

'That was just as well,' I was not in the mood for talking about Stanley and Beatrice.

'How long are you home for?' Aunt Lily changed the subject.

'As long as I am needed.'

'Don't say that, May won't ever let you leave,' Aunt Lily said. 'You girls catch up, and I'll fetch the tea and some bread pudding.'

'Oh wonderful,' I smiled.

May and I sat down next to one another on our favourite seat by the fireplace and she cupped my hands, 'I am so happy you are here, Betsy. That you'll be here when this one arrives.'

'You know I wouldn't miss it for the world. Married life really does suit you.'

'Roger is wonderful. Aunt Lily and Matthew are very fond of him, though it is a bit crammed all living here. He works so hard and saves as much money as he can so we can have our own place. They are building new homes near our old school, all installed with electricity and indoor bathrooms. It would be wonderful if we could afford one of them, but I don't think we will. Anyway, he wants to wait until I am settled with the baby, not to rush into moving now, and the longer we stay here, the more we can save. Aunt Lily doesn't mind, she likes having us here and she can't wait to have a baby around the house.'

As I listened to May I was ashamed to admit it to myself, but I was jealous and I was angry for being so selfish, for wishing I was in her shoes; married, happy and with child. I held no grudges though, she deserved to be happy, but I could no longer shield the tears that began to trickle down my cheek. As much as I forced a smile, in the hope she would not notice, a tear stained trail was left behind.

May soon realised I was upset and the smile faded from her face. She wrapped her arms around my shoulders and, from the comfort of her touch, I could no longer hold back my sorrow.

I tried to sob quietly so as not to alarm Aunt Lily and my cries were muffled in my sister's arms, feeling safe as she cradled me, 'it's all right, Betsy, I'm here. You're home, everything is going to be fine. Let it all out.'

With one arm around me, the other stroking my head, May kept hold of me and said nothing more until I had finished crying. I pulled myself up to sitting and May handed me a clean handkerchief from her sleeve to dry away my tears, 'I was so wrong, May, so very wrong.'

'What happened, Betsy?'

I told her everything; from my misunderstanding with Mr Bradshaw and my encounters with Miss Jenkins. When I retold the story, some things seemed petty, others obvious, but May just listened. When I had finished, she thought for a moment, searching for the right words I assumed, 'I am so sorry, Betsy, I have let you down.'

Her choice of words surprised me and I shot her a confused gaze.

'I was not there when you needed me, you've been on your own all this time. I should have come to see you, but you should've written and told me. I would've been there for you.'

Her face looked guilty and she lowered her head as though she was now ashamed. It was my turn to console her and I placed my hand on her shoulder, 'May, you are a married woman, with a baby on the way, I was not going to burden you. It was my choice to move away and I wouldn't expect you to travel that distance to see me.'

'I always said I would look after you and protect you, I neglected that promise.'

'This is life, May, I'm just experiencing life. I am fine, it's coming home that brought all the emotions back, knowing how much I have missed you. I have felt worse pain.'

May lifted her head up, she understood and smiled slightly. Until I saw a change in her expression, as though she had an idea, her eyes widened and glistened, her smile grew wider and she looked excited. 'Move back here! You've been away too long. Come back home permanently. It would be lovely to have you here, this little one will have its aunty around,' she stroked her stomach, 'Aunt Lily would love it, I would love it. We all miss you; you've been away too long.'

'Where would I stay? I can't stay here, there's no room for me,' I laughed at her suggestion, though part of me was tempted to return home. I waved my arm around the room, 'sleeping in this room is fine on a temporary basis.'

'We could get one of those fold down beds, store it over there,' she pointed to the wall, where Aunt Lily's display cabinet was. 'It'll be part of the furniture.'

May's wonderful ideas were cheering me up, and perhaps if May and Roger had their own place, I would have come back, but the house would be too chaotic with five adults and a baby.

'What about work?' I asked.

'You could have my old job at the tea room, Mrs Robinson is desperate for someone.'

I shook my head, still smiling.

May gave up trying for the time being, but I knew for as long as I was there, she was not going to give up. She placed a kiss on my forehead, 'I love you little sister, you'll always be my first baby.'

I was not sure if May was serious or teasing me about being her first baby, 'I love you too.'

'Always remember what father said, that *things always work out in the end,* it may not be the way we intended it to happen, but one day you will look back and think *why did I worry?* Things always work out *in the end.* Just wait and see.'

It was another week before May went into labour. It began in the early hours of the morning; the contractions were few and far between to begin with and she battled through them in silence. No one, not even Roger, knew they had begun and everyone continued with their day oblivious to May, but it was only a matter of time before May could no longer conceal her pain from Aunt Lily.

The labour was slow and continued through to the next day and the following morning I was asked to help Matthew at the shop. Roger went to his work as normal.

When Matthew and I returned home that evening we were expecting to hear the cries from a new-born baby. Instead, we were welcomed with cries of pain from May, coming from the open window upstairs. In a state of panic and sense of urgency I ran upstairs to her.

She was stood with her hands pressed against the wall and her body crippled over. Aunt Lily stood by her side and she soothingly rubbed the lower area of her back.

Aunt Lily saw me enter, 'Betsy is here now.'

'Betsy,' May's voice was weak and she panted for breath, 'Betsy!'

'I'm here,' I approached her. She turned to face me and pressed her arms on my shoulders. Her loose hair was all tangled and draped across her frightened face, her forehead drenched in sweat and her nightie clung to her skin. The colour had drained from her cheeks, her mouth was painfully dry and her lips were barely visible as they matched her pale skin.

'It hurts so much,' she cried.

'You're doing really well,' I reassured her, 'it will be over soon and you're going to have a baby at the end of it all.'

'What time is it?' She asked, 'is Roger back yet?'

'Not yet,' I said, knowing it would be another two hours before he was home.

May's hands didn't release my shoulders and she gripped me tightly through another contraction. At the start of the contraction, she was in control and focused on her breathing, until the pain peaked. The intense agony showed in her eyes as they filled with tears and I helplessly watched her scream, until it eventually passed.

'You're doing really well,' Aunt Lily reassured her and slipped out of the room. If I had taken notice of her, I would have seen the fear in her eyes, sensed her worry and detected the panic in her voice, but my attention was completely on May.

It was not until she returned and said, 'Matthew has gone for Dr Oxley,' that I realised.

My eyes shot up in the direction of Aunt Lily, searching for answers, *'what was happening? Why did May need a doctor? Aunt Lily had delivered all of our mother's babies, what was going on?'* She looked back at me and shook her head, it was not the time to explain, not wanting to frighten May, but the look in her eyes filled me with dread.

There was no change in the two hours it took for Dr Oxley to arrive. During that time she seemed to be losing so much blood, but all I could do was hold her and offer her words of encouragement through each contraction. I was relieved to hear the sound of a car pull up outside.

'They are here,' I said, as I peered out of the window to see Mr Bradshaw's car. Dr Oxley was quick to exit the passenger side and Matthew was quick to follow from the back seat. I could hear the sound of the front door opening below and their footsteps passing through the house.

Mr Bradshaw stepped out of the car and as he closed his door, he glanced up and caught sight of me watching from the window. He touched his hat and I nodded back in acknowledgement, feeling gratitude towards him for bringing his uncle to my sister's aid.

I turned away from the window the moment Dr Oxley entered the room rummaging through his bag and immediately attending to May.

As he did, he called out for items he required Aunt Lily to bring to him, but I paid no attention; by the time his words reached my ears they were gibberish. May was all that mattered now.

'I can't do this,' she said, shaking her head.

'You can,' I told her, 'you're doing really well.'

'Where's Roger?' she cried out.

Roger should have been back from work by now. Aunt Lily and I passed a glance at one another.

'I'm sure he'll be home any minute, May,' Aunt Lily said.

I ran downstairs. Matthew was sat on the edge of the chair, with an unlit cigar balancing in between his rigid fingers as he stared at it intensely.

'How is she?' he asked, when he heard me approach.

'She's struggling,' I said, 'but where is Roger? May is asking for him.'

Matthew thought for a moment, 'Sometimes he goes for a drink on his way home from work. He may have gone to celebrate.'

I sighed and pulled open the front door. Mr Bradshaw was leaning against the bonnet of his car, his arms folded and staring aimlessly out at the field. He heard me approach him and stepped towards me.

'Roger should be home by now,' I said.

'Do you know where he is?'

'Gone for a drink, maybe?'

'I will find him.' He wasted no time in climbing inside the car and starting the engine. The window was open and before he drove off I leant inside the window, 'Mr Bradshaw, thank you for doing all this.'

I really did appreciate the time he had given to help my family.

'There's no need to thank me.'

I slowly walked back towards the house and took a look behind as the car turned around in the road and sped off down the street.

In the bedroom, the exhausted May was lying down on her side, her legs curled up. As much as Dr Oxley gently nudged her shoulders to push her back into the bed, she resisted and sprung back.

As Dr Oxley examined May, her fingers became rigid as though she was grasping an invisible item, her jaw dropped back and her teeth clenched.

I would have done anything to relieve her from her pain, I was strong enough, if only I could do the impossible, I could share her pain, while her body rested and recovered; but that could never happen.

'I can't do this anymore,' her face screwed up in agony and discomfort, her upper body twitching and tensing. I fell on my knees next to the bed and took both her hands.

'Yes, you can, May,' I said, 'yes, you can.'

Her head dropped down to look at me, her eyes were heavy and barely able to stay open. I could see the pale blue of her eyes through the narrow slits of her eyelids. Her tongue kept creeping out of her mouth to moisten her dry and chapped lips.

May's grasp grew weaker in my hand. I rinsed out the flannel in the basin beside her bed and gently dabbed her forehead and around her face.

'Her body has given up,' I heard Dr Oxley say, but I already knew. There was no strength left in her now.

The long, delayed labour caused her to haemorrhage. She was losing blood faster now and her cervix was not dilated enough to deliver. Dr Oxley explained our choices but we could not make that decision.

Aunt Lily slumped down in the chair and buried her face in her hands, her shoulders shook, but she made no sound.

May hardly struggled now. Her eyes closed for longer intervals and her hand wilted over mine.

'Please May, don't give up,' I pleaded.

'We need to get the baby out,' there was urgency in his voice. We had no choice.

The room fell silent and I looked at May. 'I love you,' I said as clearly as my breaking heart enabled me to and I pressed a kiss on her forehead.

May opened her eyes slightly and smiled weakly, just a twitch of her mouth was all she could manage.

Dr Oxley sliced through her stomach and May looked at me for the last time.

'Come on, May,' I begged, shaking her limp hand, 'not now. Your baby needs you.'

But she was gone.

Gone too early to hear her baby cry and gone too early to know she had a baby boy.

There was so much blood. It had spread across the perfectly white sheets, an unsettling contrast I could not bear to look at. I reached for a clean towel and covered May's torn body to conceal the stain.

Dr Oxley attended to the new-born, cleaning him with fresh towels and the healthy baby was passed on to Aunt Lily, his cries softened in her loving hold. Through her sobbing, she spoke softly to him.

I didn't leave my sister's side and I held her hand, not accepting she was gone.

Aunt Lily lowered the baby onto the bed to lie next to his mother, close to her still warm face, his arms and legs kicked in quick jerky movements, breaking free from the blanket he was wrapped in. He was so tiny, with mottled skin and tiny strands of dark hair flattened across his head. His tiny lips pouted and his wrinkly eyes blinked quickly as they became accustomed to the new light.

I could not accept she was gone, that she would never see or hold her baby. That this new-born child would never feel his mother's love, never hear her voice and never feel her hold.

I could not believe that I would not see May again.

'Your mummy would have loved you,' Aunt Lily struggled to say, as she leant over to kiss his hand, curled up in a fist. 'This is your mummy little man. May this is the little boy you always wanted – this is Alfred.'

It was only when the door flung open and Roger stood in the doorway, his eyes urgently flickered to Aunt Lily, Dr Oxley, me and down to his son, and lastly to his wife. When he realised, he crumbled. Like a heavy weight, he fell to his knees.

For the first time in my life, I heard a grown man cry. A deep, loud roar from the pit of his stomach that shook through his body and *I felt it*.

My eyes scanned from mother to child, May could have been sleeping, her body still warm. The image of the mother and her child ripped out my heart; in one breath, life was given and in another, life was taken.

My whole body began to ache and the pain in my chest was

so intense I felt as if a knife had punctured my heart.

I had to escape.

I broke free into the open air and seeing the fields as my only path, I ran, but not far. My body surrendered and I collapsed, slumping to the ground on my knees.

I screamed.

The unbearable ripping feeling inside my stomach, the pain of my suffering and the anger building up inside me, filled me with rage. Screaming was the only way I could release it.

My fingers raked through the grass, ripping up fistfuls from the ground. When that failed to tame my anger, I slammed my fist down, over and over again.

I didn't hear the sound of feet running across the grass towards me and drop by my side. Arms wrapped around me and pulled me closer to their body. I continued to scream, wanting to break away as I pressed my fists into the body, but the hold was too strong.

My body stopped fighting, no longer rigid or tense and I cried in the arms of Mr Bradshaw. My hands gripped his shirt and my head nestled under his chin. He didn't let go.

Chapter Seventeen

May's funeral was arranged quickly. Roger could not bear to stay in that house and he moved back home to his parents, taking baby Alfred with him.

I was numb to it all. Each day that came, I wanted it to end, hoping the next day would be easier, but it still brought the same pain and emptiness. I felt no hunger and food was tasteless, so I chose not to eat. I was tired, my body struggled to function, yet I could not sleep and I often found myself, in the middle of the night, visiting the room she died in.

The bedding was stripped and the mattress had been thrown out, but I could still smell the blood and I could still see her lying there. I would lie on the bare bedspring base; it was uncomfortable, but it was the only way I could be close to her and imagine she was still there. I would fall asleep, only to be woken by her screams that haunted my dreams.

I didn't leave the house until the day of her funeral. I walked through the streets, following the horse and cart that bore my sister's body. The only sounds came from the hooves clicking along the cobbled road and the quieter sound of the footsteps behind.

Many attended the service, but to me their faces were just shadows with no identity. I sat like a statue, still and cold at the front, with Roger to my right and Aunt Lily to my left.

The vicar spoke many words and familiar hymns were sung, but I only heard distorted mumbling. I was living under a thick black veil that blurred my vision and kept me isolated from the rest of the world.

Everything was hazy, the walls and the ceilings were caving in on me, the floor moved in waves and the noise around me was muffled. The only thing that was real, the only thing that was solid and that I could focus on, was her coffin. The simple wooden box presented at the front of the church, waiting to be offered to the earth, to decay into nature, while her soul was received by heaven.

I could have been floating towards the coffin, my body had no weight, as I walked down the aisle towards the rectangular box. My hand brushed across the soft wood and the tips of my fingers traced its entire outline, knowing that within lay her beautiful sleeping face.

The service stopped, everyone was still, everyone was quiet, everyone was watching, but I did not see them. The sound of a small quiet cry, that was more of a low wail than a heartaching weep, came from May's baby, but it failed to wake me from my trance. Neither did I hear the gentle words of the vicar as he placed his hand on my arm, encouraging me to sit back down.

I slowly walked up the aisle, past the mourners who had known May at various stages of her life, and I asked myself, *'who really knew her? Who really understood her?'* I knew her at every stage of her life. I knew her as a child when life was simple; I knew when she had to grow up too soon; I knew her as a mother to me; I knew her as a woman when she first found love, and I knew her as a wife and becoming a mother.

I pushed open the door and stepped out into the cool air, taking the several steps down onto the gravel path and waited until the others began to leave the church. How long had I stood there for? I had no idea; I just waited and watched an empty world in front of me.

'I know it's difficult for you, Betsy, and I send my sincere condolences,' the gentle words of Mr Bradshaw spoke to me.

I felt nothing.

The warmth of Aunt Lily's arm slipped around my shoulder.

I felt nothing.

In the graveyard, we stood around her freshly dug grave and watched her coffin being lowered into the earth. Almost identical to the burial of my father, but the resemblance didn't touch me.

I felt nothing.

In my head I said goodbye, but in my heart, I could not.

I was first to turn my back on the burial and I weaved through the gathering of people behind me. Sympathetic eyes met mine, but my face was stone; the only time I bore a noticeable resemblance to my mother.

I came face-to-face with Mr Irving, his mouth parted ready to speak, but no words came out. By his side stood Beatrice.

I walked on.

I headed towards the town, to feel lost and camouflaged amongst the people who carried on with their day. I didn't notice the clouds were closing in and beginning to darken.

The rain burst down from the sky, falling heavily in large droplets. Within a few minutes the ground was completely soaked and puddles formed before me. My clothes were drenched and clinging to my skin.

I had no destination in mind, just allowing my feet to lead the way. Hours passed, evening was upon me and eventually I found my way back to the church and back to May.

Everyone had long since gone and the hole was filled.

My knees gave way and I fell down beside her grave. My cheek pressed against the mud, as the rain splashed down around me, dirt sprayed in my face and I could taste the gritty soil in my mouth. My arm outstretched and I pushed my hand through the freshly laid earth. It felt cold, wet and soft, as I compressed handfuls into the palm of my hand.

At that time, I would have welcomed death. It would have been easier than feeling the emptiness that now suffocated me. I didn't feel the cold attacking my bones and the chattering of my teeth, neither did I notice the shallow puddle that I lay in.

My eyes grew heavy and everything went black.

Chapter Eighteen

My father carried me; his spirit had come for me. My eyes opened long enough to recognise his outline, before they closed again. He didn't look down at me, it was dark, but I knew it was him. I was wrapped in something; it was a coat. I was frozen; I could feel the cold in my bones. I wanted to open my eyes again, but my eyelids failed to lift. He was walking quickly, I could hear the heavy panting of his breath and the sound of his feet slamming against the hard ground.

I was safe and I drifted off into unconsciousness.

When my eyes opened again, my vision was still blurred and all I could make out were different shapes in a brightly lit room. I wanted to focus, I wanted to see him, but the light stung my eyes, I couldn't keep them open.

I knew I was safe.

I could feel the softness and cosiness beneath me, as if I were on a cloud. I could feel the weight of a blanket pulled tightly across me, but despite the attempt to keep me warm, I still felt chilled to the bone.

Voices surrounded me; voices I knew; but their words were jumbled up and I failed to understand what they were saying. Shapes moved about the room, breaking the blinding light, but one shape caught my attention. I tried to concentrate on the face closest to me, but it was like looking through opaque glass.

I was too tired to keep my eyes open any longer, my body too sore to move; every part of me ached. It was easier to sleep.

'Betsy?' A voice softly spoke, some while later.

At last I could see when I opened my eyes. I felt warmer and my body no longer ached.

I glanced around the room, recognising the furniture, the wallpaper, the ceilings, the chandelier that hung in the centre. I was in Dr Oxley's spare bedroom, the room Mr Bradshaw used. Then I saw Mr Bradshaw on the chair beside me. His hand reached out and touched my forehead.

'You look much better today,' he smiled.

'I –' I tried to speak, but my mouth was dry and my throat felt as if I had swallowed knives.

'You've been here for three days. You made yourself ill staying out in all that rain, you have really worried us. That's all over now though, you just have a bit of a temperature. You're just exhausted and in need of some good food. The rest has done you good.'

I wriggled myself up the bed to a more upright position and my eyes searched the room. 'Where's my father?' I asked. He had to be real – it had felt so real. I could still see his image in my head.

'Your father? Perhaps the fever was worse than I thought,' Mr Bradshaw said. 'How are you feeling, Betsy?'

Mr Bradshaw stood up and walked across to the dresser and poured a glass of water from a jug sitting on the top. He fetched it over to me and continued to hold the glass while I took several mouthfuls. The water was cool and refreshing, it trickled down my throat, relieving me from the razor-sharp pain I had previously felt.

'I feel well,' I said, but my thoughts were elsewhere. 'Mr Bradshaw, it was my father, I saw him, he carried me.'

'No, Betsy, it was me. I was the one who carried you and brought you back here. You were freezing and barely conscious.'

'It was you?' I asked doubtfully.

Perhaps I had not seen the face after all. Perhaps the

silhouette was familiar because it was Mr Bradshaw and in my poorly state, my mind had tricked me into seeing someone else.

'Yes, it was me. Matthew came here when you didn't go home, he was worried and I guessed where we would find you.'

For a moment I had forgotten about May, I had hoped it was a bad dream, but the memories of that evening by her grave came flooding back to me, filling me with sadness. My eyes dropped to the floral cover on the bed.

Mr Bradshaw's hand reached out for mine, 'I am sorry, I know how much May meant to you, but she would want you to be happy and not make yourself ill. It is very difficult when you have to say goodbye to someone you love and some days are going to be harder than others.'

I looked up at Mr Bradshaw. His words seemed sincere and seeing his supportive face gave me a sense of hope and the motivation to try to move forward.

'Are you hungry?' he asked.

Mr Bradshaw left me alone in the room. The bed was comfy and soon I had drifted back into a light sleep. I felt as though my eyes were only closed for a minute when there was a knock at the door and an older woman stepped inside carrying a tray. The room was filled with the delicious smell of broth. My stomach welcomed it. For the first time since May's death, I felt well, but I felt guilty for feeling better.

'Good afternoon, Betsy,' she smiled, 'you look brighter.'

She placed the tray on my knee and flicked open a napkin. I took the napkin from her and tucked it into the top of my nightgown. Presented before me was a large bowl of thick vegetable soup and a slice of bread.

'Thank you, Madam,' I said, my words lost and hesitant as I realised, I did not know her name. 'The soup looks delicious.'

'That will give you some strength,' she said, 'I am Mrs Tolley. You had Mr Bradshaw worried, he's not left your side the whole time you've been here you know. He was supposed to return home last week, but when your –,' she paused and decided not to continue with the sentence, 'well, he changed his plans until after... until he was content you were... Oh dear, I do talk and will get myself into trouble. Let's just say, he was very worried and I might say, there seems to be some unusual master-servant relationship going on between you two. Just look at the beautiful flowers he sent you and he was very specific. Not even my husband brings me flowers like that. Do you know what a purple hyacinth means?'

I shook my head, staring at the vase on top of the dresser, displaying the fresh flowers and she explained, 'it means to be sorry, to want forgiveness. The sprig of holly, I can understand that – it means *hope*. What has he done that he's sorry for, I wonder?'

I stared at her blankly. She was a friendly woman, very chatty and hard to keep up with when she chattered on, but she did raise a valuable point. *'Why did Mr Bradshaw want forgiveness?'*

She laughed at my ignorance and shook her head. I tore away chunks from the bread and dunked them into the soup while she busied herself, flapping her arms about and fussing around the room. I was unsure if she was actually doing anything or just trying to create the illusion that she was busy.

Mrs Tolley walked over to the bag waiting on the chair in the corner of the room. I recognised the bag as Aunt Lily's and she removed my belongings from inside. My cream floral dress came out, which she neatly hung over the back of the chair. She placed my brush on top of the dresser and held my toothbrush in her hand.

'Your aunt has been to see you and brought some of your belongings,' she explained, and I smiled, slurping my soup.

'Sorry about your sister, Betsy,' and she placed a comforting hand on my arm, 'it is a cruel world we live in and often unfair, but time is a healer and what doesn't kill you makes you stronger.'

Her words, though they sounded abrupt as she said them, held the truth. I had to heal now that I was stronger.

'After you have eaten, you should have a nice bath. I think that will do you wonders,' she said. 'I will bring you a fresh towel. I would leave it a while though, Mr Bradshaw is in there at the moment. Like I said, he's not left your side in three days.'

Mrs Tolley left the bedroom and I finished the soup in peace. I mopped up the remains of my soup with the soft, crusty bread. My hunger was satisfied.

I placed the tray on the table next to the bed and rested my eyes. When I opened them again, my cup of tea was lukewarm, but I drank it all the same, finding comfort in the familiar flavour.

I grabbed a change of clothes, the toiletries and towel Mrs Tolley had left out for me, which she must have dropped off in the room while I slept. I crept across the corridor towards the bathroom. My legs were shaky at first as they tried to support my body weight, but with each movement I regained my balance and strength.

Mr Bradshaw stepped out of the bathroom at the point my hands reached for the doorknob and the tip of my fingertips stroked his bare stomach. In a startled yelp, I stepped backwards and out of his way, clutching my belongings tightly to my chest.

He stepped over the threshold and stopped in front of me, his blue eyes staring down at me.

My eyes wandered down to the towel that was wrapped around his waist, leaving the rest of his naked body exposed. Realising what my eyes feasted on, I turned my attention back to his face feeling ashamed. I clutched on to my belongings so tightly, my body trembling and only muttering the words, 'sorry, sorry, sorry,' that left my mouth quickly.

I took a deep breath and swallowed hard.

'Good to see you up and about, Betsy.'

'Absolutely,' I edged my way to the bathroom door, 'I am much better and I hope to feel human again after a bath.'

'I've just had a bath.'

'*I know,*' I thought, '*I can see the dampness of your flesh.*'

He continued, 'I will call Mrs Tolley to clean the bathroom for you, before you use it.'

'No need, I can do it.'

'I will be going back home in the morning,' his hands on his hips, his chest gently moving as he breathed making it difficult for me to concentrate. 'I don't expect you to come back with me. I know your aunt will need you. Just take all the time you need and when you are ready, your job will still be waiting for you, if you want it.'

I thanked him for his understanding and compassion, but felt more relieved when he turned away and I could escape into the bathroom.

In no time I was relaxing in a lovely hot bath. The warmth engulfed my whole body and the steam cleared my head. Baths weren't like this at Aunt Lily's, they took many boiled kettles to fill and once it was ready, I only stayed in for as long as necessary, finding it too uncomfortable to stay cramped up in the tin bath for long.

The water was beginning to cool when I finally stepped out of the bath and Mrs Tolley was right, it did work wonders. When I was clothed and heading downstairs, I felt human again, like a large part of my old self had come back. There was still some emptiness, and always would be; May had left a hole.

I was told by Mrs Tolley to wait in the sitting room for Mr Bradshaw, while he ran a few errands across town with Dr Oxley. I sat in one of the comfy chairs and enjoyed several cups of tea. It felt strange to be waited on in a room I once cleaned and I even glanced at my reflection in the mirror, making sure I was not in a different body.

It was early evening when Mr Bradshaw returned with Dr Oxley, both men looked tired as they walked through the door in deep discussion.

I watched them remove their hats and coats and place them on the coat stand in the hallway. Mr Bradshaw entered the sitting room as he unfastened his tie and loosened the top of his shirt. He rolled up his sleeves and slouched down in the chair opposite me. He looked exhausted.

'Good evening, Betsy, sorry to keep you waiting. How has your afternoon been?'

'Fine, thank you, Mrs Tolley has looked after me well,' I said.

'Ah Betsy,' Dr Oxley greeted me, as he stood in the doorway with his arms folded, 'nice to see you with a bit of colour in your cheeks.'

'Dr Oxley,' I stood up to greet him, 'thank you so much for everything you have done and for letting me stay here.'

'You have my nephew to thank for that, it's not a normal procedure for a doctor to allow his patients to stay in his home. After all, it's not a hospital.'

I smiled awkwardly.

'Anyway,' he stepped back in the hall, 'I am tired, it's been a long day. I will have my supper in my bedroom, if you could inform Mrs Tolley?'

'I will do just that,' Mr Bradshaw assured his uncle, before the old man said his goodbyes and wandered upstairs for the evening.

'I called by your aunt's house before and told her you are much better,' Mr Bradshaw said when we were alone. 'I told her you will be home tomorrow.'

'I feel much better now, I can go home today, I have outstayed my welcome already.'

'It's no trouble. Don't run before you can walk. Besides, Mrs Tolley has cooked you a nice meal, at least I know you'll have some decent food in you.'

Mrs Tolley served the meal and placed a carafe of red wine between us. It was surreal to sit at the dining table where I once served Dr Oxley and watch Mrs Tolley carry out the same evening tasks I once did not so long ago.

'Have you taken my uncle his dinner?' Mr Bradshaw asked Mrs Tolley.

'Yes, Mr Bradshaw, he received his first.'

'Thank you. If want to finish off in the kitchen you can go home.'

Mrs Tolley nodded, appreciating her early dismissal for the day and quickly vanished into the kitchen.

I began to tuck into the delights before me; slices of cooked ham, boiled potatoes, carrots and broad beans. Mr Bradshaw poured out a glass of wine for us both.

'Mrs Tolley seems nice,' I was making small talk.

'Yes, my uncle is satisfied with her.'

There was a moment of silence, apart from the sound of our cutlery clanking against the plate and clinking of the glasses, as they were lowered back down onto the table.

'Thank you for looking after me, how much do I owe your uncle for his care?'

Mr Bradshaw laughed and cut through his potato. I calculated in my head an estimation of the amount I would owe Dr Oxley for the past few days and it terrified me. I thought of various solutions and I decided that my only option was to work for free. If Mr Bradshaw would allow me to do that for a month, he could send my wages back to his uncle and my debt would be cleared.

I tried not to ponder over the finances and enjoyed the saltiness of the ham and savoured the flavours of the vegetables. The meal was delicious and the rich taste of the wine equally matched it.

Mr Bradshaw swallowed his mouthful and said, 'Betsy, there's nothing for you to pay. I have settled it.'

I froze, holding my wine glass in mid-air and with surprise gaped at him, *'did I hear him correctly?'* As though he read my thoughts, he nodded at me and rose his glass in a salute, 'it's the least I could do, you have been an asset to me.'

'An asset?' I continued to lift my glass and take a sip, my head seemed to feel lighter after a few mouthfuls. I was not drunk, neither was I tipsy, I was just relaxing to a level I didn't think was possible.

I raised my eyebrows and repeated the words, 'an asset?'

'An asset,' he echoed and downed the last swig of wine in his glass before topping up our drinks, 'it's a compliment! It means I value you.'

'I feel privileged,' I blushed, I couldn't remember being considered of value before. The compliment made me feel strange inside. I lowered my glass and rested both my hands on the table, as I stared down at the plate of food. The words were kind and made me feel appreciated, but they didn't bring me any joy, in fact they had the opposite effect and I felt hopeless.

Mr Bradshaw's hand reached across the table and covered mine. It was the warmth that came from his touch that snapped me from my stare and my eyes met his.

'Betsy, I feel so sorry for you and all you have been through these past two weeks. You looked so helpless and bereft at the funeral.'

'Has it really been two weeks since she died?' I asked in disbelief. 'It still doesn't feel real. Being here, I can pretend she's still at home, because nothing in this house or being with you reminds me of her. It will be tomorrow, when I go home and see Aunt Lily in our home of memories.'

'It's not going to be easy,' his hand affectionately rubbed mine, 'take everything one step at a time and you will make it through. Things will work out *in the end.*'

'A sentence I have heard many times before.'

I nodded and forced a weak smile, a single teardrop broke free and dripped down my cheek. For a moment longer, Mr Bradshaw held my hand, until the kitchen door opened and Mrs Tolley passed through the dining room. He was quick to pull his hand away and grasp the wine glass. But she noticed. Of course she noticed, the smirk across her face and her raised eyebrows told me just that.

Once we had finished eating, Mr Bradshaw and I stayed at the table to drink the last of the wine. I still felt lightheaded from the lack of food over the past two weeks and recovering from my illness. Though it was very comforting, I felt as though the rich red wine had healed me and numbed my feelings; my head was clearer and I felt merry.

We left the plates on the table and made our way into the sitting room. Mr Bradshaw switched the wireless on and the soft, relaxing sounds of an orchestra came from the speakers and I listened to the gentle symphony.

Mr Bradshaw stood by the cabinet next to the fireplace. From the cupboard underneath he retrieved two crystal cognac glasses and a decanter full of brandy. He removed the glass teardrop stopper and poured the dark liquid. When he had resealed the decanter, he paused with his hands clutching the rim of the cabinet and his back arched, he stared down, letting out a huge sigh, before he spoke, 'I am sorry my uncle couldn't save May.'

'It was no one's fault. He did all he could.'

'He was too late.'

I walked over to Mr Bradshaw and my hand reached out to touch his shoulder. I pulled away before my fingers reached the fabric of his shirt and sensing I was close, he tilted his head sideways to look at me.

I had seen that look before in his eyes; an intense look that made me stop dead as I was drawn into his stare.

He straightened his back and faced me fully. The tip of his fingers glided down my arm, across my hand and his fingers entwined around mine. His other hand he pressed on the arch of my back and pulled me closer to him.

My face lifted and I felt the stubble of his beard brush against my forehead. He lowered his head and our mouths touched. Neither of us moved.

His warm lips parted and I imitated his slow gentle kiss.

He was quick to pull away, 'I'm sorry, that was wrong of me.'

'No,' not wanting him to apologise.

'You are grieving, Betsy, and it's late.'

Mr Bradshaw switched off the wireless and walked across the sitting room to leave. I ran ahead of him and pressed my back against the door.

'Betsy, what are you doing to me?' he said in a whisper.

I reached out and pressed my hands flat on his chest. I could feel his heart beating faster beneath the palm of my hand. I stepped closer, our bodies touched and I moved my arms around his neck.

There was a moment of hesitation, where his eyes searched mine and eventually he surrendered, he succumbed to my desires. He lowered his head and we kissed again. He wrapped both his arms around my back and pulled me closer, our moment grew in passion. My whole body was awake with new sensations, new urges and new longing. I hadn't been kissed before.

For the second time he broke away from me, 'It's getting late and you need your sleep.'

He brushed past me and opened the door. I didn't stop him, and as he disappeared into the hallway, he said, 'You're not well. What am I doing?'

I listened to the sound of his steps fade as he went up the stairs and the creaking of the floorboards as he walked across the hallway to his room, not his usual bedroom which I occupied, but the box room at the back. My feet were grounded on the spot and I stared blankly at the darkness in the hall, as my mind processed what had happened.

When I was convinced he was settled in his room, I made my way upstairs, careful not to make a sound. The whole time, my head was swimming with confusion and thoughts battered my head as I tried to make sense of it all. It continued to baffle me until the early hours of the morning, when I finally gave in to my tired eyes and fell into a deep sleep.

The bright light of the sun woke me from my sweet slumber. Mrs Tolley had drawn back the curtains and stood at the foot of the bed carrying tea and toast on a tray.

'Wakey, wakey, sleepy head,' she said, 'I don't think you have a head for wine do you or whatever else you were drinking last night?'

I pulled myself up, my eyes squinting from the bright light. I was not ready to wake up, my eyes refusing to open.

'What time is it?' I croaked, looking at her with one eye open.

'Late, Betsy. Mr Bradshaw insisted you sleep and have breakfast in bed.'

Hearing his name caused my eyes to shoot open. *There were questions I needed answering, questions that only he could answer.*

'That got your attention,' she said, handing me the tray, 'but I am afraid he's already left.'

'Mr Bradshaw has gone?' I was aghast, 'without saying goodbye?'

'He was in a rush this morning. He has been away from his work too long and needed to get back but I am *sure* you said your goodbyes last night.'

Mrs Tolley left me alone to finish my breakfast and I was left feeling disheartened that Mr Bradshaw didn't wait to see me.

Chapter Nineteen

'The questions could wait.' I made that decision when I returned home to my family; they needed me more. I stayed with my aunt for another month, I felt we needed that time together and I wrote to Mr Bradshaw updating him of my plan. I had hoped he would send me a personal reply, but instead a short note from Miss Sharp followed. Until I returned, she had taken over my duties around the house, and Mr Bradshaw was unwell with *another* chest infection.

As much as I was concerned for his health, it didn't persuade me to go back sooner as there was one important thing left to do, but I had been avoiding it. The headstone was in place; I had to see *her*, as difficult as it was going to be.

I walked the longest route to *her* resting place, deliberately following the wrong footpaths through the graveyard and distracting my mind with the beauty of the nature that surrounded me. It was the thought of seeing *her* gravestone I feared, to see *her* name, forever chiselled in the rock and the short years of *her* life – 1908 to 1934 – engraved at the bottom. Too young; a beloved mother, sister, friend, and with everything to live for. It was too official.

After I circled the grounds of the church several more times, I finally convinced myself I was ready and I headed over the graveyard; the rows of headstones standing out of the ground. I inhaled deeply, and slowly released my breath as I counted the graves, my eyes briefly catching information about somebody else's loved one, whether it be a year or a name; anything that stood out; anything that kept me from looking up.

I knew how many gravestones I had to pass until I reached May and when I was almost there, I glanced up. My insides froze. I stopped walking. I stopped breathing. I stopped blinking and I stared at the figure of the man kneeling by *her* grave who was too old to be Roger.

His hands clung on to his hat that rested on his knee and his grey head of hair bowed down. He was in distress; I could see he was grieving, but his face was out of sight and he was unrecognisable.

I approached him slowly, careful not to disturb him, as my feet shuffled along the grass, and I paused behind him.

My eyes widened in disbelief. I knew who this man was and he sensed my presence. He looked stunned when his red, weeping eyes met mine.

I stared dumbfounded at the man.

'Why are you visiting my sister's grave?' I asked Mr Irving.

'I should have known I would find you here one day,' he said and rose to his feet. Still amazed at him being there, I watched him fumble in his pocket for a handkerchief to blow his nose and wipe his tears.

'Mr Irving, did you know my sister well?'

He looked around the grounds and I wondered if he was making sure no one else was close by. He was no longer the powerful and confident man I remembered from my childhood, he looked weak and troubled. The dark rings around his eyes suggested he had not slept well for weeks, and his face looked thinner than it was when I last saw him at the funeral almost six weeks ago.

'I suppose it's time you knew the truth,' he said weakly, unable to make eye contact with me. He was looking down at his fingers that twiddled with the rim of his hat.

I waited for him to speak.

'I remember the first time I met your father, we had moved into the house next door but one, on the street where you used to live.'

'Yes, Mr Irving, I remember.'

'I was a newlywed then, my wife was expecting Mark and your father introduced himself to me. He was a friendly man, a true gentleman, he told me he and his wife were expecting their second child.'

'*Bert,*' I thought, '*Mark and Bert are the same age.*'

Mr Irving continued, 'in those few minutes I spoke to your father, I knew he loved his wife and I envied him.'

I bit my tongue, preventing myself from saying something.

He looked around again; he was troubled. 'I don't love my wife. I've never loved her. My parents encouraged me to marry her, they thought she would be good for me, but I loved someone else. Someone else I wanted to marry, but my parents didn't approve of her because she was an orphan and her background was unknown.'

'That's a shame,' I said. 'My mother was an orphan and like you said, my father loved her, I think they had a happy marriage.'

Mr Irving shot me a look, a knowing look.

'*Surely not.*'

'Betsy, I met your mother when I was nineteen, before she married your father.'

'No,' I shook my head, I was not going to believe this.

'Yes, Betsy. We were young, happy, at times foolish, and,' he paused. 'I wanted to marry her, to make things right, but my parents wouldn't allow it. She was pregnant.'

I looked at him in horror, but I said nothing. He needed to explain.

'She sorted herself out, your mother. She married someone fairly quickly and I was relieved she was going to be looked after. The baby was born, a little girl I was told. My baby girl.'

'May?' I wanted to be wrong and to hear him say no, but I already knew the answer. May was named after the month she was born, and she was born in 1908, our parents were married in the autumn, the year before.

Mr Irving continued, 'your father invited my wife and I round one afternoon, and I wasn't to know when I accepted his offer, that his wife was *my* Florence. The shock I had when I saw her with this beautiful toddler on her knee. My daughter. As soon as I saw May, I knew she was mine. I could see the resemblance in her eyes. Florence just looked at me like I was a stranger, she gave nothing away; she was good at that. Whereas it took me all my strength to hide my love for this child, and a different strength to not fall at your mother's knees.'

I shook my head frantically, not wanting to believe him. May looked different to the rest of us. I always thought her hair and eyes were like our mother's, but seeing Mr Irving now, I could see they were his. Looking into his pale blue eyes, so similar to May's, I knew, to my despair, he spoke the truth.

Mr Irving went on to say, 'I don't think your father ever knew it was me, but he must have known the truth about May. Yet whenever I saw your father with the four of you, he loved you all the same.'

'What about Mrs Irving?' I asked.

'She figured out the truth, eventually. I think after the death of your father and the attention I gave your mother, that brought everything out in the open.'

I lowered my head, remembering all too well the regular visits soon after my father was buried.

'What about the baby?' I asked, 'before my mother left, she was pregnant.'

'I know, I told her to leave town and I helped her. I made the plans for the boys to go to Canada and I suggested you girls stay with your aunty. It was selfish of me but I couldn't risk your mother sending May away. It was the only way for me to still watch May grow up.'

I took in a deep breath. My hand spanned across my forehead and, with my thumb and middle finger, I applied pressure to my temple. It was too much to take in.

'Our boy, he will be fourteen in November.'

My head shot up and I repeated his first two words, '*our boy?* Does that mean you still see my mother?'

'Yes, most Saturday's I visit her. She lives in the next village, just a short train journey away.'

I was horrified. For all these years my mother had been living in the next village. I felt anger build up inside me.

Mr Irving pulled from his wallet a crumpled-up piece of paper with a scribbled address on it. The paper was tatty and discoloured, the writing had faded and the fold showed tiny shreds of paper fibre, where it had worn away. It had been kept there for fourteen years, safely tucked away with his money.

He took my hand and tucked the piece of paper inside before closing my palm, 'you should go and see her.'

'She didn't try to see May or me!' I snapped, and I screwed the paper up in my hand, but I had no intention of parting with it. 'Thank you for your time, Mr Irving. If what you said about May is true, it's too late now, she has left this world believing Alfred Colborne was her father and named her son after him. That will never change. I don't understand how you can cry at her grave when you have never connected with her, other than once being our neighbour.'

Mr Irving stared back at me, he didn't respond to my outburst. He just listened, and I took the opportunity to say more, 'do you know what I have gone through, because of you? I was bullied by Mark, he made my life hell as a child, all because of you. Beatrice has made my life hell and even today I am still suffering with it. I loved Stanley, but lost him, all because of you. *You* and *your family* took everything from me, but you are not having May. She was *never yours.*'

'I accept that burden, but there's just one thing you are wrong about,' Mr Irving cut in, 'it's you who has made Beatrice's life hell.'

I could have attacked him, but I controlled myself and firmly said, 'Can you leave, so I can pay my respects to my sister's grave – alone?'

Mr Irving walked away and I fell to my knees, facing May's gravestone. I held my breath until the footsteps of Mr Irving had faded away, and then I cried.

Chapter Twenty

Mr Irving was right, the journey to the next village was short, the train barely built up any speed before it was slowing down again for the next station.

The village was small, with only several necessary shops and a gathering of homes branching off into small streets leaving the main road. I called into the post office to ask for directions and handed the gentleman the piece of paper I had tucked away in my purse. He smiled when he saw the address and said, 'ah Mrs Colborne. If you turn right out of here, fourth road on the left and it's the second house.'

I thanked him kindly and repeated the directions in my head as I counted the streets towards my mother's house. My heart was heavy with many emotions, but the most suffocating was the fear and anxiety which heightened when I stood at the end of her street.

I had many arguments in my head; to turn back and head home, or to face what had become my demon. I needed to know, but was I ready for the truth? Would I ever be ready for the truth?

After fifteen minutes of this battle, I knew it was now or never and I stood outside her door. I rapped my knuckles against the hard wood sending an echo through the room inside, followed by the sound of footsteps drawing nearer.

I held my breath as the doorknob slowly turned. In a moment's hesitation I considered running, hiding, anything to avoid the confrontation, but whatever doubts I had, my body remained rigid.

It was too late now, the door opened.

There she stood, exactly as I remembered. The same blue eyes and the same light brown hair, loosely pulled back from her face. She had developed a few wrinkles across her forehead, deeper ones shaped in a V between her eyebrows and fainter ones curled around her eyes.

She looked at me through squinted eyes and studied my face, but not for long; she recognised me. The realisation in her eyes was apparent from the slight rise of her eyebrows, but she didn't smile, her face was vacant, neither surprised nor pleased to see me.

She opened the door fully and stepped aside, 'for a moment I thought you were Lily. I don't need to ask who you are. You'd better come in.'

The room was small and dark, with a window allowing a small shaft of sunlight through and it reminded me of our first home. It was laid out in a similar way, with the same table and stools, and her wooden chair situated next to the fireplace.

My father's favourite chair was positioned beneath the window, with a loose cushion pushed into the back. Mother sat down on this seat and picked up her knitting from the basket by her feet, she was still a beautiful knitter, just as I remembered. Her fingers twitched quickly with the needles, her eyes focused on her craft and she did not glance up at me.

'Sit there,' she said, nodding her head in the direction of another chair. I slipped my cardigan off and hung it from the hook on the back of the door, before I followed her request.

The room felt cold and uninviting, apart from the colourful rug that lay in the middle of the floor; the same rug my grandmother made as a wedding gift all those years ago. Everything about it was familiar, the colours, the way the wool had been woven and I could still remember how it felt to touch. It was looking worn, faded in places and frayed around the edges, but I found comfort in the memories attached to it, taking a moment to reflect and admire it for a while.

My mother continued to concentrate on her knitting, the sound of the needles clicking brought back memories of my childhood. I felt I had been taken back in time. I could have been that six-year-old again; all that was missing was the sound of my brothers and sister.

Not allowing myself to sink into grief, I glanced across at my mother, her head bent over the blanket folded many times on her knee and I noticed how sore her hands looked. They were extremely dry and deeply chapped. Some of the thin cuts were red with dried blood, and her yellow nails were brittle and splitting in places.

'You look like your father,' my mother eventually said.

'Mr Irving told me quite a story,' I blurted out. I had been practising what to say and how I would say it on the walk to Mother's, but this unpractised opening just slipped out.

My mother shot a quick glance up from her knitting, I was hoping to see sorrow and guilt in her eyes, but she showed no shame. She turned her attention to the pan that hung over the fire, 'it's not long boiled, if you want a cup of tea?'

'Shall I make it?' I offered. I was under the impression she wanted me to anyway and I set about making a pot. It was easy to find my way around the room, everything was displayed on the shelf and she had very few belongings. I placed her cup down by her feet and returned to the chair.

'I suppose you know the truth?' my mother asked.

'Is it the truth?' I challenged her.

She flashed me a quick look.

'That's why I'm here, is it the truth, about you and Mr Irving before Father? You may as well tell me the truth now.'

Mother placed her knitting down in the basket and picked up the cup from the floor. She took a sip and pulled a face, as though finding it too hot to drink. She held it in her hands, then rested it on her knee and stared down at the liquid as she spoke. 'I was working as a domestic servant for Mr Parkes and his wife when I met your father. I always saw him on a Monday; that was the day he delivered coal there,' a smile spread across her face, as she recalled. 'I knew he was fond of me, he looked at me differently and always spent longer than he needed to. He was shy and for a long time that's all it was, secret, short conversations.

Then, there was Wallace. I met him at a similar time. He was the opposite to Alfred, so full of confidence and he was a real charmer. We met when I was sent to have Mr Parkes' shoes repaired, and he wasted no time in getting to know me. We met whenever we could, stealing half an hour to half a day together. I was taken with him. That's how he made me feel and when he asked me to marry him, I was over the moon.

I got into trouble not long after and I soon found out that he was not going to marry me. Then your father found me, upset and you don't need to know the rest, what does it matter now? Your father is dead, May is dead, all that can be taken to the grave.'

'So you know about May?' My hand squeezed around the cup, I could feel the anger building up in my stomach, but I bit down on my bottom lip in an attempt to remain dignified.

'Yes,' her voice lowered, 'Wallace told me.'

'Did my father know the truth?'

My mother paused to take a few sips of her tea and buying herself some time before she answered. I could taste blood in my mouth, I had split my lip, but the pain distracted me from saying something I would regret. I wanted to shake the full truth out of her. She looked weak and it would have been so easy to get the answers I wanted. The answers I needed.

'I told him May was his and he believed me. He didn't question the dates when they didn't match. To him May arrived very early, but to me, she was on time. Perhaps he did know the truth, but he still carried on as the proud father. Maybe he was too ashamed.'

'Did you love him? You were destroyed when he died. I saw you. I remember.'

'What else could I do? My life was ruined. He left me alone with four children to clothe, to feed and we had no money. I was frightened, how could we live? We were this close to living on the streets.' She signalled an amount by showing an inch gap between her thumb and finger. 'I was angry with him. He made me a promise to look after me. I thought everything would be fine if I was a dutiful wife. I behaved exactly how I should behave.'

My blood was boiling and I felt infuriated; she had not answered my question. She had distorted my illusions, a memory that I had held onto for so long, that we were once a perfect, happy family. Only we weren't. It was all pretence, a game Mother played so she was safe and secure, and not an outcast in society for having an illegitimate child.

'What could have become of May, if it was not for the kindness of my father?'

'How could you live here knowing your daughters were only up the road? What type of mother are you? Did you think of us at all? What about Frank and Bert? What about my father? Did you weep when you heard about May?'

'Betsy,' her voice was sharp. 'I don't expect you to understand, you're not a mother and from what I can gather, you're not a wife. The choices I made were best for everyone. Bert and Frank would have a better chance of a life than I could offer them. I knew you and May were better off with your aunt, be grateful I did that for you. I could have left you on the streets or in a home. Just think what your life would have been like once another baby came, people would know he was not Alfred's. I would have brought shame on you all. At least here no one knows me, I don't see anyone from town apart from Wallace and I have a job, it pays, it keeps the roof over our heads.'

'And the boy?' I asked, 'does he know about us?'

My mother shook her head, 'he doesn't know Wallace is his father, he thinks he's his uncle and his father died before he was born. They are both very fond of one another.'

'Do you care about us, Mother?' I asked, a question I was not sure I wanted to know the answer to.

She didn't blink when she looked at me, her eyes wide and her tone was cold, 'I cried when Wallace told me about our daughter.'

I had heard enough, I placed my unfinished tea on the ground and rose to my feet, stamping towards the door. I wondered why I had bothered to visit her; she was as I remembered, cold and detached. I realised she didn't care about Bert, Frank and me, the children of her husband, but at least there was love for May and her son with Mr Irving.

I was ready to grab my cardigan from the door, when her tone softened, 'sometimes Betsy, the past is best left forgotten, people are so desperate for the truth and sometimes the truth can hurt the people dearest to you.'

I saw a tear roll down her cheek and she pulled a dirty rag from the sleeve of her cardigan to wipe it away. She tried to disguise it by clearing her throat with a cough. She placed her cup down on the floor and gathered up her knitting. She spoke, her voice was shaky, 'your father must have known the truth, but he didn't search for it. Nobody else knew, it was my secret, and when Wallace moved on the street, it was our secret.'

I wanted to leave now. I reached up to unhook my cardigan and I caught hold of the garment underneath. Feeling the soft material in my touch and the thickness of the material, I studied it further. It was my father's brown coat, his only coat that kept him warm in the cold months and I recalled how much he loved that coat. The same coat Mother held on to after the funeral.

'You kept father's coat,' I said in a shocked whisper.

'It was a nice coat,' she responded.

As I clung on to the material, not wanting to let go, it felt surreal to be holding something of his and a flash of a memory came into my mind.

I looked at my mother with an accusing glare and exclaimed, 'it was you!'

I remembered the familiar figure stood at the back of the church on May's wedding day, that disappeared just as quickly as it arrived, wearing the very coat I was clutching in my hand. 'I saw you. You were at May's wedding.'

My mother bowed her head. Her hands clutched tightly around the blanket and her knuckles turned white from the grasp. One of the needles, slipped out of the row of stitches and fell to the ground. She didn't pick up the needle to salvage her knitting.

I fell to my knees before her. My eyes pleaded with her for a sign, for an indication that she was not a heartless mother. I wanted to see her look into my eyes, to see into her soul. She loved all of us once, I know she did. I had not imagined those years before my father died, but she looked through me, as vacant as she was when I arrived. She turned her face away and stared at a spot in the corner of the room.

'Why did you come here?' she asked weakly.

'Because after all is said and done, you are my mother.'

'Please don't come again. Life was simple when it was just Frederick and me.'

Her words cut through me like a knife.

I rose to my feet and made my way to the front door. I still had more questions to ask, and I could have lost my temper with her, to make her realise what she had put us all through, but instead I thought, *'what is the point?'* I had suffered enough. I had lost my sister, my wonderful sister, I was not going to cry any more for this heartless woman. After all, I still had Aunt Lily and that was the one good thing my mother did for May and me, passing us over into the loving arms of Lily.

'Goodbye, Mother.' I said and pulled open the door, reaching for my cardigan as I left, 'I will not see you again.'

Florence

Chapter Twenty-One

As the door closed shut, Florence listened to the sound of Betsy's footsteps fade away. She quickly rose to her feet while her knitting carelessly fell to the floor. She dashed for the door, her long fingers wrapped around the knob, clutching it tightly ready to swing it open, ready to call Betsy back inside.

She froze, staring down at her hand and her breathing was quick to increase.

'No, no, no!' she said out loud, shaking her head frantically listening to the conflicting voices in her head, commanding her to do something; *go after her; stop her; let her go.*

She did nothing. Too overwhelmed with emotions, it had been too long since she last saw her daughter; her baby girl who she once held tightly in her arms, who she once fed from her breasts and who once lovingly called her, 'Mumma.' She had imagined this day would come, but had not wanted it to; it was easier for her life if it didn't.

Florence's gaze turned to the rug in the centre of the room and she could see, as clear as if they were real, her four children as they were back in 1919. Alfred was there too, looking like he always did, while he sat in his favourite chair. Only now she saw him differently. She was too afraid to blink in case their images would disappear.

'*I had it all,*' she thought, as she looked on at her forgotten family. Frank and Bert were shoving and annoying one another, and Alfred with his charming ways diverted their attention back to him and his story. She could hear the softness of his voice as he continued to feed the children's imagination with adventure.

Inside she was smiling and she looked at her daughters; how different they were to one another. Betsy was hanging on every word, her mouth wide open as she shuffled closer and closer to her father's feet, until she was underneath his nose and he scooped her up in his arms. May sat cross legged, her back straight and she stared into the distance, absorbed in the story and lost in her thoughts.

'Such beautiful children, such a wonderful man and wonderful husband.'

Florence's mind wandered back to an earlier time, when she was seventeen, a naive young woman with little experience with men. In her childhood she was brought up by nuns in the girls' orphanage until she began work and met Alfred. The first man her age she had ever interacted with.

A warm feeling built up inside her, as she remembered his shyness and slight stutter whenever he was in her company, not realising he was growing increasingly fond of her at the time. She was equally nervous, but with each visit they became more at ease with one another and a pleasant friendship was formed. A perfect relationship, which should have been the start of a happy future together.

Things would have taken a simpler path if she hadn't met Wallace. The opposite to Alfred, he was confident and handsome; he knew the right words to seduce Florence and she was instantly attracted to him. His charm blinded her into believing everything he said, filling her with enough curiosity and longing that she succumbed to those new-found feelings and desires. He promised to marry her and for many months she was his, but he didn't marry her and probably hadn't intended to. He was betrothed to Doris; an arrangement made by his parents that he claimed was out of his hands. This truth only came to light when she announced she was expecting his child.

Over the years Wallace had made her many promises which he didn't keep, but through her love for him, she continued to believe and wait for him.

There was only one promise Alfred failed to keep. Florence

could feel the lump forming in the back of her throat as she thought about those words he said to her that night when she came to him heartbroken. He didn't know her heartache was over Wallace and the baby she carried. He didn't ask questions, he just wanted to comfort her and wrap his arms around her, to take the pain away, while she cried into his shoulder.

She made the first move, looking up at him with her bloodshot eyes. She knew how to play him; she knew he would not resist. Her time with Wallace had taught her well.

Everything happened so quickly and Alfred, feeling ashamed of himself for taking advantage, fooled into believing he had stripped her of her virtue, did the right thing. He had loved Florence since the first day he saw her. 'I promise I will look after you and love you forever,' he said, 'if you marry me?'

When they first married, everything was going to plan and she was able to deceive him into believing the baby she carried was his. Even after May was born, he didn't question his paternity, although he realised the truth the moment he first set eyes on the baby. The colour was quick to drain from his face, removing the proud sparkle of a first-time father from his eyes.

Florence held back her tears, as she recalled remembering it was then she truly wished May was Alfred's child, and how frightened she was, for hers and the infant's life, if Alfred disowned them. She watched and waited, and to her surprise Alfred took a deep breath and smiled down at the new-born in his arms, kissing her gently on the forehead. Nothing was ever said and for eleven more years he kept his promise to look after her and to love her, until the day he died.

Out of all the broken promises, this was the one that angered her the most. His choice of words was foolish, *'I promise I will look after you and love you forever.'* It was as though he didn't think he could die young and leave her alone to struggle with their children. Not realising that in death, his promise was null and void, and he was punishing her for what she did. For a long time she hated him for it and his children.

'I did love you, Alfred,' Florence's voice cracked, as the images of her past faded and she was aware of her surroundings once more. He had given her a home, provided food for the table and what is more, he loved her, *'even more than Wallace.'*

She regretted not once telling him that she loved him during their marriage. She always behaved how a wife ought to behave, but at the back of her thoughts was Wallace. How could she forget him when she saw him in May and he lived two doors down?

Florence was not strong enough to resist Wallace after Alfred died. He finally gave her the companionship she had yearned for. His kind words eased the emptiness she felt inside and he filled her head with more promises. One promise she was still waiting to be fulfilled; that he would leave his wife and be with her.

Florence scoffed at the recollection.

She knew why she was so angry with her children. She was filled with anger and resentment knowing in her heart she should have been with Wallace and it pained her then to see him married with children, which should have been their children. She would not have been widowed so young, they would have had May, maybe a Bert and Frank and Betsy, but looking more like an Irving than a Colborne. She would have been happier, but that life didn't happen.

'His children,' Alfred's children were a reminder that he broke his promise; a reminder that her life could have been different. A reminder she could not escape.

Wallace understood Florence. He arranged for Frank and Bert to be sent away, reassuring her it was the right thing to do, as it was to give May and Betsy to Lily. He found her work out of town and a home to live in, telling her this was a chance to start again; she could pretend she was carrying her late husband's baby and no one would know any different. It was the right thing to do for all of them.

'What have I done?' Florence's pressed her forehead against the door. Every part of her insides ached and she pushed her hand hard into her stomach to relieve the torture.

She was horrible to her children and she hated herself for it. She had been trapped in a vicious spiral that she could not escape from. When Alfred died, she felt lost; she feared for her life and the children were a burden. With no money coming in, they were on the brink of starvation, becoming homeless and being shamed. It was a suffocating time in her life, she fell deeper and deeper into depression and her children began to hate her. Her love affair with Wallace was her only reason for living.

'If only she had died and their father had lived, at least their children would have stayed together.' A thought she came back to many times, and she reminded herself, *'I did what I had to do, for everyone's sake.'*

'Betsy!' Florence cried out, as she pulled open the door and ran to the edge of the road. She continued to call out her name, but it was too late. She looked down the main street, but she was gone.

Florence fell to her knees and wept, her face buried in her hands as she gave in to her repressed emotions, allowing them to finally release after all these years. She had done well to forget, to raise another son as though he was an only child and pretend her other four didn't exist.

Betsy's words repeated in her mind, 'How can you live here? Knowing your daughters are only up the road? What type of mother are you?'

'What kind of a mother am I?' she asked herself, before she answered the questions she should have replied to Betsy.

'Did you think of us at all?'

'Yes, all the time, not a second goes by when I don't think about you all.'

'Did you weep when you heard about May?'

'It broke my heart. For so long I thought she was my favourite and I always kept her close to me. Now, my first-born child has gone and I never managed to make amends, or say goodbye.'

'Do you care about us, Mother?'

'Many times I have watched you and May from a distance, wanting to find the strength to approach you both, to say sorry and to beg for your forgiveness, but I always held back. I was there when May married, and I could see you looking at me. I was there at the funeral, but you didn't see me. You didn't see anyone that day, but in you, I saw me.'

'Florence, what are you doing?' Florence looked up to see

Wallace standing over her and he offered a supporting hand to help her to her feet. 'What is the matter?'

'Betsy came to see me,' she sobbed.

He waited patiently for her to continue.

'I sent her away and told her not to come here again.'

'I think you have done what is best, sweetheart?'

'Yes, too much pain and we must think about Frederick.' Florence lied, *'things were easier when it was just me and Frederick and Wallace.'*

Wallace placed a gentle kiss on her cheek, wrapped an arm around her shoulder and led her slowly in the direction of the house.

Betsy, my sweet little girl, you were always your father's angel. I do love you and I am ashamed of myself, but I don't want you to forgive me. I want you all to hate me. I knew it would be easier for you to leave me and forget about me if you hated me. I had no choice; I did what I had to do and you have done better without me. Forget about me but I won't ever forget about you. I will continue to live the rest of my life suffering in regret. I have made my bed, I will lie in it; you can live your life and enjoy yours, to the end.

Part Five

Chapter Twenty-Two

The short journey back to the train station gave me a sense of closure, though I was filled with heartache. Was there part of me that wanted my mother back in my life or was it that I just wanted to see remorse? Yet she was everything I knew she was; heartless.

After all these years, I had finally seen my mother and realised my life had been better without her. It also created a new sense of falseness. After all this time, the one thing that kept my sister and I close was our love for our father and each other. I was thankful she never knew the truth and one thing I was certain of; she was my sister and that was all that mattered.

I caught the one-twenty train back to town, finding privacy in a carriage on my own, allowing me a few minutes to be lost in my thoughts as the scenery sped past the window. As we left the village, I watched it disappear around the bend and I vowed that I would never return again. I would forget my mother, as she had so easily forgotten the four children she had left behind.

The train had only been travelling for a few minutes when it came to a sudden halt. The sharp braking caused me to jolt forward and I held my hand out to stop me from falling into the seat opposite.

I looked out of the window and realised we were in the middle of the track, and the station was nowhere in sight. I pulled open the carriage door and listened to the commotion from the other passengers as they wandered the aisle, frantic to know what had happened.

Within a few minutes, a man's voice called above the rest urging people to return to their seats. He walked briskly up and down each carriage, repeating the same calming instructions and although passengers approached the man with more questions, he had no answers.

Twenty minutes had passed and I had occupied the time gazing out of the window. I watched the workers at the front of the train wandering around aimlessly and not making progress to resolve the problem. Shortly after, another train joined the track carrying ten or more men. Their voices were booming out as they called out their instructions to one another, all of which was gibberish to me. Several of the men boarded our train, calling out to the passengers, 'please, everyone off,' as they walked in separate directions, 'another train will take you into town.'

As requested, I left the carriage and joined the back of the queue of passengers leaving the train. It took twice as long to exit, as each passenger found the need to ask the railway worker a question, and the next passenger repeated the same question the previous person had asked.

'Yes ma'am another train will take you to town.' 'No, sir, not tonight, there's a problem with this end of the line.'

A large man before me said with haste, 'a problem with the line? You said it was with the train! Does no one know what is going on here?'

'We are sorry sir. There is a problem with the track ahead and to continue would risk derailing the train. There's a train on the next line that will take you to the next station.'

'But I am not getting off at the next station.'

'I'm sorry for the inconvenience,' the worker remained calm. 'No trains will be passing through tonight until the problem is resolved.'

'When will they be back on?' The man continued to ask questions.

'We hope trains will be running as usual in the morning,'

he replied calmly, 'we will be working on it all night. Our main priority is making sure the passengers are safe and you will be looked after at the station. Please sir, if you would make your way to the next train.'

The man stepped down on to the track and I followed behind, focusing on the gravelled ground.

'If you walk across the sleepers, you will feel more stable,' I heard the railway worker say to me. He held out his hand to support my step down, and as my foot touched the uneven ground, we made eye contact. I should have recognised his voice, but as my thoughts were still with my mother, it didn't register with me.

We said each other's names at the same time, surprised to see each other and I asked Stanley, 'what are you doing here?'

'I work here.'

'Since when?'

'Ah, a while now. I am so sorry to hear about May.'

'Thank you,' I knew I had to walk away, but my body remained still, 'congratulations, a new baby on the way.'

'Betsy, I...'

'I'm really happy for you and Beatrice, though you have taken a bit of a gamble, changing jobs when you have a wife and a child on the way; that's not like you.'

'No, it's not, but...'

Realising Stanley still had hold of my hand, I pulled it away, 'lovely to see you, Stanley. Take care.'

'Betsy...' he called after me as I walked away. I quickly balanced along the sleepers and with every step I told myself not to look back. I had been through enough these last few weeks and he was the last person I wanted to see.

'Right this way, ma'am,' another railway man directed me to the entrance.

Once in my seat, I glanced out of the window to where I'd seen Stanley, but he had gone.

Chapter Twenty-Three

Before I left for Mr Bradshaw's, I said goodbye to my nephew. He was beautiful; his tiny perfect hands and feet with adorable fingers and toes; his chubby legs that gave jerky little kicks and his chubby arms that waved around; his eyes that opened and closed, looking constantly surprised by the light and forms around him and his pouting lips. He was delightful.

I sensed Mrs Flemming was reluctant to hand him over to me; it pained her to be parted from him. He had become hers since May had passed away and she had grown possessive over him. As I cradled Alfred in my arms, she sat on the neighbouring chair, leaning towards me, invading my space. She would pull the blanket up to his neck, checking his hands were warm enough and place her finger in his mouth, making sure he was not hungry. I was glad of the few minutes she left me alone with him while she fetched some cold beverages.

Roger was at work during my short visit. I had hoped to see him, but according to his mother he worked all the time and he took on any extra hours available to him. It was all for the future of his son, but Mrs Flemming feared that his grief kept him away; Alfred being a constant reminder of his lost wife.

I fully understood his grief. I cuddled Alfred one last time before it was time for me to leave and I said to Mrs Flemming, 'please tell Roger, that Lily and I are always there for him and Alfred, he knows where we are if he needs us, and he's not alone.'

A huge part of me looked forward to seeing Mr Bradshaw again, although it pained me to leave Aunt Lily, knowing it would be a long time before I saw my nephew again.

When I arrived, Miss Sharp opened the door to me. She looked like a piece of the furniture, back where she belonged.

'How is Mr Bradshaw?' I asked, stepping over the threshold.

'Mr Bradshaw is much better now, he is having his tea at the moment.'

'I shall tell him I am here,' I said, dropping my suitcase by the door.

'Perhaps wait until he has finished, Betsy.' Miss Sharp blocked the doorway to the dining room and her jaw dropped, I thought she wanted to say something, but her mouth closed and she stepped aside.

The door creaked open and Mr Bradshaw came into sight, sat at the head of the table, his cutlery clanking against his plate. He was looking up and smiling at something across the table. The smirk remained when he glanced across to see me enter. He placed his cutlery down and dramatically threw his arms in the air, 'Betsy, you have returned.'

He was not alone and as I advanced into the dining room, pushing the door fully open, I saw Miss Jenkins, sat on the other side of the table. She didn't glance up at me, her stare was fixed on Mr Bradshaw, but I could tell by the thinness of her pressed lips and the disapproving look that she was annoyed by my arrival. She crisply said, 'so this is how things are run in here?'

My insides pulled at the sight of her, a discomforting tugging sensation in my stomach. I paused for a moment, just long enough for my disappointment to go by unnoticed, while I composed myself as a member of Mr Bradshaw's working household.

'My apologies, Mr Bradshaw,' I quickly said taking the door handle ready to back out of the door, 'I didn't realise you had company, good evening Miss Jenkins. I shall go now.'

'Miss Sharp,' he called out, peering past me at Miss Sharp standing sheepishly in the hallway, 'please bring some food for Betsy, she must be hungry after her long journey.'

'That won't be necessary,' I stopped Miss Sharp, 'I have eaten, thank you, Mr Bradshaw.'

'Wonderful to have you back,' he said to me, raising his wine glass and ignoring Miss Jenkin's hard stare.

'Thank you, Mr Bradshaw,' I politely said, 'I believe you have been unwell, I am pleased to see you are your normal self again.'

'That I owe to Miss Jenkins,' he turned his wine glass in her direction and flashed her a smile, 'she has nursed me back to good health.'

'If you would excuse me, Mr Bradshaw, I am tired after my long journey and think I need an early night so I feel refreshed to begin my duties tomorrow,' I said, feeling as though my inner self was sat on my shoulder mocking me.

'As you wish.'

As I closed the door behind, Miss Sharp handed me my suitcase and whispered, 'Miss Jenkins has been a regular guest while you have been away. She has fussed over Mr Bradshaw like I don't know what and thrown her orders around as though she was lady of the house. We've had doctor after doctor round here the past month.'

'What has been the matter with him?' I asked, feeling a sense of worry.

'He doesn't talk about it. You know Mr Bradshaw, he doesn't like the fuss and he's better now, that's the main thing.'

I agreed. Feeling a lump in my throat, I swallowed hard, but Miss Sharp could see my struggle, 'you unpack and I'll bring you up a glass of brandy later. That will help you sleep.'

My arrival was not how I envisioned it would be, or how I had hoped. The last time I saw Mr Bradshaw was so very fresh in my mind and was the very reason I returned to him, but while there was Miss Jenkins, my hopes would never come to be.

I was up early the next morning, ready to start my day. Daylight was breaking through the window hinting that it was going to be a sunny, but chilly, day.

When I entered the dining room, the clock chimed seven. Miss Sharp was in the kitchen preparing breakfast and my cleaning brushes and cloths were ready and waiting for me in the doorway. I was definitely back at work.

After I had wiped the surfaces and fluffed the cushions, I began to brush down the soft furnishings. The sweeping sound of the brush dragging along the chair coverings distorted the sound of Mr Bradshaw creeping into the room. I let out a yelp at the sight of him and my heart leapt into my throat.

He laughed at my fright. In his smile, I could see the edge of the illness he was combating, the tiredness in his eyes and the grey tinge to his skin.

'I hope you are feeling better. Miss Sharp said you had a chest infection; you've had one of them before.'

'And I will have many more of them. I had pneumonia as a child, Betsy, I'm grateful to be here, but unfortunately I am prone to chest infections.'

'Miss Jenkins has looked after you well.' The words sounded more bitter than I intended them to.

'Miss Jenkins insisted I had the best care.' Mr Bradshaw straightened his posture, his hands held behind his back and his chest pushed upwards. There was something authoritative about the way he stood and he lifted his chin. 'I'm surprised you came back. I thought you would have stayed with your family.'

His words shocked me, making me feel as though I should not be there and worry quickly grew inside me. I became anxious, especially as his eyes locked on mine, seeking my reply. This sudden change in character confused me, but I tried to brush it off as Mr Bradshaw still felt unwell and I remembered him being a difficult patient for me that time. I also saw Miss Jenkins to blame, filling his head with venomous nonsense.

I took a deep breath and somehow, found the confidence to remind him, 'Mr Bradshaw, the last time I saw you?'

Only he was quick to cut me off, the tone of his voice halted me from saying any more; perhaps he wanted to save me the embarrassment of saying too much about that night. 'Betsy, you have worked hard for me for three years and I am fully satisfied with your standard of work. Even Miss Sharp commented on the condition of the property, the organisation of the cupboards and maintenance of the garden. I've not had such a delightful garden to admire and enjoy.'

The doorbell rang and Mr Bradshaw let out an annoyed, deep sigh and rolled his eyes. I advanced across the room, but the pattering sound of Miss Sharp's feet across the tiles in the hallway told me she was answering the door. I faced Mr Bradshaw again, waiting for him to continue.

'As I was saying, Betsy. It's all well and good that you enjoy working here. That's if you do enjoy working here?'

I frowned, not sure I was following what he was saying.

'What I want to know, is why are you here?'

'To work,' I answered, what I thought was the correct answer.

'No, Betsy. Why are you here? What is there here for you? What keeps you here?'

I understood what he was asking me, but I stood statue like, my mind empty and lost for words, unable to find the correct way to answer him. Thankfully, Miss Sharp entered the room and disturbed the awkward silence.

'Tell them I will be a moment,' Mr Bradshaw said to her.

'No, Mr Bradshaw,' she replied and looked at me, 'someone is here for Betsy.'

'For me?' I asked, puzzled by whom it could be.

Mr Bradshaw hesitated; I think he too was surprised and then, unexpectedly said to me, 'take the morning off, Betsy, to think about what I have said and see to your visitor.'

He briskly left the room and I noticed him glance down the hallway, as he passed the threshold, perhaps to have a glimpse at my mystery visitor.

'It's not every day you have a visitor and it's rude to make people wait,' Miss Sharp took the brush from my hand and I removed my apron.

The visitor was no longer at the door, and as I made my way outside, I saw the back of him. He was leaning against the garden wall, his hands in his jacket pockets and he wore a hat, but I knew who he was. I stopped in my tracks, only for a moment while I took a deep breath.

'What does he want?' I asked myself, while making my way up the gravel path towards him. The sound of my feet crunching on the ground alerted him of my presence and his head darted round to look at me.

'What brings you here, Stanley?' I said, sounding annoyed, *'to torture me more, ask me to be godmother?'*

'I – it was a surprise seeing you the other day,' he seemed nervous.

I looked back at the window unsure if Miss Sharp was there, behaving like a curious cat watching, but the net curtains made it impossible to tell. I glanced up at the first floor, just as the figure of Mr Bradshaw moved away from the window.

'How did you know where to find me?' I asked.

'I called by your aunt's after work yesterday, but you had already left. She gave me this address.'

'Does Beatrice mind?'

'Do you have time to for a walk?' he ignored my question.

At first, I wanted to refuse; I felt awkward going for a walk with a married man and I wanted to protect my feelings, but as I spoke, the word, 'yes,' slipped out instead. I returned to the house to collect my handbag and coat from the bedroom, while Stanley waited for me on the street.

On the walk back down the stairs, Mr Bradshaw was waiting, 'and who was your visitor?'

'Stanley, he's an old friend.'

'Ah, Stanley Rhodes, I remember, married Beatrice Irving. Why is he here?'

His words made me feel guilty for agreeing to spend time with Stanley, 'we were good friends once,' *'like you and Miss Jenkins,'* and I justified my actions, by adding, 'we've not seen each other in a while and since May has passed away, I assume he's here to see if I'm all right.'

I waited for Mr Bradshaw to respond, but instead he turned around and walked away. It was a further few seconds before I joined Stanley outside.

We followed the footpath along the side of the canal, it made for a pleasant stroll, with the slow flowing water and watching the ducks swimming close by. Not many people passed by, but from the streets overhead we could hear the commotion of traffic and mumbling of voices.

I broke the silence, 'now are you going to tell me why you're working for the railway lines?'

He took a moment to answer the question, 'as you know, I've thought about doing it before. I found out they were recruiting and I went for it. It doesn't pay well, not as well as having my own business, but it pays.'

'What about Irving's?'

Stanley stopped walking and looked at me perplexed, 'do you not know?'

'Know what?'

'I am surprised, I thought everyone knew – nothing stays a secret for long. He's bankrupt; he's lost everything as he didn't keep up the rent.'

'I didn't know. When did all this happen?' *'How did I not know this? I had spoken to Mr Irving a week ago.'*

'June.'

'June, not that long ago.' I thought back to when I last saw him, and recalled how troubled he looked, I had presumed it was over May, but there was more to it. He was a man living in his own hell.

'Oh Stanley, I am sorry. You've lost everything too.' I was sincere.

I was sympathetic towards Stanley, he only ever wanted the best out of life, to make the right decisions, just a shame it ended up being the wrong one. After all he married someone he didn't love for it.

'At least you have found alternative work and have a baby on the way,' I reassured.

'Baby?'

'My aunt told me, am I wrong?'

Stanley's eyes narrowed and the lines above his nose were deep from frowning. He was processing what I had said and while he studied me, my mind wandered back to the afternoon when Aunt Lily told me, hoping I had heard her right.

'You do know I didn't marry Beatrice?'

'Pardon?' *'Did I hear him right?'*

'I didn't marry her, Betsy,' his frown had lifted.

'Why didn't you marry her, she's pregnant. You should have married her; her life will be ruined now. Think of that poor baby, Stanley. What are you playing at? What have you done?' as I ranted, I realised it was because of May and what could have happened to her if my father hadn't married my mother.

'The baby is not mine. Beatrice is married to a man called Donald Robinson.'

I stared in astonishment. I felt my head ache as I absorbed this new information. Many questions rolled around in my head; my world, my logical world, had flipped over, but the one question that sprung forward was, *'why did I not know?'*

'The baby is not yours?'

'No, Betsy, the baby is not mine.'

'When did you end it? Why did you not marry her? Why do I not know this? Why now?' The questions just tumbled out.

'When I last saw you, you said something that made me think about my life and what I wanted.'

'What did I say?' feeling defensive that blame was being pushed on me. From my understanding I had only ever been supportive about his marriage to Beatrice and offered him my best wishes.

'You told me to be happy. It played on my mind for days. I was not going to be happy with Beatrice and called off the wedding immediately. She took it well, apparently there was someone else lined up and she married him in February this year.'

'Why did you not tell me?'

'My life was a mess; I was in a bad place. I had no job so had no money coming in. I was lucky they needed railway workers, when they did.'

'Why did you not tell me?' I repeated the words again. I was running over some calculations in my head; *it was a year ago when he changed his life path, why was I hearing about it now. Why did Aunt Lily and May not tell me, they would have known. Aunt Lily told me that Beatrice was pregnant, she could have mentioned it then and why did May shake her head at her to say no more.'*

'I wanted to sort myself out first,' Stanley explained. 'I spoke to May about getting in contact with you and she said I was wasting my time. She wanted me to leave you alone, that your life was better here.'

'When was this?'

'Early in the year, when I started work again.'

It frustrated me that I couldn't confront May and ask her why? To understand her reasoning behind this secret; had she been trying to protect me? I would never know her side of the story.

'What about Mark?' I asked. 'You've put your life in your own hands not marrying his sister.'

Stanley raised his eyebrows and chortled, 'you're absolutely right. Luckily, I managed to avoid him the times he came home and once Beatrice was settled with Donald he got over it. I have seen Mark since Mr Irving lost his business and I think with the humiliation of it all, he kept his head down.'

'That's lucky for you,' I smirked. Then, using the same words Mr Bradshaw asked me, I said 'why are you here?'

Stanley placed his hands firmly on my shoulders, making sure he had my full attention, 'I have nothing to offer you, only me,' he said. 'I have a return ticket for you tomorrow morning. If you want to come back, I will be waiting for you at the other end.'

There was doubt in me that kept me on my guard. After all, I had misread and made a fool of myself before.

'Stanley, you're asking a lot from me. I have made a life here for myself and you have complicated things, expecting me to drop everything at your call.' A lump formed in my throat and an inside battle to hold back the tears failed, as my eyes began to fill, 'it's a lot to take in.'

Stanley offered to walk me back to Mr Bradshaw's house but I refused, needing some time on my own. He pressed the ticket into my palm and curled my fingers around to seal the hold. He bowed his head and kissed my hand, 'I will be there tomorrow afternoon.'

He walked away and I stood stationary, watching him disappear as the path curved away. I didn't examine the ticket in my hand, I tucked it safely into the pocket at the back of my bag.

I struggled to process the change of events and for several hours I wandered the streets, trying to make sense of it all. An internal battle began as I tried to reason with the over-complicated thoughts swimming around my head. I was drowning in confusion and doubt; I was being suffocated by reason and decisions. My feelings for Stanley were deeper than they were for Mr Bradshaw and our connection was much stronger; we were the same and would be accepted by others as the same. Our life would be filled with contentment, love and happiness, welcomed by almost everyone, which I wouldn't have if I stayed with Mr Bradshaw. With Mr Bradshaw, there would always be Miss Jenkins somewhere in the background.

I was lost in my worries and wandering around in circles, delaying my return. My feet were aching, my heels were stinging and the top of my toes burned from the large blisters gradually forming. The pains in my stomach could have been hunger or my troublesome thoughts niggling at my insides and my mouth was dry from thirst. I felt unwell.

The handle of the front door seemed heavier than usual and the door was an even heavier force to push against. With difficulty I stepped inside the hallway, where the walls appeared to be moving together, closing in on me. The corridor became long and narrow, pushing the stairs too far away for me to reach. I moved slowly, my arms outstretched and pressed against the walls to steady my balance as my leaden feet dragged along the floor.

My vision quickly blurred into billions of tiny, colourful dots and my temperature rose rapidly. My body's defence system kicked in as a pool of cool sweat formed on my back and across my forehead, accompanied with a profound feeling of nausea; my eyes closed into darkness.

When I opened them again, my sickness had passed and

everything in the room took focus. I was lying down on the settee in the sitting room, Mr Bradshaw was stood leaning against the fireplace and Miss Sharp was stood over me, 'Oh Betsy, you had me worried, I didn't know what to do with you. You were as white as a ghost and out cold for five minutes. That's what you get when you gallivant off without any breakfast. I'll fetch you a sandwich and a cup of tea.'

'Thank you, Miss Sharp,' Mr Bradshaw said to her, and with the sound of the door shutting as Miss Sharp left the room, his eyes fell on me, 'where have you been all morning?'

'Walking,' I responded, swinging my legs round, my feet met the floor and I raised my body to a sitting position.

He picked up a teacup that was perched on top of the mantelpiece and gulped the last of his drink. He aimlessly examined the bottom of the cup, swirling the loose tea leaves around, 'and how is Stanley Rhodes?' I wondered if I detected a hint of jealousy in his voice, 'that was a nice surprise for you. What was his purpose here?'

'It was a surprise, I give you that.'

Mr Bradshaw sat down on the chair opposite me, staring into the distance, his foot resting on his knee and his fingertips pressed together. He listened to me as I briefly explained my morning with Stanley. It was difficult to know what he thought, his expression didn't alter and perhaps he was not jealous, just curious.

When I finished, he did not respond; his focus remained on the same spot he had been looking at the whole time. Miss Sharp returned and I sensed she felt uneasy with the silence. She quickly placed the sandwich and drink on a table next to me, whispered some words I barely heard, but guessed she said, 'tuck in, it'll do you good,' before quickly leaving the room and closing the door behind her.

'Betsy, I asked you a question earlier. Why are you here?'

I nodded.

'Let me elaborate. Where do you think your future lies? At home you have your family. You now have Stanley. You can't be a maid forever and I don't want you wasting the best part of your life trapped inside these walls. I have thought about this for a while and I can't see what reason you have to stay here, other than,' he paused, 'me?'

I gulped.

'I hope I am wrong, Betsy. I hope I am not the only reason because you really have no future here. Nothing will go beyond employer and employee; that's all it will ever be.'

His words did not come as a surprise, deep down I knew nothing would ever develop. He had said in the past he would never marry. Even if he wanted to, I knew it would be to Miss Jenkins, not me. After all, in society we were very different.

'I am sorry about that night at my uncle's, I should not have overstepped my position, that was very wrong of me.'

I shook my head and smiled weakly, as if to say no need to apologise.

'Just ask yourself why you are here? And where will you have a future? A happy future, that you deserve,' he rose out of his chair and stood over me, 'Betsy, I know what I would do.'

Mr Bradshaw was not there the following morning to say goodbye, he had left the house earlier than usual with the excuse he was meeting a client. I left what had been my home for three years, not sure if I would see Mr Bradshaw again.

Miss Sharp stood by the front door knowing she would be there for longer now I had gone and, personally, I think she was glad to be back on a more permanent basis. She held me close and said, 'all the best and please write, I would like to keep in touch.'

I promised and left for the short journey to the train station, uncertain if I was making the right choice, but knowing it was my only path with a future.

My hand rummaged around my bag for the ticket and when I removed the small paper, another piece that was attached to it, fluttered to the ground and landed by my feet. I crouched down to retrieve a folded-up piece of white paper. I hadn't noticed it the day before when Stanley handed me the ticket and I quickly tucked it away, knowing I didn't have much time.

The station was busy with a large number of people rushing around and I boarded the train just as the whistle blew to signal the time for departure.

When I was alone in my seat, I pulled out the paper. My finger traced along the top and I felt excited to open it, like a child looking inside her stocking on Christmas morning.

Slowly, I lifted the fold and the words written neatly and clearly read, 'I love you.' The words warmed my insides and I smiled at the simple note that meant so much.

When the train pulled into my station, I returned the note to a safe compartment in my bag for safe keeping. With my suitcase in my hand I stepped down onto the platform and, feeling a million butterflies fluttering in my stomach, I eagerly scanned the crowd searching for Stanley.

It was busy, many people were darting around and dodging others in their path. All the men wore similar hats and it was hard to identify Stanley. Finally, I spotted him, stood against the wall. He had not seen me, his eyes were frantically flitting around the crowd and a disappointed look was developing on his face.

I picked up speed, almost knocking into a few passengers that crossed over my path and when I was a few steps away, he caught sight of me.

My pace slowed down as I made the last couple of steps to him and my case dropped by his feet. Our eyes locked, neither of us knew what to do, we were both nervous and both stood in disbelief.

'I didn't think you would come,' he said.

He stepped forward, his hands slowly reached around my neck and the touch of his fingers brushing below my ears sent shivers down my arms and spine. He held my neck firmly, gently raising my head to meet his and the tip of his nose brushed against mine.

His lips met mine once and placed a gentle kiss. He didn't pull away, our mouths touched and in an apologetic whisper he said, 'I have nothing to offer you.'

'*You have everything to offer me,*' I thought and I tilted my head up to kiss him. Aware that we were in public, Stanley took a small step back and his hand lowered to grasp mine.

'Will you marry me?'

'Yes,' I beamed.

It had been three years since I had first known he would be the one I married and I felt so overjoyed that, at long last, I was completely happy. Stanley had only ever been the right one for me.

Part Six

Chapter Twenty-Four

Stanley and I were married in February 1935, and early in January 1936 we were blessed with our first daughter, Margaret, followed by Victoria, two years later in February 1938.

We were very happy with our small family and we lived cosily in a one-up, one-down house. Stanley continued to work for the railways and although many times he wished we lived differently, I didn't complain, I was grateful he still had work. For once, things were going right.

Of course, the minute you feel content with your life, something comes along to test your resolve and strength. This time, with the underlying threat of another war breaking out it affected everyone and our worst fear came true on Sunday 3rd September 1939.

We had been to church as usual, Stanley was sitting in the living area with the girls. Victoria was toddling around the room, her legs wide apart, feet stomping on the floor as she rocked from side to side, with her arms outstretched for balance; she had not quite worked out how to bend her knees. While Maggie was running in circles around her, showing her how it was done.

I was preparing dinner in the kitchenette and I could hear the wireless playing. It was quarter past eleven in the morning when the announcement was made. Stanley hushed the girls and he listened intently to the voice of Neville Chamberlain crackle through the speaker.

This country is at war with Germany.

Those words rattled through me, filling me with dread, horror and sorrow for what was about to come. We had been expecting it; since Friday the whole country was living in darkness when the new blackout regulations were imposed, but there was always a glimmer of hope that conflict would be resolved.

Stanley spent the rest of the day listening to the wireless and at 6 o'clock that evening, for the first time in our lives, we heard our King speak.

King George began, 'In this grave hour, perhaps the most fateful in our history, for the second time in the lives of most of us, we are at war.'

The realisation of it all hit me and I was petrified, and when I saw Stanley's face, I knew what he was thinking. I wrapped my arm around his shoulders and sat on his knee. He didn't say anything, but I knew what he was mentally preparing himself for; the inevitable, just like our fathers did before us, and I thought about Stanley's father who died at war. I understood why Stanley would sign up.

The day came when Stanley left to join the war. I tried to be brave and not cry because whatever happened, he was braver than me and most of the women were experiencing the same painful goodbyes.

It was a foggy morning when he kissed all three of us goodbye. We stood in the doorway and watched him walk down the street with his bag over his back. It was difficult to see him at the end of the road and I prayed the thick blanket of mist would not take him too early.

The children didn't fully understand, Maggie clung to my dress shouting, 'see you soon, Daddy,' and Victoria waved as she said, 'bye.' They both thought Daddy was going to work and he would be back in time for dinner.

I waved and swallowed hard, fighting to conceal my aching heart, wondering if that would be the last time I would ever see him and wanting to run after him for one last kiss goodbye. He reached the end of the road and glanced back, smiling as he waved. He did that for the girls; that would be their last memory of him for a while. On his final wave, before he disappeared out of sight, he didn't smile and took a few seconds to capture the last image of us. My heart snapped in two.

In the weeks after Stanley left, I discovered I was pregnant and the news came as a frightful shock. I feared I was bringing another child into a mad world; a child that may never know its father, a child that Stanley may never meet. But our son, Stanley James, was born on 18th July 1940.

The years that followed gave me a new-found strength. The population of men decreased in the town as they joined the war effort and women began to take over their roles. We became a strong community, working together and helping one another more than ever before. We lived through blackouts. No one dared walk the streets at night; you could barely see your nose in front of your face let alone anything else. Cars drove around in darkness without their lights to show the way and there were a few near accidents. Our protection from a bomb attack was a large cupboard in the living room, it was only big enough for the children to hide in comfortably and I would wait under the open stairs until the sirens signalled the all clear. The children were really scared being alone in that cupboard and I struggled to keep them calm from my own safe haven. It was during these attacks you really did fear for your life.

Food became rationed, several items at a time and we all worked together to grow our own. The field next to where Aunt Lily lived was turned into a huge allotment, which many helped maintain. The soil was perfect for growing and there was a good supply of vegetables, which still needed to be rationed, available for everyone. Our main diet was Oxo and bread, and the children often complained about it, but they preferred that to powdered eggs.

Many nights the girls climbed into my bed and I liked the comfort of feeling them close by. Little Stanley slept in his cot, oblivious to where his sisters were. They wanted to hear stories of their father and I glorified his adventures. I had no photo of Stanley, just my memories, and I often portrayed a detailed description of him, not wanting to forget what he looked like; he had been away for so long.

Every night I would light a candle and say a prayer for Stanley and the other men, praying that war would be over soon. I prayed that I would not receive that dreadful telegram the next day and be grateful in the evening when another day passed without that news, only to relive the worry the next day. I often heard the names of people from our town who lost their lives. Roger was amongst them and the dreadful news of his death reached Aunt Lily in July 1942, just a couple of days before Alfred's eighth birthday.

Alfred had been living with Aunt Lily since 1940, after his grandma passed away. His grandfather could not cope with raising a child and with Roger away at war there was no one left to look after Alfred. She was overjoyed and welcomed the child with open arms, taking him in at an age not much younger than I had been when I first went to live with Aunt Lily. Alfred had been through more than his fair share of loss, but he was a resilient boy. He was strong and brave, embracing each day through his pain and I saw so much of his mother in him. I wished I was as strong as Alfred.

In September 1944 I received an urgent letter. My initial reaction was one of fear that it was news regarding Stanley and I delayed breaking the seal. Then I realised it was not a telegram, but a handwritten note that was posted through my door.

To Dear Mrs Rhodes

I am writing to inform you of my nephew's poor state of health. He resides at my home and requests the immediate presence of your company.

Yours sincerely,

Dr E Oxley

I made plans to visit him the following day. It felt like a lifetime ago since I last walked down the road to Dr Oxley's house and yet it was so familiar. The surreality of it all was quite overwhelming as I hesitated before knocking on the door. I remembered it all too well.

I took a deep breath and rapped the knocker twice. The sound echoed within the house. Mrs Tolley pulled open the door and it took a moment for it to register that it was me. It had been ten years since I saw her last and I was just as surprised to see she was still working there as she was surprised to see me.

After we passed our greetings I said, 'Dr Oxley sent for me.'

'You have come to see Mr Bradshaw?' She bowed her head, where she would have once smiled to tease me with the mention of his name; now, she looked concerned.

Mrs Tolley ushered me inside and directed me to the living room where Dr Oxley sat still looking the same. In all the years I have known him, the man I saw in front of me still looked just the same as the man I saw as a child; he had not seemed to age at all.

'Mrs Rhodes,' his voice weaker and croakier than it used to be, 'do come in.'

'How are you, Dr Oxley?' I asked, taking the seat he signalled me to sit down on.

'I am well and thank you for coming at short notice.'

'How is he?'

'You will see for yourself. There's nothing left for me to do for him now, other than to keep him comfortable.'

Dr Oxley detected my vacant expression and realised I had no idea what he was talking about.

'When he was a child he caught pneumonia, he was very weak and very close to dying. His mother, my late sister, did everything she could to save him. Of course he recovered, but over the years it has left him vulnerable to chest infections. Now, his body is too weak, he can't fight back anymore. I have tried, believe me, I have tried, but he's not responding to the medicine this time.'

'Does he have another chest infection, will it not pass?'

'No, pneumonia. I pray for a miracle.'

I took the familiar stairs to Mr Bradshaw's room. My hand trailing the soft wooden handrail that felt so smooth as my palm glided across it.

The door to Mr Bradshaw's room was shut, emphasising the divide that now existed between us. I knocked gently before entering the room that held many memories of when I first nursed Mr Bradshaw and when he returned the favour by taking care of me some years later. The same thick curtains draped the window, the floral-patterned wallpaper and the scenic pictures that hung from the picture rail.

I expected to see Mr Bradshaw unaltered and exactly how he was in my memories. I wanted to see him stood by the fireplace or sat in the chair engrossed in a book, with a glass of brandy in his hand. I wanted him to be smartly dressed, clean shaven and looking a picture of health. The man I saw bore no resemblance to the Mr Bradshaw I remembered.

I moved closer to him. He was resting his eyes, his chest moved up and down slowly. His body had become weak and frail, his arms that were uncovered looked thin and his fingers like tiny twigs at the end of his hands. His face shocked me the most. The youthful plumpness it once possessed now gone, his skin now so thin it barely covered his bones making him look like the skeleton Dr Oxley had in his surgery.

There was a chair next to the bed and I sat down waiting for him to wake up. I took his weak hand and held it lightly as an overwhelming cloud of sadness swept over me; I pitied this man.

'Betsy?' his eyes opened and he found the energy to slowly turn his face. I looked into those eyes, the only thing that I recognised of the man I once admired.

'I'm here.'

'I wanted to see you again,' he spoke with great difficulty.

I made a hush sound and stroked his face. There was no need for him to talk, I was with him and that was all that mattered.

'Miss Jenkins was right; those who stay alone, die alone.'

'No, Mr Bradshaw, don't talk like that.'

'Still the same, Betsy,' his mouth twitched a smile, 'are you happy?'

'Yes, I am,' I said, but I felt more grateful, than happy. Grateful for my children, for their health and for mine. Grateful that we have a home and that we are safe. Grateful that somewhere in the world, Stanley was still alive. I would be truly happy again when the war was over.

'Tell me about your children,' he spoke slowly, 'about your life.'

He closed his eyes and listened. It was strange at first as I spoke about my children and Alfred, then after a while I found myself lost in my subconscious and trailed off at a tangent. I spoke about everything and everyone that had touched my life good or bad. One memory triggered another and sparked a different thought. I was relaxed with my open discussion, mainly because I thought he was asleep and I found satisfaction in complaining about Miss Jenkins.

I eventually paused, my throat was dry from my talking and my palm was sweaty from clutching on to Mr Bradshaw's limp hand. I sat with him all morning, waiting and watching as he drifted in and out of sleep.

He had been sleeping for a long time and I was certain he had fallen into a deeper sleep. I slipped my hand from underneath his and crept to the door.

'Did you find my note?' he asked, before I opened the door.

'Your note?' I questioned. I turned around to face him and from the slits of his eye lids, I could make out the striking sky blue of his iris peering at me.

'I wondered if,' he paused, 'you saw it.'

My eyes flickered around the floor, trying to recall a note and as much as I rattled my brain, the only note I remembered was the one I found from Stanley saying 'I love you.'

My eyes shot up at Mr Bradshaw, and he said, 'the words I couldn't bring myself to say out loud.'

I stood dumbfounded. All these years I believed Stanley had written me the note and I kept it treasured in a drawer at home. The small token that I had treasured for all those years were the written words of Mr Bradshaw.

'What about Miss Jenkins?' I asked in disbelief, 'I thought you loved her.'

'Maybe once, a long time ago,' he coughed out a short laugh and it took a few seconds before he could speak again, 'I was trapped.'

'Trapped, how? You told me I had no future with you.' My legs beginning to feel like jelly, I took the seat again next to his bed.

He began to cough, his eyelids pressed tightly shut and he grimaced in discomfort. I felt his pain; the same illness that took my father; only it took my father very quickly. I felt so sorry for him, wishing there was something more I could do. I patiently waited until he could speak again, 'we were too different, she would have made things difficult?'

'Who, Miss Jenkins?'

'Her father was my main client, he owned everything.'

'Mr Bradshaw, when you said you would never marry, what you meant was, you could never marry?'

Mr Bradshaw laughed, which only aggravated his chest and it ended in a splutter, 'after all these years and you still call me Mr Bradshaw.'

'Do you have regrets?'

'Stanley is a good man, Betsy, you made the right choice.'

I tried to conceal my tears, but the more I fought them the more I began to weep. I took a few deep breaths and my crying gradually eased. I removed a handkerchief that was tucked up the sleeve of my cardigan and dried my cheeks.

'I still mean it, Betsy, I love you.'

I leant over his bedside, planted a painful farewell kiss on his lips and whispered, 'I love you too.'

'*I always have.*'

'Until next time,' was the last thing he said to me before I left the room. I knew there wasn't going to be a next time.

Chapter Twenty-Five

His funeral took place back at Mr Bradshaw's home church, Dr Oxley travelled there, with his body, by special arrangements. It was too far for me to travel, but on that day I managed to have an hour alone to walk through the local park, to mourn and reflect in my own way.

As I followed the paths, scattered with fallen crisp leaves of deep red, brown, yellow and orange, crunching and rustling beneath my feet, a misty sun broke through the trees and lit the way ahead. It had been an icy morning, patches of white glistened on the ground, until the rising sun melted it away.

The day was pleasant and fresh, and the cool air filled my lungs, helping to rejuvenate my thoughts.

'He was no longer in pain,' I told myself.

Completely distracted with my memories, I didn't notice Beatrice walking in the opposite direction. I was aware of someone pushing a wheelchair towards me, and I politely stepped aside to allow them to pass.

She stopped in front of me and there was a moment of awkwardness, when neither of us knew what to say to the other. We had succeeded in avoiding each other's paths for so long and even though our children went to the same school, we had not seen each other. I felt uneasy in her presence, after all I was married to the man she was supposed to marry. I was so distracted that at first I didn't acknowledge the man in the wheelchair.

I smiled awkwardly at Beatrice and then her company. To my horror, I realised it was Mark; he was almost completely unrecognisable. I scanned his whole body to fully register the state of his health. He was very different to the young, strong and cocksure man I had last seen. Both of his legs had been amputated and his left arm and the left side of his face scarred with burns. Even though he wore a hat, I could see a large area of his scalp visible around his ear where part of his hair had been scorched away.

I failed to find the right words to say.

Mark tilted his head to look at me from his right, through his good eye and uninjured side of his face, 'Beatrice, would you give me a moment with Betsy?'

Beatrice threw her brother an annoyed glare, 'I'll go over there,' she said and wandered over to a bench in the distance.

'Would you mind?' Mark flicked his head back, signalling me to the push his wheelchair back in the direction I had walked from, and away from Beatrice.

'Not at all, Mark,' I replied.

'It's nice to feel the air on my face,' he raised his chin to welcome the breeze.

We moved for a minute or two in silence, with just the sound of the thin wheels of his chair pushing through the gravel.

Mark raised his hand for me to halt and his eyes searched the ground, 'can you see those conkers over there?' he asked pointing to a cluster of several on the floor, 'can you pass me the biggest two?'

I crouched down and gathered a selection of conkers. The shiny mahogany nuts shone in the sun, like precious gems or recently polished wood. Cupped in my hands I presented the collection to Mark and he selected the two he wanted, the rest I slipped into my pocket for my children.

'They're for my nephew,' he explained. 'He's been bringing conkers home all week, and I love to play with him.'

I tried to picture Mark as a playful uncle, being so caring and considerate. In his tone, I sensed he cared very much for his nephew, Peter, a boy born a few months after Alfred, and it dawned on me. *'Peter and Alfred are cousins.'*

Mark tucked the conkers inside his jacket and let out a grunting sound. The position he twisted himself into had caused discomfort and he grimaced in pain.

'I am sorry, Mark. Are you hurting?' I asked.

His expression softened, 'not so much now. This is nothing compared to what it felt like in the beginning, I would have welcomed death. I still do at times.' His voice trailed off, into a murmur, as he recalled a recent memory, 'I relive that day, so many times. I'll be safe at home and in the blink of an eye I'm lying in a field. There are explosions everywhere. Men, my men, are running, some are crawling, some are screaming in agony and body parts are scattered all over the place. There's this smell, I can still smell it, that sort of smell won't ever leave you, you know? The smell of burning flesh; it was my flesh.'

My face screwed up in disgust. The image he created was so vivid in my mind, I could picture the men running for their lives, some making it, but many falling and only a few surviving.

'I have never been so frightened before in all my life,' then realising, Mark said, 'my apologies, Betsy, a too detailed account for you?'

I began to push the chair again.

'You looked sad before, no news about Stanley?' Mark said.

'Oh no, not Stanley, someone I knew very well passed away recently, and today is the funeral.'

'I see. In battle?'

'No, natural causes. Like there's not enough death with this war.' As soon as I said it, I instantly regretted my tactless choice of words, 'sorry Mark, that was thoughtless of me.'

'Not at all, I agree. I must look a frightful sight.'

'No,' I said softly, 'not a frightful sight.'

'Who's going to want me now? My life is ruined. I thought I had all the time in the world. I enjoyed life, enjoyed women and now look at me.'

'Mark, you still have all the time in the world and you are very lucky to be here. You have your nephews.'

Nephews slipped from my mouth accidentally, but he didn't notice my use of the plural.

'Lucky!' he scorned my words, 'what about the men that died, who had a wife and children at home? I have so much guilt, Betsy; why do I deserve to live when so many men, with so much more waiting for them at home, have to die? What if Donald doesn't return home to my sister and nephew? What if Stanley doesn't?'

Hearing Stanley's name stabbed my heart. In a moment of fear, I pictured him being amongst the men on the field, suffering, close to dying and being so far from home and never to see it again. My feet rooted to the ground, the energy to push Mark any farther was drained from me and my hand firmly gripped the handles.

'I am sorry, Betsy, that was insensitive of me.'

It took me a moment to shake away my vision, before I could speak again. 'Mark, it's only natural you feel the way you do. I know this does not compare to what you have seen, but when May died, I would have done anything to trade places with her, so she could live to see her son grow up. At the time, I had no one who needed me. The difference is, you do have people who need you. Think about the conkers in your pocket and who they are for?'

He contemplated what I said and I hoped found some form of comfort in my words. Whatever he was thinking he didn't say and changed the subject to the one he wanted to talk to me about, the reason we were on this stroll. 'When we were children, I hated you, all of you, but I think you were the smallest and easiest to torment. You were so weak looking and easy to make cry. I liked making you cry.'

'Mark, I'm not sure if I want to discuss this now.'

'Please, let me finish, I have to. You see, I wanted you all to suffer, like me. Did you know I saw them?'

'Saw who?' I was still thinking about his earlier words about hate; such a strong word.

'My father and your mother,' he sounded disgusted. 'He had been acting differently, so had my mother, and I knew something was wrong. I followed him one day and saw him go into your house. They didn't hear me come in, the door was unlocked and I saw everything. I was nine, Betsy.'

'That's awful for a child to see,' I was sympathetic, realising how disturbing that must have been for a child, no wonder he was filled with so much hate and resentment.

'It was your family that was the enemy that was destroying my family. Do you know that day when we found you and Stanley in the fields?'

'Yes!' My teeth were clenched to together. *'How could I forget that day?'*

'I did it for my mum,' he continued, 'I thought she would be proud that I was teaching you all a lesson, and to know that I was on her side. She didn't see it like that. Your uncle came round and I will spare you the details about what happened, but afterwards my dad gave me such a beating. He held me by the neck and said, *you never, ever, lay a finger on them Colborne girls again.*

'I didn't understand why he was bothered about you two, not until much later, but it was the look my mum gave me that upset me. It was full of disappointment and disgust. She turned her back on me and didn't speak to me for days. That hurt the most, and do you know what she said to me? She said, *Mark, if that's how you treat women, then I have been a terrible mother.* It made me think differently. Yet you weren't the enemy, it was your mother I wanted to attack...'

'I know...' I said softly. If anything, it might give him closure to know I bore no grudges.

'I know about May,' I felt broken when he said her name. 'It all made sense.'

I walked around the front of the wheelchair and crouched down in front of him. I cupped his hands, they were hot and clammy, but I could see he was aching inside. I could see he had changed, I felt that reassurance from deep within. I felt a connection, we shared May, she was both of ours' sister.

'I always knew there was something different about her,' he looked down at my hand. 'Did you know my father left ten years ago and we've not seen him since?'

I nodded, recalling a conversation with Stanley.

'I wasn't there when it happened, but apparently he spent a great deal of money; so much was unaccountable for.'

I wondered if some of that money was used to help my mother and their son, but I was not going to say that to Mark.

Mark continued, 'he grew nasty and was horrible to my mother. Not long after May died, he became so bitter and left. My mum was not surprised by it at all, luckily she had Beatrice and Donald, and now she is the happiest I have ever seen her.'

'It must still have been a difficult time for your family, Mark.'

'Do you think he has gone to your mother?'

I shrugged, as I didn't know, but I thought of my mother's last words of hope that one day they would be together again. Perhaps after all this time, she finally had her wish.

'Things must have been difficult for you too, Betsy; you lost a sister.'

'We both lost a sister,' I said and that was the first time I admitted out loud that May was an Irving.

'And I have another nephew?' Mark's voice was soft.

'Yes, Alfred, he is the sweetest boy who has seen too much.'

'Does he know about us?'

'No, no one knows, I've not told anyone. Sometimes the past is best left in the past, less people get hurt then.'

He nodded and I knew he understood my reasons, 'perhaps I will see him one day playing with Peter.'

'What will you do now, Mark?' It was my turn to change the subject and to sound positive, to give him hope. 'Your nephew needs an uncle and you could always restart your father's business?'

He laughed at my suggestion, 'what use will I be in this thing?'

'You're an Irving! Besides, your arms still work don't they?' and I dropped a hint, 'maybe one day, soon enough, your ideal partner will come home; fully trained to your father's standards – after all there's not a cobblers in town that mends and makes shoes quite like an Irving.'

Mark tilted his head and he looked at me thoughtfully, as my words digested. A smirk appeared across his face, followed by a slow considered nod.

Chapter Twenty-Six

In December 1944, despite the lack of money and rations, we managed to create a wonderful Christmas day for the children. The weather was frightfully bitter and the snow fell heavy with a risk of being snowed in. The children and I spent Christmas Eve night at Aunt Lily's just in case the predictions were accurate.

We sat around the fire while we waited for Matthew to return home from work; Aunt Lily and I drank a small glass of sherry, and the children enjoyed hot chocolate. They were so full of excitement, with high pitched voices, laughter and speaking too quickly to comprehend what they were saying. Their bottoms barely stayed still as they wriggled and bounced around, flapping their arms like little birds. Aunt Lily and I watched the four children in absolute delight.

It was difficult not to think about the people that were missing from our gathering, but I could see they still lived on in the children. In Alfred, I could see May's smile and the shape of his eyes matched hers. He shared her caring and gentle nature and, as a result, he was a positive leading force in charge of the others. My three looked up to him and I was as proud of my nephew as if he was my own. I knew his parents would have been too.

My three filled me with so much pride. The girls had changed so much since their father last saw them, and he hadn't even seen Little Stanley. He had been gone for five years, Maggie was eight now and Victoria six. Maggie looked more like her father than the other two; she was the female version of Stanley, but her eyes were dark like mine.

Victoria was only a toddler when Stanley left, a similar age to me when my father left for war all those years ago, and like me, her memories of him were vague, like a distorted shadow she could no longer see his face clearly. I promised her, one day she would see his face again.

She was more confident than Maggie, her head was full of strong ideas and at times she was very opinionated. Nothing bothered her and I admired her bravery, she was the complete opposite to me. She had Stanley's green eyes and every time I looked at them, I could see him looking back at me. It brought me comfort seeing him in our children, but it also brought me pain as I was reminded of what I missed.

Little Stanley was mine; he had my dark eyes, my thick mass of hair and likewise his similarities resembled his grandfather. But, on occasion, I would be taken off guard as sometimes I would see Stanley in some of his facial expressions and mannerisms.

From the minute I arrived at Aunt Lily's there was something that felt special about that Christmas. My insides filled with a warm sensation of hope and wonderful things to come. There was nothing notably different about the day, I just knew it would be a Christmas I would treasure forever.

Like every year, I had been saving since January to cover the cost of Christmas, slowly building a pile of copper in a glass jar on the top shelf of my pantry. Unfortunately, due to the hard circumstances, many times I needed to dip into the jar and begrudgingly watched the small pile dwindle away.

However, between Aunt Lily and I, there was enough to provide for a family Christmas and we each took a role towards the Christmas meal. I had made the pudding earlier in December following a recipe I found in a magazine that used ingredients that were available during rationing. It could not match my mother's recipe.

I baked bread in the morning, but due to rations it would be served without butter. The fields that year had produced a good supply of potatoes, carrots, onions, rhubarb and beans.

Aunt Lily was determined she would serve creamy, mashed potato with the Christmas dinner and the butter was saved for this purpose.

Aunt Lily surprised us all with a goose she had bought from a farm that Matthew was to collect on his way home. It had been so long since we had eaten meat, I had forgotten the taste.

The children were making paper chains to hang on the wall when Matthew appeared in the doorway carrying a goose by its legs, its poor head swinging. In his other hand he carried a cedar tree branch. He wore a huge smile on his face, his cheeks and nose red from the cold. There was a covering of snow on his shoulders and cap that fluttered off onto the floor as he came across the room. We all squealed in delight at the sight of him.

He greeted us with 'a Happy Christmas all.'

'Happy Christmas,' we called back in chorus.

Aunt Lily stayed in the kitchen plucking, beheading and gutting the goose, while we remained in the living room. The branch was for the children to decorate as a Christmas tree, twirling their paper chains and carefully cutting out snowflakes, stars and fairies to rest on top of the branches, and by the time they had finished, all the green was covered.

One decoration stood out differently from the rest.

'What have you made there, little man?' I asked, peering over Stanley's tiny shoulders as he studied a blue paper cut out of a man no bigger than his hand. He held it so delicately and looked at it with wonderment.

'It's Daddy,' he whispered, 'so he doesn't miss Christmas.'

I choked; his gesture was so heart wrenching and I was speechless. His words silenced the room, until his siblings and cousin came over to praise his craftsmanship.

'Oh Stanley, that is Daddy, I remember,' Maggie said.

'Stanley,' Alfred gently took hold of Stanley's hand and admiring his jagged cut out. 'Where do you want him to go so he can see us on Christmas morning?'

'At the top.'

No one minded when Maggie's fairy was removed from the top of the tree and the paper figure of Stanley was put in its place. A tear dribbled down my cheek and I quickly brushed it away before anyone noticed.

After a supper of bread and milk, the children sang Christmas carols to us and a chorus of joyful spirit-lifting tunes filled the room; we cheered after each one. We joined in with the singing when we were asked to, but most of the time we listened; their voices were like angels in the room. When it came to bedtime, it took the children longer than usual to fall asleep. They were squashed into what was once mine and May's old bedroom, but it now belonged to Alfred. Maggie and Victoria slept head to tail in one bed, Alfred and Little Stanley slept on the floor on a bed made up of blankets and spare cushions.

Matthew kept them entertained; I could hear the booming of his voice from downstairs. Eventually they fell asleep, but Little Stanley was the last to drift off.

Matthew sat in his chair listening to the wireless with a glass of sherry by his side and drifted in and out of sleep. Aunt Lily and I focused on the children's stockings; four old socks waiting to be filled with presents from Father Christmas. Each stocking was to be filled with a shilling, a satsuma, which Matthew had kept aside before they were all bought, and a bag of nuts. We had warned the children in the previous weeks that even Father Christmas had to ration. Whilst I filled the stockings, Aunt Lily brought out a box and placed it down beside me.

'I thought these might be useful,' she said as she started to remove the contents. I watched with curiosity as each item was placed on the table in front of me and the memories of Christmas 1919 came flooding back. Laid out before me was the soldier, train and teddy that Aunt Lily had given to Bert, Frank and me, all those Christmases ago.

I stared at the items in amazement, each looking just how I remembered it; untouched, undamaged and still as bright in colour as they were when we first received them. I hadn't expected to see them again, I always thought they had disappeared with Mother or had been left discarded at our old home.

'I couldn't bear to part with them,' Aunt Lily said.

'They are perfect, Aunt Lily,' I replied awe-struck, 'thank you.'

'There's something else.' Aunt Lily's hand slipped back inside the box and when it resurfaced, her fingers were wrapped around the body of a hand knitted doll. My hand covered my mouth and I gasped. I looked at the button eyes, brown woollen weaved plaits in her hair, and the knitted red dress and boots she wore.

'Dotty,' I whispered, carefully taking the doll from her. I stroked her hair; she was smaller than I remembered. The last time I saw her, I had thrown her onto the floor with the stocking, vowing never to play with her again. Yet many years had passed and many new memories had been made, so that holding her now brought me comfort and not the heartache I had anticipated.

'Aunt Lily, it's been so long since I saw these.'

'We always thought it was kinder to you both if we kept Bert and Frank's toys out of sight and I remember how much you loved this doll. Perhaps it would be nice for the children to have them now?'

'Yes, I think it would.' I knew exactly which toy belonged to which child as I squeezed them into the stockings, knowing they would be delighted with their findings in the morning.

That night, I camped downstairs, curled up on the settee. It was not ideal, but I was that tired I didn't notice and soon drifted into a deep sleep. It only felt like minutes had passed when I woke up suddenly to the house shaking as a herd of elephants stomped down the stairs cheering with delight.

'It's Christmas!' the children cried out in chorus, 'he's been!'

My eyes flickered a few times, the room was dark and freezing, and my face poking out of the blanket felt cold. I could hear them surrounding me, their shadows circling and I yawned, and thought, *the children are awake.*' Within minutes I heard Matthew creep down the stairs and Aunt Lily followed behind.

Matthew lit the fire and the room came to life with the dancing orange flames brightening the room. We embraced each other with 'Happy Christmas,' and kissed. The children were untouched by the cold, while we adults rubbed our hands together blowing on them with cold breath that came out in misty clouds.

The clock pointed to six o'clock and Matthew twitched the net curtains to see how deep the snow had fallen through the night, but he was faced with darkness and the windows were too icy on the inside, as well as on the outside, to see beyond the glistening white spiral pattern.

We huddled close to the fire, the heat slowly warming the room and the children, filled with happiness, began to remove their presents from their stockings. My attention moved across all four of them, not wanting to miss any of their faces as they retrieved each of their gifts. Their eyes wide, smiles shining brightly, I saw an overjoyed Alfred with the wooden solider; a delightful cheer from Maggie as she cradled the teddy in her arms; a high pitched squeal from Victoria to discover Dotty and happy shunting sounds from Stanley as he immediately pushed the train across the floor.

Maggie's expression changed and she looked deeply at the teddy, fascinated by the rotating arms and legs, circling them a full 360 degrees. Her eyes dropped as her delicate hand stroked the soft fur, her hand running across the head, ears and back.

I crouched down beside her and said softly, 'do you like him?'

'Yes, Mummy,' her reply was earnest, 'he's so soft.'

'Have you named him?'

'I don't know what to call him, that's the problem.'

I looked to Aunt Lily and Matthew for ideas, and they suggested a few. The other children were keen to call out many names but at each suggestion Maggie's face screwed up in disapproval and she shook her head.

'What about George, after our king?' said Alfred, 'or Winston?'

'Winston,' Maggie smiled brightly, her face lit up and she cried out, 'he's Winston.'

'I like Winston,' Victoria said, sitting by her sister's side and looking at the bear before she thrust her doll under his nose, 'look Maggie, a doll. I wanted a doll.'

'She is lovely.' Maggie showed an interest in the blurry doll frantically waving inches away from her eyes, I doubt she could see her clearly.

'Mummy, look,' Victoria said, waving the doll under my nose.

'You are a lucky girl, what are you going to call her?'

Victoria thought for a while and after careful consideration said, 'Ivy, because it's Christmas.'

'Oh, what a lovely name,' I told her and pleased with her decision she went around introducing Ivy to the rest of the family.

Stanley was very quiet, crawling along the floor and pushing the train along. He didn't contribute to the naming suggestions for Maggie; he was content in his own world. He knew his father worked on the trains and I was certain he was thinking about him while he played.

'You know what, Stanley,' I said, 'that train is very special, I know a special boy who once had a train just like that.'

'Was it Daddy?'

'No, not Daddy, he was a special boy called Frank,' and I sensed Alfred stop to listen, 'and I also remember a very special boy who owned a solider like yours too, Alfred. He was called Bert and they were two very, very nice boys; good boys.'

'Your brothers?' Alfred asked, familiar with the names.

I nodded and patted Alfred on the back for his great thinking, 'look after them.'

I had hoped the solider would be special to Alfred, a memory of his father; a brave soldier who fought for his country.

We went to church mid-morning and met most of what was left of the town folk. The snow had fallen thickly during the night and snowballs were being thrown in fun as we walked. The children continued to play in the snow when we returned home, building snowmen and making snow angels.

'When I was a child, we would have the freedom of the fields and build snowmen, and I would make snow angels in the pristine snow,' I said to the children, as I stepped out on the street to join them and nudging my head in the direction of the fields, glistening white in the daylight.

'Can we play in there?' Victoria asked.

'Please,' the children cried out in chorus.

'No, they serve an important purpose at the moment,' I reminded them, 'we can't go treading all over the crops, can we? Anyway, it looks as though you have done a brilliant job right here with this snow.'

I admired the unfinished snowman that stood proudly outside the house. As I circled their creation, a snowball landed on the back of my head, followed by huge roar of laughter from Alfred, his head leaning back and his hand clutching his stomach as though preventing it from splitting open, 'Sorry, Aunt Betsy.'

'I'll show you sorry,' I laughed, scooping up a small ball and patting it firmly into shape before throwing it back to him.

Alfred laughed as he managed to dodge my white missile and it triggered off a snow war, unfortunately, I was a team of one and the children targeted me. After a few minutes, I surrendered with powdered snow splattered all over my coat and in my hair, while they remained almost untouched.

'Let's finish our snowman,' Maggie suggested, 'Mum, can you help?'

'I certainly can.'

They had rolled two balls and wanted me to help lift the head on top. With careful hands, and the help of Maggie and Alfred we slowly raised the smaller ball into place.

'Who wants to go around the back and get some coal?' I asked.

'I'll go,' Victoria ran up the steps to the front door.

'No, Victoria,' I said, 'side gate please, Aunt Lily won't appreciate snow walked in through the house.'

'Sorry, Mummy.'

She returned minutes later with pile of coal in her hands. Each child took one piece and found a spot on the snowman. He was given two wonky eyes and several buttons were placed that made an almost military coat style, as Alfred insisted his coat would be double breasted.

I held a piece in my hand and took a moment to appreciate

it, feeling the roughness of the rock, the light weight and the dark stain that it left in my hand. I closed my eyes and inhaled deeply; the smell of coal would always take me back to a childhood memory that would never fade.

'Mummy, what are you doing?' Victoria asked.

I opened my eyes and looked at the four children staring at me bemused and puzzled.

'Just thinking about your grandfather,' I smiled and stroked Alfred's face, 'he was called Alfred too. He delivered coal for a living and the smell reminded me of him. The smell of coal before it was placed on the fire.'

I held it in the air to show the unlit coal and I passed it to Alfred to smell. He mimicked my actions, examining and exploring the coal, from touch to smell and passed it along to Maggie to follow suit.

'Coal before it is lit,' I continued, 'he carried bags of these on a horse and cart through town delivering sacks to all the homes. He would come home smelling of coal, his face, hands and clothes covered in the black dirt. He believed in the many good properties of coal.'

'Don't forget he brushed his teeth with it,' an unknown male voice spoke from behind me.

I turned around to greet the stranger. He was stood a few feet away, keeping a distance between us. His face was friendly, wearing an uncertain smile and looking not much older than me. I heard the children behind whisper amongst themselves, asking one another, 'who is it?'

My whole body stiffened, I was frozen to the spot, not sure if who I was seeing was real or a figment of my imagination. There was something extraordinarily familiar about him, other than his broad shoulders, the strands of thick dark hair that curled from underneath his hat and dark eyes that I recognised. Yet it could not possibly be who I thought it was.

I was trembling, my bottom lip quivered and my knees gave way, as my body dropped to the ground. Thankfully I was cushioned by the snow as I landed on my knees. I stared at him in disbelief and awe.

'*So many years have passed.*'

'Mummy,' I heard my children cry out.

'Aunt Lily, Uncle Matthew!' Alfred's voice called, his feet crunching across the snow, running towards the house.

'Betsy, it's me,' he said in an accent I did not recognise.

At first glance, with all that was familiar about him he could have been my father. He had his eyes but his face was different and I could see a glimpse of the boy he used to be.

He was apprehensive to take a step towards me, anticipating that his arrival would come as a shock. He remained still, giving me chance to believe he was really there.

I asked in a shaky voice, 'Frank?'

'Yes, it's me, Betsy.'

He shuffled forward and slowly crouched down beside me and I reached out to touch his face, to feel he was real. I felt the outline of his jaw in my touch. It truly was my brother. My big brother had finally come home after nearly twenty-five years.

I didn't notice the wetness from the snow had drenched through my skirt, until he pulled me to my feet, and I felt the numb, coldness in my knees. 'You are real,' I cried and flung my arms around his neck. I was not letting go and I squeezed him tightly, saying again, 'you're here; you are really here.'

'Yes, Betsy, I'm here.'

The children stood around bemused that their mother welcomed a stranger with such love. Alfred stood in the doorway, unsure whether to come out or wait for Aunt Lily.

'Are these yours?' Frank asked, admiring my three children stood like statues behind me.

'Yes,' I said, wrapping my arms around my three and presenting them to their uncle. 'This is your Uncle Frank.'

The children's eyes widened and they looked at each other with amazement.

'I have your train,' Stanley was eager to say.

'My train?' Frank looked at me confused.

Stanley continued to explain the train in great detail and succeeded in reminding Frank of his childhood toy.

'Do you still have it?' Frank sounded almost as excited as Stanley.

'Father Christmas found it and gave it me. He rations too, you know,' Stanley explained.

Alfred slowly moved to my side, his head was to my shoulder and he looked up at Frank. He was anxious about meeting his uncle and I sensed his nervousness.

'Another nephew?' Frank asked me, he strained a smile, but I could see the reunion was overwhelming for him.

'Yes, my nephew, Alfred. He's May's only boy,' my voice broke as I said her name.

'Pleased to meet you, sir,' Alfred politely said, offering his hand.

Frank took his nephew's hand and shook it, then turned to me with a concerned gaze. He had sensed my sorrow, 'and May?'

I swallowed hard before answering, 'May passed away during childbirth,' protectively I wrapped my arm around Alfred and kissed the top of his head.

Frank didn't respond. He looked at the ground and I thought he said to himself, 'I'm too late.'

Hearing of his sister's death for the first time, ten years after it had happened, he took a few deep breaths and carefully processed the news. The family he had hoped to come home to, had one vital member missing; it was not the family reunion he had imagined for so many years.

Matthew ran outside and I held up my hand to him, as I heard his feet pounding towards me. From the expression on his face, he was expecting to fight away some intruder, but this slowly dissolved when his eyes fell on Frank and he came to a halt.

Following behind and peering over his shoulder was Aunt Lily. She clung to Matthew's arms and looked on.

She didn't blink and she slowly left the guard of her husband to advance towards Frank. Like me, she went pale, thinking she was looking into the eyes of the dead, and both hands rose to cover her mouth and nose. I thought she was going to scream at first, but then she reached out to touch his face.

'Frank?' she said his name first to be certain, before she threw her arms around him. Afterwards she cupped his face and looked at him intensely. 'Frank, you look just like your father, oh, for a minute you could have been dear Alfred.'

'Happy Christmas, Aunt Lily,' he kissed her on the cheek.

Matthew approached, placing an arm around Aunt Lily's shoulder and shook Frank's hand with the other, 'welcome home chap.'

'What a wonderful Christmas present,' Aunt Lily said, 'we've not had our dinner yet, you're just in time. You are staying, aren't you?'

'As long as you have enough.'

'Of course I do. Let's get inside out of the cold and I'll make you a cup of tea.'

'I think he wants something stronger than tea, Lily,' Matthew said. 'I have some whisky I have been saving for a special occasion.'

'Tea is fine,' Frank smiled, 'maybe later, Matthew.'

Aunt Lily led the way and we entered the house. Frank looked about the living room and I could see his eyes exploring the room he had not seen since our childhood. He smirked to himself as he glanced at the settee; not a happy smile, but a smile to suggest he was thinking of that Boxing Day memory, when there were four of us. Frank took the seat in front of the fire and I sat down beside him; now we were grown we left only enough room for a child. The children were fascinated by their uncle, they didn't say a word, but sat by his feet and gazed up at him.

'How on Earth did you remember where we lived?' Matthew asked, 'you must have been eight when you were last here.'

'How long are you here for? You can stay here for as long as you like,' Aunt Lily spoke over Matthew.

'Thank you, Aunty, only if there's enough room for me tonight. I have to be back tomorrow.'

'No question about it, this is your home,' at the mention of the word home, I heard Frank inhale deeply and held his breath. Aunt Lily continued, 'back, where?'

'The army. I have to be back tomorrow evening; I am being picked up in the town centre by one of the guys.' Frank spoke to Matthew, 'you wanted to know how I remembered your house. I vaguely remembered the direction here from the centre of town,' then he looked at me and smiled, 'I remembered what Betsy used to say about the house being at the very edge of town, on the last street and the very last house.'

I was deeply moved. After all these years he remembered and I murmured, 'still is.'

'It was only in October that I was stationed so close to here,' Frank continued, 'I didn't think I would remember, but the memories came flooding back and I knew where I was. One of the guys offered to drive me here for Christmas.'

Aunt Lily wandered through into the kitchen and soon returned with a tray of hot drinks, that she placed on the coffee table. She took one and held the saucer in her hand, while she perched on the arm of the chair next to Matthew, a smile of happiness and disbelief spread across her face.

'Are you based with the Canadian camp ten miles west of here?'

'Yes, I am, but –' Frank looked at Matthew quizzically and sounding as though he was taken back by the comment said, 'how would you know I am in the Canadian army?'

The question threw Matthew and wide eyed, he looked at Aunt Lily, wondering if he had said something wrong. In a splutter, Matthew replied, 'I just assumed when you were sent to Canada.'

'How do you know that I was sent to Canada?'

The room fell deadly quiet, even the children failed to make a noise and the only sound came from Aunt Lily when she lowered her cup down on the coffee table. She eventually said, 'Frank, your mother told me she had sent you there.'

Frank glanced down at his hands, his whole body had become tense and he began to slowly, but forcefully, rub his fingers together in circular motions. Suddenly, the mood seemed to have shifted, I rose to my feet and quickly sent the children outside to play. The conversation had taken an unexpected turn and Frank's reaction worried me. I took my seat next to him again and rested my hand on his arm. He didn't respond to my touch, as though he could not sense my presence. He continued to stare down and I could see his teeth were clenched.

Aunt Lily's hand reached out for Matthew's and she carefully said, 'Frank, your mother told us she had arranged for you and Bert to go to Canada.'

'She knew,' his tone was quiet, but harsh, it was difficult to know if he was upset or angry. 'We were told if we were lucky someone might come for us,' he flicked a look at Aunt Lily, 'we were told, you might want us after all.'

Aunt Lily shook her head. She looked sick with the news, the colour had drained from her face and tears filled her eyes, 'no Frank, no. I wanted you, all of you. It broke my heart when Florence told me. She said it was too late, you had already gone, she waved you off on a ship.'

Frank stared at the fire, 'No, she didn't. That morning, we went on a bus and then a train, but there was no ship, not then. They didn't tell us where we were going or what was happening.'

'They?' Aunt Lily questioned.

'Mr Irving and our mother. He came with us. We left Mother at the train station,' he scoffed, 'she couldn't even say goodbye. She turned her back on us and stayed there, too guilty to look us in the eyes. Mr Irving walked us to this building and a woman was expecting us. We still didn't know what was happening. Mr Irving then said, *if you're lucky someone might come for you, your Aunt Lily might want you after all,* and then he said to the woman, *they don't have anyone.* We didn't know anything about Canada, not until we had been in the home for three months, but Mother must have known all along.'

'Three months!' Aunt Lily shrieked, she rose to her feet and faced the wall. She had one hand pressed against her forehead and the other clutching her stomach, while she arched her body. She was shaking. The room fell silent again. My body was numb, staring dumbfounded at the side of Frank's cheek and then I looked at Matthew. He often knew the right words to say, but he was just as lost, gazing intently at the ground. I had no words to say, my mind was spinning with confusion; all I could do was listen and slowly comprehend the news.

'*That woman* lied to me,' for the first time, I heard real hatred in Aunt Lily's voice. 'She knew I would have taken all of you in. I begged her and begged her to tell me where you were, and I can still hear her words, *too late, they're halfway across the Atlantic, I saw them leave.*'

Aunt Lily dropped to the floor beside Frank's knee and cupped her hand around his. Her eyes red with sorrow, 'my dear, Frank, I am so sorry. If we had known, we would have come for you both. I am so angry and so upset. You poor boys, you were in this country for three months thinking you had no one, believing no one wanted you. There was plenty of time to come and get you. If only we had known. We could have come for you!'

'Aunt Lily, don't be sorry,' Frank replied softly, 'we can't change the past. I haven't forgotten how much you cared about us. I didn't believe what Mr Irving told me. It just took me by surprise that you knew about Canada.'

'What about Bert?' I asked, 'did you two stay together?'

'We travelled over and spent a few nights in the same distribution house. I hoped Bert and I would stay together, but we didn't.' Aunt Lily's head lowered as she listened to Frank, his news was too much for her. 'The farmers would come and pick you like cattle; the strongest boys first. No one cared if you had a brother.'

Frank paused. This was difficult for him, just as it was heart-breaking for us to listen to. Mother had yet again proved just what a monster she really was, she had denied us being a proper family; we could have been close to a real family with Aunt Lily and Matthew. Only something stopped Mother from giving Aunt Lily what she wanted.

'Bert was collected first,' Frank eventually continued, 'and they wouldn't tell me where he went. I was alone and afraid. In four years, I was moved to three different farms and I didn't know where Bert was. I –' he paused. He took a deep breath and closed his eyes, the memories of his past were torturing him.

It was one thing knowing Bert and Frank were sent overseas,

but another to learn they were separated. All I could see in my mind was this frightened eight-year-old boy, all alone, not knowing where he was, what was happening, almost stripped of his identity and childhood.

All I could do was let out a comforting groan and stroke his arm. I could only imagine his pain and I swallowed hard. He needed me to listen and to be strong, while Aunt Lily was beside herself and in pieces. Matthew sat silently in his chair, almost not present in the room, but I was there. My touch made my presence known.

'Finally, I arrived at Caffrey Farm and for the first time in four years, I was shown some real kindness.' His voice broke.

'Frank, we don't have to talk about this now.' I assured him.

He took a deep breath and continued, 'Mr Fawding and his family were very nice to me. He understood me. He wrote to the Home to see if Bert could be located and after a year, we received a letter; Bert was transferring to a farm close by. It had been five years since I last saw him. I was glad we were together again and we continued to live close to one another until I joined the army. We've not lost touch this time, we made sure of it.'

'And where's Bert now?' I was careful to ask.

'Bert is very well; he's a farmer, married to Frances with two daughters, Norma and Jane. The girls are twelve and nine now,' Frank reached inside his pocket and pulled out a photograph which he passed over to me. I glanced down at the square photograph; a sepia image of a smartly dressed family. The man, I recognised as Bert, was stood proudly at the back, his wife sat at an angle on the chair in front of him. The older daughter stood next to her mother, her hands crossed over and resting on the side of the chair, and the youngest girl sat on the floor with her legs curled to the side.

'My goodness,' Aunt Lily said, her voice still frayed as she turned my wrist to peer at the photograph. 'Bert looks like your grandfather, my father.'

I studied the photograph for a long time, staring the longest at the man and searching for the boy I knew. It brought me comfort that I could see his face again, to remove the veil that clouded my memories. Out of the sadness, I was relieved

Frank had brought good news about Bert, to know he was happy and with a lovely family.

'Do you have a family?' I asked.

Frank shook his head, 'no, my life took a different path to Bert. I always knew one day I would make my way back here. If I had a wife, how could I come back?'

After a moment he asked, 'can you take me to May's grave before I leave tomorrow?'

The children and I took Frank to the graveyard the following morning. The snow had melted slightly during the night, making it easier to trudge through, but May's grave was still covered and Frank brushed away the white powder to slowly reveal her name.

Once it was all uncovered, he bowed his head, his eyes closed and his hands together as he said his own prayer. I had grieved, missed and accepted my sister's loss for ten years and it was heart-breaking to see Frank mourn for her for the first time. It ripped my heart out to see him bow down at her stone to say goodbye; ten years too late.

I walked my three children around the footpath to keep them warm in the cold and to allow Frank some time alone. I asked Alfred to join us, but he insisted on staying with his uncle and the mother he never knew. Alfred stood at his side and Frank wrapped a supportive arm over his shoulder. He was a broken man, there was just a glimpse of the child I once knew. As children, both had experienced their own pain, one left alone in another country treated unfairly by the people who swore to look after him; the other born without ever knowing his mother and to later lose his father. An unbreakable bond formed between them; one that would bind them together; one that could repair the broken pieces.

When Frank and Alfred were ready, we left the churchyard and walked slowly towards the town centre to where he had arranged his lift. Then, he asked me the question I was prepared for, but not wanting to answer, 'have you seen our mother?'

I hesitated before I replied. No one knew about my visit, but I could not lie to Frank, 'I saw her once, just after we lost May.'

The hopeful look Frank gave me told me how much he wanted to see her. That, after all these years he still loved and cared for our mother. Whereas I felt nothing but emptiness for her.

'Where is she?' he asked.

I reached into my pocket and pulled out a piece of paper, not the one Mr Irving had given me, but a fresh sheet I had written on earlier that day. I was prepared for this conversation and I had scribbled down her address should Frank have wanted it. I passed him the note, 'I went to see her, perhaps you will be more welcomed than I was. This is her address, I am sure she still lives there.'

Frank didn't say anything. He took the note and slipped it inside his jacket. For a few minutes we walked in silence watching the four children running ahead, laughing and calling out for Frank to watch them. Eventually he broke the silence and said, 'So, you married Stanley, such a great kid. I remember Beatrice being besotted with him.'

I just laughed, knowing he was not far from the truth and I decided not to mention what might have happened. 'When you two had gone, Stanley looked out for me and he was my best friend. Beatrice was too intense for him.'

'You must really miss him?'

'Everyday. I thought the war would have been over by now and yet another month passes.'

'Hopefully it will be soon.'

Before we said goodbye, he made one promise that was mainly aimed at Alfred, 'when all this is over, I will come back to stay. I belong here now.'

Chapter Twenty-Seven

On Tuesday, 8th May 1945, on what would have been May's thirty-seventh birthday, after five years and eight months, the war in Europe was finally over. It was a day to celebrate as a community, showing humanity at its greatest, rejoicing together at the well-fought victory; a day that was to go down in history.

The children didn't go to school and from morning until the evening we gathered in the streets. Everyone brought their tables and chairs outside, joining them together to create a long line, filled with whatever food we could contribute. It was a line of exhilarated faces, bursting with happiness as we cheered and sang. Everyone knew the lyrics to Vera Lynn's, *There'll Always Be an England* and *Land of Hope and Glory*, which we sang many times during the course of that day; it only took one to begin singing and we all joined in. We were our own choir, the words to the songs had so much meaning that we all felt and could relate to. It was difficult to reach the end without being overwhelmed with a tear in our eyes.

The years that had brought us together as a community and as a nation were expressed in the memorable and magnificent atmosphere felt everywhere across the country.

One of the neighbours pulled me close, her grasp so tight, my arms were pinned to my side and she exclaimed, 'It's over, it's over, it's over! Our boys are coming home.'

It was a joyous and victorious day for people who had sons, fathers, brothers, nephews, grandsons, husbands, fiancés and friends finally coming home. Yet it was also a heart-breaking and difficult time for the many who struggled to share in the glory, knowing their beloved would never return.

Alfred had said goodbye to his father five years before in the hope that one day he would see him again, yet he would be one of the many children who would not see their father return. My heart went out to the people who had lost someone.

I thought of Mark, his fear had come true; Beatrice lost her husband just months before the war ended. On learning this sad news, I went to Beatrice to offer my deepest condolences, half expecting her to close the door on me, but instead I was welcomed into the home. I sat with her while she wept, listened to her pain and, with empathy, I cried with her.

From her grief, the wounds of our past mended and we found a friend in each other. I made regular visits to her house, seeing her strength build up little by little, her son being the reason she kept going; he needed her.

Mark dealt with the news as anticipated, overwhelmed by guilt, wishing it was him, but the loss encouraged him to take action to rebuild his father's business. He was to be the main bread winner for the Irving's. It was to be a long journey for him, but it gave him hope, something to work towards and a future for his nephew.

Both Beatrice and Mark often asked after Alfred. At times I took him along with my children to play with Peter. I could see how they genuinely cared for Alfred, to see the two cousins play together like best friends, but to never know they had the same blood running through their veins, like Mother said, 'sometimes Betsy, the past is best left forgotten, people are so desperate for the truth and sometimes the truth can hurt the people dearest to you.' This was to be another generation with secrets, like our parents had watched May play with Mark and Beatrice, with the truth hidden; that lie now continued through their offspring.

Frank was true to his word and returned home within a fortnight after the war was over, with the intention of never leaving again. He found work at the flax mill, which amused me, remembering what Stanley once said back in 1925, 'everyone starts off at the flax mill.' He stayed with Aunt Lily until he found his own property, though he was in no rush to move out; he wanted to stay close to Alfred. My predictions were right, the two were destined to find one another; in Frank, Alfred saw a father figure; in Alfred, Frank saw the son he never had and his lost childhood.

Bert and I wrote to one another and in his own words I had an account of the missing years. He was content and most of all happy, and I thought of father's words, *'things always work out in the end,'* and for Bert, it did. I was looking forward to the following year when he planned to travel over for a visit with his family.

Gradually, over the weeks, the men returned home a few at a time and our streets began to fill once more. The town seemed to swell with people as the summer days became more frequent.

I was still waiting for Stanley and as each day passed, my concerns grew into worry and panic. No news had been sent to me, good or bad and a dark cloud still hung over me, reminding me that nothing was guaranteed.

It was a Thursday evening and we had just finished dinner. I was in the kitchenette washing the pots, Maggie was reading her book, while Victoria and Little Stanley were playing a game together on the floor. It was one of those rare, quiet times when the children were unusually quiet and content in each other's company, without the need to squabble.

The calm atmosphere in the house made the loud knock on the door come as a shock. The children glanced at me with their innocent and startled eyes, as I scurried across the floor, drying my hands on the apron on my travels. I brushed a hand over my hair, tucking any loose strands behind my ears, making myself look presentable before I unlocked the door.

It didn't register that it was Stanley at first; he looked drained, his face was slimmer and a few grey hairs had grown through his beard. He stood in the doorway, a broad, but tired, smile spread across his face. It was seeing the familiarity of his smile that I realised it was him. My senses woke up, my arms fell round his neck, my body collapsed into his and I cried in hysterics at the sight of him. Reunited at long last with my husband; we had been parted for almost six years.

His arms tightly locked around my waist and his face brushed against mine. He was real, I could feel the stubble from his beard and his warm cheeks. He lifted my feet off the ground and spun me around as he stepped into our home. Once inside, he kicked the door shut and no longer exposed to the street, we kissed.

'Hello, my love,' he said, sounding as though he had only been out to work for the day.

'You're home! I have missed you so much.' My hands cupped his face, admiring him before me once again.

The children were by my side; none of them spoke, but they were intrigued to meet the father they only remembered through my stories. Little Stanley kept out of sight, the weight of his small hands clinging to my skirt as he hid behind me.

Victoria, being the more confident child, stepped forward first and when his eyes dropped to acknowledge her, she leapt into his arms and cried, 'Daddy.'

'Victoria,' he spun her around and held her tenderly. 'Beautiful, just like your mother.'

'Stanley,' I chortled, 'she's every bit of you.'

Stanley slowly lowered her to the ground, kissing her forehead before his attention fell on Maggie. He outstretched his arms to welcome her, but she stood still, shaking her head, unsure what to make of the stranger she no longer recognised before her. She was overwhelmed. I could tell she was nervous by the way she nibbled her bottom lip and how she reached out to grab my hand for reassurance.

Stanley was patient and he bent down to her level. He picked up her tiny hand in his and kissed it gently.

'Maggie, my angel, you have grown so much,' he carefully said to her. 'Do you remember me? When you were about this high,' he demonstrated with his hand, 'you would sit on my knee and we would tell each other stories.'

She released my hand and took a step towards him, she hesitated for a moment before she took him off guard and sprung, her arms around his neck. Stanley let out a chuckle at her sudden show of affection until he realised her body shook in his arms as she cried into his shoulder. He rose to his feet, carrying her in his arms and soothed her with gentle rocking. He buried his face in her hair and he too struggled to contain his emotions, and with eyes shut tight, he managed to say in a whisper, 'Daddy is home now. I have missed all of you. Thinking about you all kept me going,' then, he opened his eyes and looked at me, 'Betsy, you've done a marvellous job.'

I coughed, feeling choked, but the tugging of Little Stanley pulling on my skirt distracted me. He was finding the courage to shuffle around me and look at his daddy for the first time. I glanced down at his awe-struck face, his wide eyes and mouth open, peering up at Stanley.

Stanley's eyes glistened with held back tears when he caught sight of his son. He lowered Maggie to the ground and she reluctantly released her hold on him, before slipping her arms around my waist to shield her face in my blouse.

Stanley knelt down in front of Little Stanley to absorb everything about him. A smile spread across his face, 'hello, fella, and who do we have here?'

'S-Stanley, sir,' Little Stanley replied, his voice shaky and he tugged my arm, 'Mummy, is this my daddy?'

'Yes,' I could barely say the words and gently pushed him towards his father, 'go on, it's all right.'

'Stanley,' Stanley repeated his son's name and held his arms out. Little Stanley slowly curved his arms around his father's shoulders and rested his head on his chest.

'Finally, my boys have met. Finally, we are reunited. Finally.'

'I am so sorry,' he stood up, carrying Little Stanley with one arm and the other he embraced me, 'I'm sorry I wasn't here. I have been away too long. I have missed you so much.'

'Don't be,' I said, 'you're home now and we have our whole future together, the five of us.'

I realised then, that in a life of misery there is always hope, and in hope, we are faced with challenges that bring us misery. But no matter how hard life is, whatever obstacles obstruct the way, things will always work out *in the end.* If I was to look back at the hardest times in my life, when I struggled, I will always see I survived it.

Like my father once said many years ago, *'things always work out, in the end.'*

In the End

1934

It had been a week since she saw Betsy, six weeks since she lost May and since then, Florence had devoted most of her thoughts to her forgotten children. She was tortured by her own regret and sadness, as she quickly declined into depression, anger and bitterness. She could no longer bear to look at her reflection in the mirror for she despised the woman that looked back at her.

She tried to focus on Frederick, to shield her feelings and carry on as though her world was unaltered, but the faces of her first four children haunted her. She saw them everywhere and everywhere reminded her of them. The village that once brought her sanctuary no longer protected her from her past and she could no longer hide from what she was; *a mother who abandoned her children.*

Even after all those years of wanting and waiting, Wallace had finally fulfilled his promise and left his wife to be with her, but it did not fulfil her. She was not certain if he was there out of love or desperation. He had lost everything; his business; his eldest child; the respect of his other children; his wife; his home. Neither was she certain if she loved him, because all she felt when she looked at this weak and defeated man was hatred.

As he sat in Alfred's chair, looking comfortable and at home, Florence glared across the room at him. She was angry, from a large build up after suppressing it for many years, going back to when she first met him. 'I want you to leave!'

Wallace looked at her surprised but he did not move.

'I don't want you here,' Florence rose from her chair and snatched his coat from the peg, flinging it across the floor to land at his feet. 'I want you to leave.'

'Come on now, Florence,' Wallace laughed at her. 'You know you don't mean it. We have wanted this for so long. Think about Frederick.'

Florence clenched her fists, her insides boiled and her pulse began to race. The adrenalin attacked, but without yelling she said, 'what about my other children? I have lost them all because of you.'

He chortled, 'well, you practically begged me to help you. You couldn't cope, remember? You said so yourself that they'd be better off without you.'

'No! *You* told me they would be better off without me, *you* made me feel like I couldn't cope. Everything I did, *you* told me to. *You* made me do it all.'

'Florence, you make it sound like I had a knife to your back. I've not made you do anything. You signed those papers for your sons, you didn't even bother to read it.'

'You ruined my life, you've taken everything away from me, everything! You've always been there, taking from me.'

'You could barely look at your own children. I did you all a favour.' There was an acid tone to his voice.

'I could not face them. I didn't know how to deal with the grief.'

While Florence's anger rose and her voice echoed around the room, Wallace remained seated. A smirk spread across his face and he brushed down the creases on the trouser legs, he behaved like he had heard her words a thousand times before; not bothered, 'Ah, you're a cold woman, Florence. You don't know how to love, let alone grieve for it. You just put up with Alfred, he was the fool that believed you.'

Florence swallowed hard before replying, 'I want *you* to leave my house.'

'What about my son?'

'Frederick is *my* son. Your name is not on his birth certificate, Alfred's is, just like his name is on May's. He is nothing to you and you can't prove anything.'

The words shot through him and in a panic, he said, 'where will I go?'

'I couldn't care less! I want you out of our lives. Alfred was the best thing that ever happened to me. You have ruined my life and I hate you for it. I *hate* you.'

Wallace stood up and picked up his coat. He stopped in front of Florence and pleaded, 'come on my love, don't do this to me, to *us*; we've just lost our baby girl?'

'*My* baby girl, that *you* took from me; she was never truly yours,' Florence almost choked on her words, but found strength to firmly add, 'This whole time you have taken me for the fool, with your lies, after lies. There has never been *us*.'

Florence slammed the door on Wallace, something she should have done in December 1919. She had finally broken the strings that he had used to control her for so many years. She was no longer his puppet. She was no longer his.

1946

Twelve years had passed since she closed the door on Wallace and her only regret was that she had not done it sooner. She was finally free, but alone. When Frederick was old enough, he moved away and soon married. He fought in the war and returned safely and, although he wrote to his mother often, he saw little of her.

In the early part of the year she received a heartfelt letter from Frank, one that took him a year to send. She replied immediately and for a few months, several letters filled with love, regret and forgiveness were exchanged between them, until Frank felt ready to visit and see his mother for the first time in almost twenty-seven years.

Florence waited impatiently in the room for his arrival and slowly watched the hand of the clock move round until it reached the time he was due. After a few minutes, a loud knock sounded on the door; so loud it boomed through the room and her body shook with excitement. A wave of fear and anxiety washed over her as she shuffled across the room to open the door.

There, in the doorway stood Frank and beside him, to her surprise, was Bert. Florence's eyes filled with tears and she wrapped both her arms around her sons and pulled them near. 'My boys,' she wept, 'my sons.'

It took a moment before they responded to her embrace and

when they did, they held each other for as long as possible, making up for all the lost years.

Florence was the first to pull away and with a loving, but painful, smile she looked at her grown boys. Until she glanced over their shoulders, just searching and just hoping, when she asked, 'did Betsy not want to come?'

'Not today, Mother,' Frank said.

'Well, I don't blame her,' Florence forced a smile, but that did not shield the heartache in her eyes, 'send her my love, when you see her.'

Florence spent the afternoon reuniting with her sons, Bert and Frank. She was happy. For the first time in a long while, she was truly happy, and in her thoughts she said, *'If you could see me now, Alfred, I am with our sons, In the End.'*

The End

Lightning Source UK Ltd.
Milton Keynes UK
UKHW011010100720
366326UK00003B/658